To A

THE
RESPONSIBILITY
OF
LOVE

With best wishes

J. DAVID SIMONS
July 2021.

Published by BackPage Press

www.backpagepress.co.uk/press
@BackPagePress

A catalogue record for this book is available from the British Library.

ISBN 9781909430518

Cover Design by Andy Bridge
Typeset by Laura Jones

Printed and bound in Great Britain by Clays Ltd.

THE
RESPONSIBILITY
OF
LOVE

J DAVID SIMONS

NOW

JAKE TULLY DIDN'T BELIEVE IN GOD. He was far too rational and cynical to possess such faith. But he did have a sense of there being some kind of universal energy, a space/time continuum far greater than his will, a place where the ego ceased to exist and a much higher (or deeper) self took over. An overarching current it was possible to plug into. Or not. That old Hippie maxim of going with or against the flow. For so long, he felt he had been swimming upstream. But today... today felt different. He felt as if all the elements of the earth were rising up to finally declare: *This is Jake Tully Day*.

Overwhelmed by this unfamiliar feeling of positivity, he sat down on the edge of the bed. It had come to this, he thought. The stars were arranged just so. The tectonic plates of his fate were sliding into place, he could almost hear them slotting together with a satisfying ... he actually made the sound out loud with his tongue. 'Click, click, click.' He could feel it in his bones, in his waters, in his soul. It was as if he had thrown a double-six as a black cat crossed his path with a four-leaf clover clutched in its mouth. Rarely had he experienced such a ... such a what? Such an alignment between who he was and his true sense of purpose in life. It was a very powerful feeling. Intoxicating. It was so intoxicating it was scary. Perhaps this was how the Buddhists felt prior to enlightenment, what the Chinese called the attainment of the rainbow body. When all physicality disappeared into the ether and all that was left were a person's hair and nails. He looked down at his fingers with their bitten-down, discoloured keratinous tips. No, no, he didn't aspire to that. He definitely wanted to be very much present today in his nearly fifty-year-old body to finally reap his reward. Or to wreak his revenge. He took another gulp of whisky straight from the flask, the fine malt sliding down his throat to fire up a stomach already lined with the ingredients of a Lorazepam nicked from Francesca's medicine cabinet. He dismissed the thought that his rare feeling of euphoria could simply be linked to the heady combination of alcohol and anti-anxiety tablet currently spreading out from his belly into his veins.

He held up the flask in front of his eyes, with difficulty read the fancy loops and curls of the inscription engraved on the side. *To Albert Tully. From his comrades.* His father, the very owner of this battered piece of silverware, sat downstairs watching afternoon TV. Jake felt a rare moment of compassion for the man. *To Albert Tully. From his comrades.* To survive a war, to dodge the German bombs and bullets, to raise two sons virtually on his own, to build up a business as a blacksmith – a rare and dying craft these days – the fingers of the poor man's hands permanently swollen like sausages from hammering and welding wrought iron for fences, stair rails, grilles and balconies. To arrive here on his son's special day as a bitter old soldier sitting in front of the television, swearing at the screen, yearning for those good old Vera Lynn days when children contracted polio and rickets, average life expectancy was barely over seventy, there were only two TV channels, the country was bankrupt, the threat of a nuclear holocaust was on the horizon, porn was on the top shelf, biscuit jars on the bottom, and alcohol came in brown paper bags. Yes, those good old days when his father's fellow citizens actually appreciated his wartime sacrifice and we Britons never had it so good. *To Albert Tully. From his comrades.* 'Cheers!' Jake made to take another swig, thought the better of it, twisted the top back on, slid the flask back into his pocket. Just as well. For here was Francesca.

'Not ready yet,' she said flatly.

Even after over twenty-five years of knowing this woman, he still could never work out whether she was criticising him or merely stating a fact. Francesca was certainly dressed herself. In an ivory, silk sheath of a gown. It must have cost a fortune, Jake thought. But then again, that wasn't his problem. Francesca was quite capable of purchasing her own designer chic with her perfectly respectable salary, far greater than his own meagre income. Although after today, after *Jake Tully Day*, that kind of imbalance might be corrected.

He smiled at her, the cocktail of drugs and whisky making him feel benevolent not only towards her but to all womankind.

She smiled back, gave just a little cock of her hip as she did so. He could see her pelvic bone move under the silk. She probably hadn't even been aware of her action, an automatic response to something buried deep in the vintage of their relationship, but to Jake that simple gesture was imbued with meaning. What did it signify? An irritation with him? A playful flick? Was it sexual? He just couldn't read her anymore. He actually couldn't see her anymore either. Really see her. Jake knew that Francesca was attractive, intelligent, successful, highly principled, a wonderful mother, a woman who took her responsibilities seriously. He knew that others saw her as such too. But he had lost the ability to view her in that way. He was like a museum guard watching others marvel at a famous painting while all he could think of was that it would soon be time for lunch.

'Need help?' she asked.

He picked up the length of black fabric from the bed. 'One thing my old man taught me was to tie one of these.'

'Very well. But you need to stop with the drinking.'

'I only had one swig.'

'I don't care. You've got a lot to get through today. I hope you'll behave yourself.'

'And why shouldn't I?'

'I know what you're like. Just don't embarrass yourself. These people are your peers.'

Jake held up the tie, then pressed it over his heart. 'I promise I shall not let them pee on me. Or I on them.'

'We are not amused,' she said, her forehead crinkling into a scowl. 'What about your speech?'

'Why bother? I'm not going to win.' He decided it was best not to admit to his dear Francesca that deep in his bones he felt victory was already his. That the winning oratory had been written for years inside his head, although only recently transposed onto paper. His ungracious acceptance speech. His retribution. His Decca List. Named for the record company that according to music legend had turned down an up-and-coming guitar group called The Beatles. But for Jake to speak of potential victories out loud before the appointed time was to tempt fate, to court the evil eye, to upset this wonderful flow, to offer himself up for yet another fall. 'Happy just to make the shortlist,' he said. 'Winner's just down to sheer luck.'

'God, Jake. You're so full of shit.'

Jake gave his practised shrug of the innocent.

Francesca persisted, as she so often did. 'The bookmakers have you down as favourite.'

'Where did you hear that?' he queried, amused to hear that bookmakers were actually calculating the odds on the winner of a prize for books. *Jake Tully Day* just got that little bit better.

'Radio 4.'

'They'll go for that black woman from Zimbabwe. Juries love these stories of oppression and survival from our obsolescent Commonwealth.'

'I don't think Zimbabwe is in the Commonwealth.'

'Good for them. Bloody good for them. Freeing themselves from the yoke of Imperial oppression.'

'I believe they suffered under the yoke of Mugabe's oppression after that.'

Jake grunted. 'How about that teenager writing from the Outer Hebrides? A remote community in turmoil. Love in the herring industry. A triumph of youth over an old hack like me.'

'She's thirty-one actually.'

'Who?'

'Your teenager from the Outer Hebrides.'

Jake stood up. He felt a bit wobbly, tried not to show it as he walked over to position himself in front of the wardrobe mirror. 'You know what?' He sucked in his stomach. 'Next time round, I'd like to come back as a professional tennis player.'

He could see Francesca's reflection in the mirror, her standing there hand on hip, looking at him looking at her. Their eyes connected. Was she able to really see *him* anymore?

'What are you on about?' she asked.

'Reincarnation.' He folded up his collar, wound the fabric around his neck. 'Another Roger Federer.' He took one side of the bow tie, brought it across and under, then up through the loop.

'And your point is?'

He made another fold, then another to make the bow. 'My point is that with tennis, if you're the best, you win. Simple as that.' He brought the loose end down across the middle of the bow, folded it back and through the loop. 'None of this being assessed by a panel of judges. Or being lucky enough to be at the sharp end of the prevailing *zeitgeist*. Or the product of a huge marketing campaign.' He pulled down on the ends to tighten the arrangement, then fiddled around with it until it sat straight. 'Just hit the ball over the net, get it between the lines, beyond the reach of your opponent. And voila!' He made a swipe with an imaginary tennis racket, nearly fell over. 'I win.

5

And why? Because I'm the best. And not because of the opinion of some self-appointed gatekeepers.'

'I'm impressed…'

'Such is the culmination of my philosophical wisdom gained from years of rejection, failure and then even more rejection.'

She flashed him one of her long-suffering smiles. 'I'm impressed you managed to tie up your bow.'

'As I said, my father's sole legacy to his wayward son.'

He gave the air another swipe, a bit steadier and slower this time, let out a hiss as the invisible ball kicked up the chalk line in the Wimbledon of his imagination. 'A father's sole legacy to his wayward son.'

'Why don't you go show him then? I'd like some space in here to finish up.'

His father sat in an armchair drawn up too close to the TV, shouting at the screen. Or at least at the young woman struggling to answer a question as a giant digital clock counted down the seconds behind her.

'Operation Overlord,' Albert barked. 'Jesus Christ, woman. Operation Overlord.'

Jake sucked on a mint as he watched from the doorway. *To Albert Tully. From his comrades.* Would he end up like this too? Yelling at a quiz show broadcast on whatever media platform the future had in store for him thirty years down the line. Technology might bound ahead but quiz shows would never change. Human beings were always so desperate to show how clever they were.

The digital clock ticked down.

'Operation Overlord, for fuck's sake.'

'Calm down, Dad. It's only a quiz show.'

His father turned to him. 'Oh, it's you,' he said, as if it could be anyone else. 'Turning point of the war and she doesn't have the decency to remember.'

'She's far too young.'

'Forty thousand Allied troops died on the beaches of France to give her freedom. She should bloody well know. What do they teach children in school these days?'

'Sex ed., software development and media marketing, I believe.'

The sound of a klaxon emanated from the television. The answer was given. Albert Tully sat back in his chair, arms folded. 'I'd be up ten thousand bloody quid by now.'

'You should go on one of these shows.' It was a sincere comment. Jake was impressed that for a man of ninety, his father could still recall facts from another millennium despite often struggling with details of his everyday life.

'Aye, I should,' Albert Tully snorted.

Jake moved into the room. His father looked him up and down. 'Off to see Her Majesty?'

'Very funny.'

'Just you and Fran then?'

'Nick too. Possibly Melissa, if she's not having one of her meltdowns.'

His father breathed in deep, his barrel chest looking set to burst the buttons on his cotton plaid shirt that he would be shocked to know had now become the height of hipster fashion. 'Never thought of inviting your father?'

'You hate these things.'

'Nice to be asked though.'

Jake bit back his irritation. After all, it was *Jake Tully Day* and he wasn't going to let his father spoil it.

'Why are you heading off now?' his father asked. 'It's the middle of the afternoon.'

'These things start early. I've got an interview to do. Then reception, speeches, dinner.'

'What about my dinner? I hope you didn't bring me over here to starve.'

Jake again felt his irritation rise but as if on cue, the angel Francesca floated into the room wrapped in a vaporised mist of exquisite perfume. 'I've left you a casserole beside the Aga,' she said in that soothing manner of hers capable of persuading a client to spend a fortune on kitchen worktops. 'All you have to do is pop it in the top oven and heat it up for twenty minutes. I've left a sheet with instructions on the counter along with a timer. There are some beers in the fridge. The ceremony is on at nine.'

'Same time as my programme.'

'Your programme?' Jake said.

'That Swedish detective series.'

'Christ, Dad. Don't you think…'

'…I know the one,' Francesca said. 'Why don't you watch Jake's ceremony live. I'll show you how to watch your programme on the computer later.'

Albert Tully leaned back in his chair, let out the frustrated sigh of a man used to moulding hot metal into whatever shape he desired. 'Tonight's the final episode.'

Francesca was not to be cowed. 'Perhaps your father would like one of those beers now.'

As Jake wandered off to the kitchen, he could hear his father's admonition wafting behind him: 'And do something about that bloody bow tie. It's as crooked as a dog's hind leg.'

He opened up the door of the too expensive refrigerator (interior designer Francesca must have an eggshell blue Smeg in 1950s retro style), felt the cold blast of air on his face. His senses were all alive. His body was tingling. He could do with a beer himself. And perhaps some of this cheese. Jarlsberg. Nothing quite like a piece of Norwegian cow's milk. After all, he shouldn't be drinking on a stomach empty but for a sucked mint, a few drams of whisky and an anti-anxiety tablet. Which reminded him that he had two other Lorazepam wrapped up in foil in his pocket just in case. He pulled two cans off the shelf, felt that delightful over-priced suction as the door closed tight. So much so that he repeated the process with a matador's flourish before sitting down at the kitchen table. He took a knife out of the drawer in order to tackle the cheese, enjoyed the cool of the can in his hot grasp, then plucked at the ring-pull. 'Shit!' The damn thing had come away in his fingers. He picked up the knife, stabbed at the metal top, then repeatedly attacked the aluminium in frustration until the blade slipped right off the rim and into his hand.

'Fuck, fuck, fuck.' It was a deep cut. He had almost sliced off his index finger. Not an unexpected outcome from the employment of a Japanese sashimi knife in some kind of can-opening *yakuza* atonement ceremony. Blood was spurting all over the place. On to the table, on to the floor, on to the instruction sheet for his father, on to his shirt. He held his hand away from his body, away from his hired dinner suit, rushed over to the sink, ran the cold-water tap.

'Francesca!'

It took ten minutes for the bleeding to stop. It must have been the Lorazepam thinning his blood. He had gone through half a kitchen roll and now Francesca was sat in front of him, an apron over her gown, wrapping up the wounded finger in bandages.

'It's almost through to the bone,' she said. 'I think the tendon is cut. Can you bend it?'

'A bit.'

'Is it painful?'

'Not really.'

'You're probably in shock.'

'I'll take some codeine.'

'We should really get you to A&E.'

'There's no time for that.'

'You'll have to do something with it.'

'I'll figure something out.' He watched as Francesca bit into the end of the bandage so she could split it in two, tie it off with a knot. She then stood up, wiped her hands on her apron, shook her head. 'Jesus Christ. What a mess.'

'What will I do about the shirt?'

'You could keep the jacket buttoned up.'

'It's a bit tight. Have I got any shirts left upstairs?'

'What? Like as a souvenir? I'm afraid all your clothes went out with our marriage.' She took a step back as she pondered his predicament. 'I'll text Nick. He must be about the same collar size as you. I'm sure he'll have a spare dress shirt.'

'He's probably got a closet-full, knowing my brother.'

'Keep your jacket closed for now. And give me that flask.'

'What?'

'Seriously, Jake. Everything always ends up being such a drama with you. And the booze doesn't help.'

Jake looked down at his blood-stained shirt, his aching bandaged finger and sighed. Perhaps this wasn't going to be *Jake Tully Day* after all.

THEN

WHEN JAKE WAS ABOUT TO BE SIX-YEARS-OLD, his mother took him and his older brother Nick by train into the city to buy him his birthday present. The plan was that they would meet their father at the toy shop, the four of them would be involved in making the purchase together as was the family ritual, then a proper afternoon tea would be had at some fancy hotel close to the station. His father was usually late for these outings for unless these birthdays fell on a weekend, he struggled to get away from his foundry work on time. Such was the case on this particular afternoon, which was no great hardship as it meant the two boys had more time to explore the entirety of the store.

Jake somehow managed to detach himself from Nick's constant needling and his mother's watchful ambit, got a bit lost and ended up all by himself in a far corner which contained shelf upon shelf of teddy bears and other stuffed toys. He found himself drawn to one particular teddy, a certain vulnerable look in its cute button eyes that seemed to demand his attention. He walked over to the shelf and began stroking the toy animal's fur as if he needed to gain the bear's trust before he picked it up. He was just about to lift the teddy off the shelf when he heard his mother shriek: 'Stop!'

His whole body jarred to the command. He dropped hold of the bear, turned round to see his mother standing there, her hand covering her mouth. She was wearing a short white cardigan of the fluffiest wool over a dress adorned with sworls of blue and yellow flowers. Over a forearm was looped the handle of an ivory-white leather handbag that matched the colour of her shoes. As she walked towards him, he could hear the swish of the fabric of her dress, the click of her heels on the floor. She crouched down in front of him so that her face was level with his own. He recalled her tight auburn curls, bright red lipstick that contained crumbs of dry skin, her eyes dull but smiling at the corners. He breathed in her flowery fragrance that seemed to match the pattern of her dress. She placed a hand on his shoulder.

'Do you want me to buy this teddy bear for your birthday?'

Jake shook his head. 'I want an Action Man.'

'And that's what we'll get you.'

'But why can't I pick up the teddy bear?'

'Because when you pick it up, its little heart will start to beat and it will come alive with love for you. Then you'll put it back down, and it will be left all alone on the shelf. You should only pick up a teddy bear if you're going to buy it and give it a home.'

Jake's hand crept back to clutch hold of the bear. He could feel the coarseness of the fabric, the slight give in the soft toy's belly from his tightening fingers, this overwhelming urge to pick it up again. His mother gently moved his hand away from the stuffed animal, then kissed him on the forehead for what seemed a very long time. 'My own mother told me that too,' she said. 'It is a good lesson. And now I have passed it on to you.'

These were the last words Jake ever remembered his mother saying to him, for a few months later he was informed by his father, also in a crouch before him, a glazed look in his rheumy eyes, that she had passed away to a far better place. A place where she was sure to have found peace and respite from all her pain.

As if to compensate for the loss of the boy's mother, Albert Tully bought Jake a dog for his next birthday. Jake had not asked for a dog or ever expressed any interest in having one. He actually wanted a Lego set. Yet here was this creature thrust upon him. His father told him he had rescued it from the pound. 'Nobody else wanted her,' his father informed him. 'She looked so lonely and abandoned.' Jake wasn't surprised she looked so lonely and abandoned for she was such an ugly mongrel. There was a bit of Jack Russell in there, a dachshund perhaps, something else too, nobody knew what she was. She had exposed pink nipples and this smooth white skin which Jake could hardly bear to touch. He was furious with his father, especially when he considered the Meccano set his brother Nick had received for his birthday. Why did he suddenly have responsibility for this dog which he didn't even like? Perhaps it wouldn't have been so bad if his father had taken him to the pound as well so that he had a chance to choose his own dog. He would have gone for a labrador or a golden retriever or a collie. Something long-haired, glowing and substantial. But this horrible runt of a thing? His father even wanted him to name her after his dead mother but he absolutely refused to do that. Instead, he called her Lassie. Even at seven years of age, he possessed a sense of irony.

Jake tried to love Lassie. He knew that was what a young boy should do with his dog. He should be petting her, letting her lick his face, they should be off on adventures together, he on his bike with his trusty companion running alongside him. They would rescue silly girls from drowning in the park pond or capture a thief robbing one of the local shops. If Jake fell down a hole in the ground, his dog would be there to assess the situation, then run off to find help. None of that happened with Lassie. The poor thing had an inbuilt fear of everything, no doubt instilled by cruel treatment received at the hands of a previous owner. Jake was not immune to the constant terrified look in Lassie's eyes. He remembered the last words his mother had spoken to him. He really did try to love that dog even if he hadn't been the one to pick her up off the shelf. But somehow it was not to be. His father must have realised that too. For about six months later, Lassie suddenly disappeared from Jake's life. He didn't know where she had gone. He looked all over for her, although somewhere deep in the darkness of his heart, he hoped he wouldn't find her. His father said nothing, took no interest in the missing dog. Then after a few days when she had not reappeared, Jake's life continued as before and Lassie was never spoken of again.

For his eleventh birthday, Jake received a copy of *The Little Prince* from his father. Or *Le Petit Prince* as Albert Tully called the book in its original language in memory of a wartime spent in northern France. This was a far more successful gift than that of the hapless puppy. Jake loved that book. He loved the exotic name of the author. Antoine de Saint-Exupéry. He loved the little prince. He loved his golden hair. He loved his scarf. He loved his asteroid with his beloved rose and the three volcanoes. He loved his adventures to other planets. But the part of the book that affected him the most was the story about the fox who wanted the little prince to tame him. The lesson of that encounter being not far removed from his mother's remembered words: 'one becomes responsible forever for what you have tamed'.

But Jake himself was not to be tamed. Although he did fairly well at school, especially in English and French, any academic achievement tended to be tempered by his bad behaviour. He came close to expulsion on a number of occasions, his more serious misdemeanours always taking place in classes with female teachers, 'as if he were in a personal vendetta against me,' declared the home report of one mistress on the subject.

In contrast, his best friend at school was a model pupil. Adam Taylor was a robust, fair-haired lad who boasted that enviable combination of possessing both academic ability and sporting prowess. Like some kind of comic book super-hero, Adam with his reading glasses was the shy and studious schoolboy, the pride of the maths department. Without his spectacles, he was a star on the running track, the try-scoring wing-back on the rugby pitch. And since Albert Tully had neither the time nor the inclination to take his own children on holiday, it was with Adam and his parents that Jake used to spend his summers, down in Cornwall where the Taylors owned a second home – a rambling old house perched on a hilltop overlooking the sea and one of the finest surf spots in the country. Jake liked Adam's parents – Rob and Trish – who were half-drunk most of the time on these holidays, often disappearing into their bedroom for 'naps' at odd times of the day.

'Only reason you're invited, mate,' Adam would tell him. 'Just so they can go off and fuck. Without worrying about social services turning up with their abandoned surf bum of an only child.'

Adam had been surfing these waters since he was a kid and was pretty skilful on a board given his aptitude for sporting prowess. Jake, on the other hand, discovered he had an innate sense of balance and was reasonably flexible so that despite being a land-locked city boy, he adapted quickly to the sport. He thrived among the waves, enjoying the adrenalin rush and sheer joy from the fear and the excitement they generated. He cherished those sunny, salty, sandy days out in the sea with his friend, paddling out the back, sitting astride his board, waiting for whatever the water gods would throw at him. And when his chance came, he loved to jump from prone to half-crouch on his six-foot fibreglass deck and ride that wave-borne energy, to feel at one with nature, to experience that sense of freedom as he glided along the face. To be totally focussed, to exist only in the present moment, to bask in that treasured release from final exams, from teenage angst and from a motherless household.

The challenge for both of them along that part of the Cornish coast was Spiky Point. On a good day with the wind just right, stacking the waves six-to-eight-foot high in a line across the bay, the surf break was a formidable sight. The danger wasn't just in the wave's sheer power and height but also in the fact it broke over a barnacled reef with a spiked high point just after take-off. It was during his second summer-time visit to Cornwall that Jake decided he was ready to take on the break.

Along with Adam, he suited up, trotted down to the beach full of false bravado, swam out past the breaking waves until they joined a whole pod of tourists hustling for position with the locals out the back. As outsiders themselves they both felt the pressure. They had to show courtesy, they had to show courage, they had to push themselves forward yet they had to make sure they didn't drop in on a local, otherwise they could find themselves being pulverised by fists as well as by waves and rocks. Jake supposed it was trying to get all these things right that made him lose concentration and he managed his take-off all wrong. Instead of skimming across the face, he got straight-off caught underneath the lip and that wave just slammed him down mercilessly onto the reef. He pushed down on his board, using it like a shield so that it took most of the frontal contact but as he was flipped over, he felt the jagged edge of rocks slice through his suit, gouge out a chunk of flesh just under his shoulder blade. He went into a churn after that, his leash and board being ripped off him and he was floundering around gasping for breath. His ears were burning, his lungs were searing from the pressure, he had been turned around so much he wasn't sure which way was up. With the lack of oxygen to his brain, he would soon either black-out or start hallucinating, his lungs would involuntarily spasm to suck in water instead of air. But then a hand gripped his forearm, dragging him upwards, until he burst through the surface into cool, sweet air. He was turned onto his back and as he sucked the life back into his lungs, his vision of pure sky was interrupted by a familiar face.

'Saved your life, mate,' Adam said.

Perhaps it was this near-death experience that fired Jake up into such a ferment of nerve-ending sensitivity that he found himself plunged headlong into his first teenage crush almost immediately after the Spiky Point incident. The target of his obsession, of his besottedness, of his lust (which, of course, he confused with love) was Denise, a sixteen-year-old Canadian girl, one of two daughters and their parents who had rented the house next to the Taylors. Denise was so unlike the other girls he knew who tended to be sullen and hostile, herded together in their impenetrable little cliques. Denise possessed a North American confidence, there was something open, wholesome but also bratty about her at the same time, a combination Jake found irresistible. She wore over-sized college sweatshirts, colourful silky shorts that showed off her long legs, turned-around baseball caps with the words *Toronto Blue Jays* emblazoned on them. Her teeth were perfect, she chewed gum and bounced along as she walked. She spent hours stretched out in her bikini on a lounger on the neighbouring lawn, letting the rare English sunshine stroke her flat teenage belly and slim limbs, then turning over onto her front, the straps of her top falling loose from her shoulders to reveal the sides of her naked, flattened breasts. He would sit for hours by his upstairs bedroom window, waiting for her to appear, this anticipation, so exquisite and tormenting in its longing. Yet there was nothing profound or meaningful contained within this obsession. There was no desire to know Denise (except in the biblical sense) or that she would want to know him. This was a bestial, hormonal yearning at its most primitive level where rationality and compassion ceased to exist. And as with most all-consuming relationships such as this where one person was the dealer of lust and the other the addict to it, Jake fell most definitely into the latter category.

'She's outta your league,' Adam told him as they headed back to his parents' property, dripping wet after an afternoon out in the surf.

Jake chose to ignore the comment, concentrating instead on manoeuvring his board between two log fence posts at the end of the sandy path from the beach.

But Adam persisted. 'I've seen you following that blue-jean babe around like a forlorn puppy. We're just fucking kids to her.'

'She must be about our age.'

'Girls our age are looking for guys with wheels, designer stubble and pockets full of *dinero*.'

'Yeah, I get that. Doesn't mean I haven't a chance.'

'If you're going to have any chance at all, you've got to act cool. Instead of pursuing her like a demented stalker.' Adam stretched out his arm, forcing Jake to stop in his tracks. 'And here's your opportunity. Our young cock-teaser has finally risen to greet the day.'

Denise was sitting up on her lounger as they passed the low wall separating the two gardens. She peered over her sunglasses and waved to them. 'See you guys later,' she said.

'What's happening later?' Adam asked.

'Your folks have asked my folks over for a barbeque.'

The Taylors' garden sloped down from the house to a wrought iron gate within a stone perimeter wall. A wooden bench sat at the bottom of this garden from which Jake could observe the many passers-by on their cliff-top walks as well as monitor the status of the daily surf. As mountaineers might look at a yonder hill and pick out an appropriate ascent among the rocks, the scree and the heather, he could sit there with Adam for hours discussing the various attributes of the sea's behaviour in a way that the ordinary cliff-top observer might not. He was doing that now, commenting to Adam on the height of the waves, the strength and direction of the wind, the way in which the water was breaking over the reef, the rip currents and the distance between sets, anything to take his mind off the imminent arrival of the object of his lust. Behind him, he could already smell the fish baking in their tin foil wraps alongside the giant slabs of meat the Canadian neighbours had brought over in a massive cooler that also contained six-packs of beer. Mitch and Jennifer from Toronto were big-boned, amiable blonde Canucks who hadn't even bothered coming through the gate but had merely stepped over the low-dividing wall in their matching purple Polo shirts and beige chinos before passing over their younger daughter Amy, a frisky six-year-old. As for Denise, she was yet to make an entrance but here she was now, coming through the gate, loping barefoot across the grass until she stood in front of Jake and Adam, hands on hips, dressed in a pair of denim shorts and a sweatshirt that announced she was 'Cute But Crazy', the ragged hem of which she had obviously cut off by herself to reveal her taut midriff.

'Who's gonna sneak me a beer then?'

It was a hot Cornish afternoon and Jake wandered around the garden in a kind of a daze, the heat, the alcohol, the smell of charred meat, the proximity of Denise creating a sort of dreamy, soft-focus effect to the day. Rob and Trish, Mitch and Jennifer – two couples bonding by virtue of their common ages and Commonwealth ties – stretched out on deckchairs on the small patio area at the front of the house, drinking beers, talking sport, politics and travel while they watched Amy splashing about in the paddling pool. Jake went over to the barbeque, piled a plastic plate high with grilled bovine and piscine flesh alongside baked potatoes and heaps of coleslaw. Denise and Adam came over to do the same. Lips became greasy. Fingers were licked. More cans of beer were nicked. It was good that Adam was there, Jake thought, it meant he could act more natural, restrain himself from behaving like a panting puppy. There was Sixties music blaring out from a cassette player and impromptu dancing from the adults, the two couples having switched partners to show off their moves. Adam's father Rob brought out bottles of spirits on a tray from which Jake surreptitiously served himself a double vodka shot and he was sure he could smell dope being smoked somewhere. His head was spinning, he drifted in and out of Denise's company, lost sight of her for a while when she went to play with her sister and then she ambled back to him with another can sneaked from the cooler. He loved that whole loose-limbed, easy-going, cute but crazy way of hers. He lost sight of her again, needed the toilet and made his way upstairs. It was on the top landing that he bumped into Adam also on the way to the bathroom. Behind him, the bedroom door was slightly open and Jake could see Denise sitting up on the bed, her T-shirt discarded to reveal a purple bra which Jake's mind bizarrely linked to her parents' similarly coloured Polo-shirts as if they were all part of a matching family set. A long, tanned leg stretched out from under the sheet and kicked the door closed.

Even as a darkness enclosed around his heart dousing forever the innocence of his teenage lust, Jake found himself giving his friend the thumbs-up sign.

Adam returned the gesture, grinning as he mouthed: 'Saved your life, mate.'

NOW

JAKE GAZED OUT AT A DAMP LONDON TOWN from the window of a black cab stuck in a jam somewhere between Victoria Station and the historic Moorgate building of their destination. The River Thames had already been crossed on one of its many bridges which was something of an achievement at this time of day and the direction of their hired chariot was now due east. He hardly recognised the London he had grown up in any more. It was all new and shiny, tall and expensive, populated by Arab princes, Russian oligarchs, bailed-out bankers, high-end escorts and reality TV stars. Throw into the mix, an extended family of royals, coachloads of gullible tourists, a parliament of useless administrators, a plethora of over-priced cinemas, up-themselves restaurants, seen-better-days Oxford Street stores, pavement stalls festooned with Union Jack tat, and that was the city centre in this new millennium. Thank God he had moved south of the river when it had still been affordable.

He took stock of his mood. Despite the rain continuing to drizzle on *Jake Tully Day*, the meter moving faster than the actual vehicle, the blood seeping through the bandages around his wounded finger, his jacket closed too tight over his stained shirt, he still felt remarkably calm, returned almost to that positive state he had been in earlier. The two codeine tablets had helped, as had another shot of whisky – purely for medicinal purposes, of course – before he had surrendered the flask to Francesca. He began to hum some random tune, his left leg started to move to his own beat. Francesca glanced over and frowned, a creasing of her brow that seemed all too common recently along with the raised eyebrow of disapproval. He fiddled with one of the buttons on the door until he could get the window to open slightly. The streets were busy, bodies passing beside and around the cab, everyone looking so young these days, the girls skinnier and prettier, the boys more lost and despairing. The only thing he envied about this present gener-ation was their youth. They could keep their lack of purchasing power, their twittering networks, their school psychologists, their burgeoning suicide rates, their social isolation, their gender fluidity, their loss of identity, their tablets, their vapers and their poor spelling.

His mobile rang. He twisted around so he could fetch it out of his trouser pocket. The name *Guy* was flashing on his screen with an urgency that only a call from his publisher could inspire. He looked across at Francesca. She was scrolling through messages on her own device. He answered. 'What's up, man?'

'You know what's up,' Guy said. 'Where the fuck are you?'

'Crawling along the Embankment.'

'Hopefully not on your hands and knees.' Guy chuckled at his own remark. 'I've got two broadsheets lined up waiting for you already. Then the BBC interview with Sylvia in the lion's den. Still to draw lots on that one.'

'What do you mean?'

'Running order not yet decided. We literally have to draw straws with the other shortlistees to see who goes in to face her first. Democratic process of the Broadcasting Corporation and all that. So better make sure you're here soon in case you're on first.'

'There's not a lot I can do. Traffic's bad.'

'You could get out and walk. Or run.' *Ping.*

'What was that?'

'Oh, I've got a new app. It lets me know when you have an online sale. *Ping.* There it goes again. Can't imagine what it will be like if you win.'

'You'll be *pinging* all over the fucking place.'

'Hopefully like a cash register. Is Francesca with you?'

'She wouldn't miss this for the world.'

'Well, give her my love.'

Jake waited a few polite seconds. Francesca hated Guy. 'She sends you the same,' he said, before tapping off.

He glanced sideways at Francesca. 'Guy. He's getting nervous.'

'I guessed.'

It was hard for him to tell from her tone if normal relations had been resumed after the sliced finger/whisky flask episode. He decided instead that it would be safer to engage with the driver of licensed taxi registered number 67692 as issued by the Transport for London, Public Carriage Office. A certain William Thoroughgood. Definitely a name to be trusted.

'What's the hold-up?' he called through the open glass partition.

The driver rolled his scarred neck from side to side then twisted his head back. 'Kids left over from the demo.'

'What demo's that?'

Jake saw William glance in his rear-view mirror, a look passing over his eyes that seemed to say *Where you been for the last few months, guv?* Totally caught up in the self-obsessed promotion of his literary career would have been his answer if William had cared to ask. 'Students,' the man grunted. 'Can't blame them really. Tuition fees are going to kill them.'

'Our generation certainly screwed them over,' Jake said, impressed with this charioteer's compassion for these young persons, especially as they were the cause of their current slow progress. William really was most thoroughly good.

'You got it right there,' William said. 'You'd think it would be the opposite. Here we are, the ones who got the benefit of a free university education...' He lifted his hands from the wheel of his stationary vehicle to make a gesture that seemed to include himself as a beneficiary of this largesse. Perhaps Jake had underestimated Mr Thoroughgood. Perhaps he was one of those people who were doctors or university professors in their real lives, driving a cab the rest of the time to pay off an expensive divorce settlement or sexual harassment suit. Professor Thoroughgood was continuing: '... and rather than think – oh, what a fantastic privilege that was, let's make sure our own little brats can enjoy the same. What do we do? We vote in a bunch of ungrateful baby boomers that tells the next generation to fuck off and pay for their own learning, if you'll excuse my language, madam, but I do get worked up by such injustices.'

Francesca looked up from some frantic texting. 'What?'

'We were just talking about the student demo,' Jake explained. 'Against the tuition fees.'

'We know all about that, don't we?'

'We do?'

'Well, I don't know where Oliver's going to find the money to pay for his education except from us. Unless we want him stuck with a mountain of debt all his life.'

'Yeah,' Jake said, having forgotten that he actually had a son these days. Oliver had decided to take a gap year after leaving school, gone off to hang out with his twelve hundred and sixteen Facebook friends in a squat in some deprived east London borough destined to be turned into an upmarket hipster paradise while they organised a new political party for under-25-year-olds called *Youth for Truth*. He hadn't heard from him for weeks.

'What did I tell you,' William said, putting the cab into first gear and shunting a few yards forward. 'Chickens coming home to roost for you too.'

Jake felt slightly chastened by that comment, especially as he was not a supporter of said government of ungrateful baby boomers responsible for bringing in tuition fees. Although dressed in a dinner suit in the late afternoon, albeit with a blood-stained shirt tucked underneath, might set himself up as one. He looked out at the rain again, youthful bodies still brushing against the side of their vehicle. He was surprised when Francesca took hold of his arm.

'There's something you should know,' she said.

'Yes?'

'Your father…'

'My father?'

'Albert knew all about watching your ceremony on TV.'

'What do you mean?'

'I saw he had marked it off on the Radio Times. Big red pen circle.'

'The two-faced old sod.'

'You know what he's like. He's a lot less forgetful than he lets on.' Francesca moved in closer, a tactic Jake knew was meant to disarm him from whatever she intended to say next. He couldn't remember the last time she had been so affectionate towards him. 'There's something else I know.'

'What's that?'

'The contents of your speech.'

Jake felt his bandaged finger start to throb again. 'You hacked into my laptop?'

'I most certainly did not. I saw the print-out on my dressing table.'

'You invaded my privacy.'

'Oh really? Don't you think that on some level by leaving it out like that, you…' William Thoroughgood leaned back and with a practised flick slid the glass partition shut. '… you meant for me to see it.'

'Just because you got an ordinary degree in psychology from

the University of St Andrews doesn't mean you can go all Sigmund Freud on me.'

'Come on, Jake.'

He moved away from her, sat up straighter, folded his arms, didn't respond. It felt good to have the moral high ground against Francesca for once. Such were the benefits of it being *Jake Tully Day*. The vehicle staggered forward again. He watched the green digits of the meter tick over. This could be an expensive silence.

Francesca let out a deep sigh. Her mobile phone beeped for an incoming message. She looked down at her screen, ignored it.

'You're not going to make that speech,' she said eventually.

'Don't worry yourself. I'm not going to win.'

'You keep saying that. But you've had a smug look on your face all day that makes me think that you think differently.'

He had no answer for that. He started to hum again.

'Jake? The speech? This whole Decca List thing. Do you have to?'

'Have to what?'

'Name names.'

'That's the whole fucking point. If I don't, those bastards won't think it's them. The names are crucial.'

'But couldn't you leave your venom for some newspaper interview further down the line? You're supposed to accept these prizes gracefully.'

'I'm sorry but I don't want to be like one of those actors who gets shafted throughout their entire career. Yet if you shove a golden statuette in their greedy little hands, they forget all the sexual and psychological abuse, the humiliation and rejection, and go on to spout a frothy "I love you all" speech to the very people who abused, humiliated and rejected them.'

'I don't know what's happened to you? When did you become so… I don't know, vengeful.'

'I'm not vengeful. I forgive. I just don't forget, that's all.'

'It'll ruin your career. Just when things are going so well for you.'

'At least I'll go down fighting.'

'Suit yourself. But I want no part of it.'

'I'm not asking you to be.'

'Don't expect me to be all smiling and dutiful then. If you win this thing, I'll be off to the loo by the time you reach the stage.' Her phone began to thrum. Her ringtone was Phil Collins' *In the Air Tonight*. She had always loved that drumming gorilla. She looked down at the screen, then picked up.

'Yes, darling. How have you been?' She turned to Jake and mouthed: *Oliver*.

He mouthed back. *Surprise fucking surprise*.

Francesca's voice suddenly moved up an octave as she spoke into the phone. 'What? When did this happen? Oh, for God's sake. Yes, of course. Where are you? Yes, yes, yes. No problem. Holborn. We're in a taxi now as it happens. Yes. As soon as possible.'

'What was that all about?' Jake asked.

'Oliver's been arrested.'

THEN

AS SOON AS HE COULD, JAKE LEFT HOME, set off to study English and Politics at St Andrews, as far away from Albert Tully's grim orbit as his slightly better than average A-level results could propel him. As for Adam, he stayed in London to study computer science at Imperial College at a time when no-one else knew what computer science was. Despite their divergent paths, the two remained friends. The incident with Denise was never discussed, Jake preferring to bury it deep in a vault that also contained the memories of his dead mother along with other slights, rejections and humiliations he had accumulated in his formative years – psychological scars that would no doubt express themselves unfavourably in his future intimate relationships.

St Andrews suited Jake. An ancient place with stone towers and Gothic arches standing resilient against the bitter winds off the North Sea. For it was a time to be resilient too. Chinese students were protesting in Tiananmen Square, the Berlin Wall was about to come down, South Africa was beginning to turn its back on apartheid. And here in Thatcher's Britain, Scotland had become the testing ground for the introduction of the Prime Minister's detested poll tax. Taking up a mantle his father would have been proud of, Jake found an outlet for the anger he always seemed to carry with him. He protested, he demonstrated, he wrote letters to the newspapers. In his spare time, he volunteered to work at a shelter for the homeless, tending to the needs of those cast adrift by what he considered to be the heartlessness of Thatcherite policies. He was determined, he was focused, he knew what he was fighting against – he just wasn't sure what he was fighting for.

He rarely attended lectures, he smoked too much tobacco and weed, he eschewed mullet hairstyles and designer stubble, he wore his hair long and lank, he paid little attention to fashion so that jeans, dark trainers, T-shirts and tweed sports jackets were his usual attire. Apart from his political campaigning, he tried to write. Poetry, short stories, first chapters, articles for the student rag, nothing substantial, nothing satisfying, nothing accomplished, he tended to channel his literary frustrations into his protest against the Tory government.

It was at St Andrews that Jake met Francesca, at a party in his own flat hosted by his room-mate Martin. He would often recount their meeting as being love at first sight (at least on his part), although being quite stoned at the time might also have contributed to his heightened emotional sensitivity. He certainly didn't expect to be enamoured by this tall, slender, elegant, dark-haired beauty who appeared at his doorway draped in a deep blue, knee-length pinafore dress over a turquoise cashmere sweater. He didn't want to marvel at her expensive snake-print boots, or be dazzled by her fake pearl earrings. And when she sat down on the sofa, and he leaned over to pour her a glass of wine, he didn't want to have an overwhelming desire to kiss the bare skin of her neck exposed by the brush-up of her hair. She was so different from him. Her accent, her manner, her grace, her poise, her clothes, her class. Her very *bourgeois-ness*. She summed up everything that he preached and fought against. Was he fiercely attracted to her because of it? Was this the perverse buzz that came from wanting to sleep with the enemy? And did she feel the same way too? Surely she must. How could such chemistry exist in a vacuum? Her effect upon him was overwhelming. He was shaking, he was perspiring, he was doing all that he could to prevent himself from spilling the wine as he poured. Having achieved that delicate task, he replaced the bottle on the dining table, and picked up a can of proletarian lager for himself. He watched on as Francesca sipped her wine, flicked over the pages of the student mag which lay on the coffee table in front of her. He was tempted to direct her to his article on homelessness which lay within the publication, but decided to let modesty prevail. She crossed her legs, the hem of her dress rising slightly on her bare thigh, as she let a foot booted in snakeskin bob away to the music on the stereo. A space beside her beckoned. He hovered then sat down beside her. He felt that the air was electrically charged. Yet she seemed immune to all this energy flashing between them. Was he imagining this? Were his body and his instincts betraying him, playing games with him. Was all this erotic fascination just a marijuana high? Was this just another immature Denise-like obsession that was going to end badly? She drew her attention away from the magazine, turned towards him and asked:

'Are you stoned?'

'What?'

'You heard me.'

Jake held up his hands in mock surrender. 'Just a little toke before the party started. How can I say? An aperitif.'

'Well then?'

'Well what?'

'Don't you think we should be on equal footing?'

Jake nodded his approval at this unexpected turn of events. 'I think that can be arranged.' He extracted from his jacket pocket an old tobacco tin with the flag of Ethiopia hand-painted on the lid. He had a half-smoked joint inside which he placed between the splayed fingers of her held-out hand. Such long, delicate digits, the skin tanned even though it was winter in eastern Scotland. He passed over a cigarette lighter and watched as she lit up. She drew on the joint between her rouged lips, inhaled deeply, stifled a cough, and as she exhaled, she returned the joint to him. He drew in a final toke for himself, feeling in his heightened state that his own lips sucking on the now red-stained filter was akin to kissing her.

'So who are you?' she asked.

'Jake. Martin's flatmate,' he stammered as he tried to recover from the shared intimacy of their joint smoking.

'I know that, silly. I meant… oh, I don't know what I meant…I'm sorry, I'm not very good at this… I'll try something simpler… What are you studying?'

Up until that point, Jake had been intimidated by Francesca's beauty and her poise. But in those few words, a gap of vulnerability and insecurity had opened up into which he felt he could pour his affection, his lust, his love. An opening into which he could pour himself. 'English and Politics,' he told her.

'So… what are you trying to be?'

'What do you mean?'

'Do you want to go into politics? Or do you want to teach?'

'Actually, I would like to write.'

'Political commentary?'

'Fiction preferably.'

She took a sip of wine, peered at him over the rim of the glass. 'I like creative men,' she said dreamily.

He scrunched the remnants of the joint into a hubcap that served as an ashtray. Some kind of test had been passed. But sadly, there was to be no relief.

'What do you want to write about?'

'What do I want to write about? Yes, what *do* I want to write about?' He held out his hands to the room, to the universe, to the infinite extent of life itself. 'We are living in turbulent times. I want to write within the context of that.'

'The definitive *fin de siècle* novel?'

'Yeah. That.'

'I think you need to be a bit more specific.'

He wasn't sure if he could, given his present state of stoned-ness. 'I want to write about injustice,' he ventured. 'And suffering.'

'Have you ever suffered?'

At least, he had a decent answer to that question. 'I lost my mother when I was six.'

'Does she ever come up in your writing?'

'Not yet.'

'She will.'

'That's very assuredly prescient of you.'

'Isn't that what motivates all creative people? Trying to find a vehicle in which to express their loss.'

'That's quite a profound statement.'

She laughed. 'Grass has that effect on me.'

'Is that what you try to do? Find a vehicle to express some kind of loss.'

'I'm not particularly creative. But my father died a couple of years back.'

'I'm sorry to hear that.'

'Don't be. I hated the bastard.'

Her venom surprised him. He wanted to take a swig of his beer, but the can in his hand felt inappropriate to the delicacy of the conversation. Eventually, he ventured. 'And you? Who are you?'

She laughed again, raised her glass to her lips. 'I have absolutely no fucking idea.'

Which as Jake would later find out was not true. Francesca knew exactly who she was and what she wanted. She was a woman of impeccable taste with a keen eye for design. She was taking a double major in fine arts and psychology with a view to becoming an interior designer with an insight into the minds of her clients. Beauty, aesthetics and self-examination were as important to her as they were as unimportant to him. And for some unexplained reason, she seemed to like him. Did opposites truly attract? This yin-yang explanation reflected Jake's own assessment of their relationship in that he believed he added some harsher edges to Francesca's existence while she softened his, that his strengths complemented her weaknesses and vice versa. But in reality, they were both quite similar, striving to fill in the gap left by an absent parent of the opposite sex, until they both found themselves merging into a comfortable mush of bourgeois apathy and smugness as they entered into a decade when the apathy, avarice and smugness of the middle-class was something to be celebrated. And paradoxically, the very aspiration that had initially inspired Francesca to be attracted to Jake – his desire to be a writer – ended up being quashed, along with his anger, by the cosiness of their relationship. *Le Petit Prince* had indeed been tamed by the fox. Or had it been the other way around?

That distant memory of his childhood book *The Little Prince* entered Jake's head right now. Perhaps because he was in France. Or perhaps because he was watching his wife. France. Francesca. The mind and memory. Such wonderful tricks they play on each other. The day was warm, the light blindingly Mediterranean. He was just a little bit stoned. As was his old friend Adam, sitting beside him. The two of them pleasantly exhausted from a morning surfing down at a nearby break known locally as *Le Sail Fish*. Francesca was returning now from her own trip to the beach with their son, Oliver. Beside her, Adam's wife Tina, and their son, Patrick. The two sun-dark boys were slapping each other lightly, laughing, playing a secret game whose rules were known only to them. Francesca was also laughing. Her skin was glowing from the sun. She was wearing a bikini, the lower half semi-obscured by a chequered cheese-cloth wrap. Her feet were bare and sandy. Their villa was in the second row back from the beach, the first row of houses being reserved for the super-rich of which Jake was definitely not one. But he was feeling rather smug about the location here in Cap-Ferret and the reasonably low price paid because he had rented slightly off-season in late September. Yet the weather had turned out to be fabulously mid-summery, the waves not too gnarly but consistent enough for ancient and unfit surfing bums like himself and Adam, and not so dangerous that the kids couldn't frolic about with their bodyboards. So here he was with a slight buzz on, admiring his wife, thinking that while Tina was definitely very attractive, he believed his very own Francesca possessed the edge in the beauty stakes. But then again, he and Adam had always been competitive with each other. If Jake were to be entirely honest with himself – a journey of self-examination he rarely entered into these days, except perhaps when he was stoned – that was always how he had measured the index of his life, his happiness, his success. Against Adam.

'Look at you two,' Francesca called out. 'Lazing on a sunny afternoon. You were supposed to be taking care of the barbecue. While we were taking care of the kids.'

'That's because I'm totally lost without you,' Jake retorted.

'Well, get your arse into gear,' Tina said because she was American and liked to show off her Anglicisation by eschewing the word *ass*. She kicked Adam's outstretched legs off a chair, rousing him from his cannabis-induced stupor.

'What the…?' Adam uttered from under his pulled-down sun hat.

Jake laughed. Then Francesca was near, he could smell her coconut sun cream, her fingers as they brushed his shoulder. All was well in the Tully household, he thought.

'I'm going for a shower,' she said. 'Then I expect great things to have taken shape out here.'

Jake raised his hand in acknowledgement of his assignment then drifted back into his reverie. Yes, Francesca had tamed him, shaped him until here he was at thirty-something feeling terribly satisfied with himself. Who wouldn't be in this lovely holiday villa in the south of France? With his healthy son, his beautiful wife, his best friend, his best friend's wife, and their healthy son. And with the money to pay his share without it feeling like too much of a drain on his resources. Although most of the expense was being covered by Francesca's salary rather than his own. But that wasn't his fault if Sunday and daily newspapers, even those as widely read and prestigious as his employers, didn't pay their columnist as well as they should. Even if what he wrote was a load of crap. He couldn't believe it really. A lifestyle column three times a week in the dailies and a full page in the Sunday colour supplement. So many hundred words basically on how he spent the day as a house-husband. He could compose one of his pieces right now. *I lay on my hammock at my rented (one row back from the) beach house in the south of France and let my wife take care of our son because she felt guilty about having such a demanding job that took her away from spending time with him during the rest of the year thereby leaving said house-husband i.e. me – to surf, to smoke a joint, drink some local plonk at four Euros a bottle, eat oysters by the bucket-load because they're as common as polystyrene pots of whelks on a Weymouth quayside in this part of the world, and basically think about nothing except his own childhood memories of another louche maverick in search of the meaning of life i.e. Le Petit Prince. Thereby bringing said sentence to a neat conclusion by starting in France and finishing in French. Voila!* All with accompanying cartoon drawing of the family in question by the in-house artist, the house-husband being represented as a rather raffish if somewhat flustered chap, the wife as a sleek, pointy-faced, office-type in tailored suit (an image which Francesca hated) and the young son not that different from the golden-haired, scarf-wearing innocent that was the little prince (an image which Oliver loved). *One becomes responsible for what you have tamed.*

Jake felt himself tipped out of his reverie and his hammock by the manual efforts of his showered and perfumed wife. Fortunately, the fall was not too great and the landing not too hard on a sandy lawn earlier softened by the operation of the irrigation sprinklers. Francesca and Tina and the young boys were laughing. He brushed himself off and sat down with them at the large outside dining table.

'Where's Adam?' he asked.

'Off to get something,' Tina said. 'Big secret.'

Adam returned with a bottle of champagne in one hand, four flute glasses bunched together in another. 'Celebration,' he shouted. The young boys cheered in unison. Jake looked over at Francesca who just shrugged back at him.

Adam set out the glasses, thumbed off the cork with a rather muted explosion which the boys cheered anyway and began to pour.

'What's up?' Jake asked. 'Promotion?'

'Patience, my friend,' Adam said excitedly as he went round the table, even tipping a few splashes into the plastic beakers of the children. 'Wait until I've poured.'

It was Tina who made the announcement. 'I'm going out on my own,' she said.

With the sun directly behind her head, Jake had to screw up his eyes to look at her. He wasn't sure what she meant. Was she leaving Adam?

'Oh, that's great,' Francesca said. 'Very brave of you.'

'What are you talking about?' Jake asked.

'I'm leaving the agency,' Tina said. 'Starting up my own firm.'

Jake pondered this information. Tina was an agent at one of London's biggest literary outfits. She had originally started out in their New York office but transferred to the UK after getting together with Adam.

'Yes, that is rather brave of you,' he said. 'Will clients go with you?'

'Not sure. Some I can't steal because it is in my contract. Restrictive covenant and all that. Others have said they'll come but in the end they won't. But anyway, I already have my first client.' Tina sipped her champagne, she looked all blown-up ready to burst.

'Who?' Jake asked.

'This one here.'

'Who?' Jake asked again.

'Adam.'

'Adam? This Adam? Your Adam?'

'Yes, my Adam.'

'Adam is writing a book?'

'Adam has written a book.'

'When the fuck has Adam had the time or the skill to write a book? He's a fucking computer programmer.'

'Perhaps I should say something here,' Adam said. 'First of all, Jake. As you well know, I'm the chief technology officer for a global IT company.' A fact Jake always chose to ignore, Adam having leveraged his early interest in computer science into a highly lucrative job while Jake had done what? 'Secondly, I have a lot of free time on the road. And in the air. I had some ideas. I started to write them down.'

'It's a good book,' Tina added.

Jake poured himself another glass of champagne. 'What kind of book?'

'A crime novel.'

'You never mentioned it before.'

Adam shrugged. 'I was a bit embarrassed really. You were the one who was always the writer among us.'

'Are you allowed to do that sort of thing?' Jake asked. 'Husband and wife as writer and agent. Isn't that a conflict of interest?'

'A cooperation of interest,' Tina countered.

'That sounds very corporate American of you.'

'You should have been my first client, Jake,' Tina said. 'But I got fed up waiting around for the one great novel you promised me. Adam just got in with the goods first.'

Jake felt himself squirm slightly. 'I need to experience life first before I can write about it.'

'Is that what you're doing now?' Adam scoffed. 'Indulging in life's great experiences? Writing all that lifestyle crap about nothing.'

'Now, Adam,' Francesca said soothingly. 'No need to get personal here.'

'Really, Fran. I can just tell from that sneering look of his what he's thinking.'

'There's nothing wrong with crime fiction,' Tina said. 'If it's well written. Which Adam's book is. There's a lot of interest in the genre these days.'

'What? Have you got him a deal already?'

'Let's just say there is a lot of interest.'

Jake fumbled for the champagne bottle but it was empty. Francesca moved across, poured him a glass of red from an earlier unfinished bottle.

'Well, maybe Adam's venture will give you a little encouragement, darling,' she said, patting his forearm.

Jake lifted his glass, tilted it towards his friend. 'I wish you fame and fortune and *mucho successo*,' he said with as much grace as he could muster.

NOW

ACCORDING TO SOME APP OR OTHER on Francesca's phone, Jake was informed it was exactly 0.9 miles from where they were stranded in the taxi to Holborn Police Station. By taking the Tube, they could get there in 22 minutes, if they walked at an average speed they could make it in 20 minutes, if they walked quickly they could make it in 18. They decided on the fast walk option even though it was still raining (albeit lightly), they had no umbrella, Francesca was wearing a long dress and heels, and he was feeling less than energetic due to his overall lack of fitness along with his intake of whisky and medicinal drugs. He paid off the taxi driver and they stepped out into a throng of students being herded down the Strand towards Charing Cross Station.

'This is typical of Oliver,' Jake said. 'We don't hear from him for weeks. And now this. Today of all days.'

'For God's sake,' Francesca said as she swung her shawl above her head to keep off the drizzle. 'Don't make everything out to be about you. Our son's been arrested.'

'I was just making an observation of fact. Did he at least say what he's been done for?'

'He only said it wasn't his fault.'

'I suppose it was police brutality then.'

'Can we just concentrate on trying to get there?'

By the time they had made it across the wave of soon-to-be-se-riously-in-debt teenagers into Covent Garden, the rain started to come down more heavily. Where were these bloody plastic umbrella sellers when you needed one? Jake thought. He was also quite seriously out of breath. He couldn't remember the last time he had done any fast walking or any exercise for that matter. What had happened to those halcyon days when he was the toned surfer with the lung capacity of a blue whale? Disappeared for ever in the blink of thirty years. Francesca was slightly further up ahead, consulting her phone to give her the quickest route to their destination, while demonstrating that her expensive gym membership had finally paid off. The rain suddenly exploded into one of those downpours that merited the definition '*the heavens opened up.*' He called out to her to come back which she did reluctantly. They ended up taking temporary shelter under the striped awning of a very expensive retail clothing outlet with a huge display window but with very little on display. Jake was just about to point out the inherent smugness of a store too up itself to even deign to promote its wares when they were joined by several other members of the public with the same desire for refuge.

'I think we should go on,' Francesca said.

'This rain'll be over in a couple of minutes,' he said, casting a glance upwards to the murky sky. 'I wouldn't worry about Oliver. He's not going anywhere.'

Francesca gave him one of her looks. 'I'll text Nick,' she said, already punching out letters on her keypad.

'About my dress shirt?'

'No, not about your dress shirt. I'm going to tell him to meet us at the police station.'

'Criminal law isn't his thing. He's more corporate.'

'He's still a fucking lawyer. I'm sure he'll know something. Or he can get hold of someone who'll help. Unless you have any better ideas?'

Jake said nothing. He knew that when Francesca started swearing, silence was the best tactic. He smiled apologetically at the seven other captured pedestrians standing under the same awning, went about brushing raindrops from his dinner suit with his non-bandaged hand.

'We know you.'

Jake turned round to locate the source of the comment. A reedy young man, perhaps in his early thirties, lank hair, thick glasses, pale skin, jeans and tweed jacket, an outfit not that remote from Jake's own attire as a student several decades previously. Jake pegged him as a junior lecturer at some university recently promoted from technical college, teaching computer programming or something more obscure like medieval poetry. The 'we' of his comment referred to his companion, an Asian woman, perhaps a colleague or his student or his girlfriend or wife, age indeterminate, always so hard to tell with women of that continent. Was that a racist thought? So difficult to know these days. 'I don't think you do,' Jake replied.

'Most definitely,' he said. 'One of those literary festivals. Hay, Chichester, something in London.'

'Oh, I see. You know me professionally not personally.' It felt good to be recognised in front of this small audience of bystanders. That could be another batch of sales right there. *Ping, ping, ping,* Guy.

'We were right then,' the man said, turning to his companion who simply nodded. He addressed Jake again. 'Which was it?'

'Which what?'

'Festival.'

'How would I know? It was certainly not Hay or Chichester. Something in London, I'd guess. I rarely venture outside the city.'

'That's possible. We did go to a lot of events here recently. And you are …? Let me see.' The man tapped his head lightly with his fist, no doubt in an attempt to dislodge the information buried there along with the specks of dandruff that fell to his

43

shoulders. 'Jack Scully. That's it. Jack Scully.' He turned again to his companion who again just nodded.

'Jake Tully actually,' Jake corrected.

'Oops, sorry. Silly me.' Then, addressing his companion again, a petite woman who appeared to be dressed to play tennis. 'Mary. Photo.' Back to Jake: 'You don't mind, do you?'

Before Jake could decide if he did mind, the young man had already invaded his personal space by moving dandruff-ridden shoulder to shoulder while Mary honed in on them both with her phone camera.

'Thank you,' the man said once Mary had finished.

'Happy to oblige a fan,' Jake said grudgingly.

'Actually, we're not fans. We didn't like your book at all. What was it called again… ?'

'Well, if you can't recall either my name or the title of the book, I doubt you remember you didn't like it.'

'Oh, we definitely didn't like it.' Again the man looked to his companion for confirmation.

'Absolutely not our cup of tea at all,' Mary confirmed in her first venture into what was becoming a rather terse exchange. The conversation was attracting even more attention from all the other huddled persons under the awning, including Francesca who had ceased her texting and was looking at him anxiously.

'What do you mean?' Jake asked. 'Not your cup of tea?'

'Exactly that,' said tennis-playing Mary. 'Brian and I don't usually read that kind of book. How do you call it? Literary fiction.'

'Sci-fi is our thing,' Brian added.

'Well, what can I say? I'm sorry you didn't find it to your liking.'

'We only gave it a one-star review on Amazon and Goodreads.'

'Are you telling me you marked me down on a review, not because it wasn't any good, but because it wasn't what you normally read?'

'Exactly,' confirmed Brian.

'That's a pretty stupid thing to do.'

'Jake…' Francesca said, with a tug at his arm. 'We really should be going. The rain's stopping.'

Brian swept a wave of hair off his forehead. 'Are you calling me stupid?'

'Yeah,' Jake said.

'I'll have you know that I'm a university lecturer.'

'Certainly not in English literature,' Jake replied, quietly pleased that he had summed up his critic rightly from the off. 'You're like a vegetarian ordering meat at a restaurant by mistake, then complaining you didn't enjoy it.'

'I thought the book was pretentious.'

'And I think you're an idiot.' With his uninjured hand, he gave Brian a push to his chest, a little harder than he might have wished. The man stumbled backwards, tripped over someone's foot, then fell to the ground in front of Mary.

'Let's go now,' Jake said, grabbing Francesca's arm. Brian must have lost his glasses as he fell, for Jake felt his foot crunch down on a pair as he walked off. He didn't bother looking back. According to Francesca's app, it would only take them fifteen minutes to Holborn Police Station. That is if they walked quickly which was something he was most definitely going to do.

THEN

JAKE'S LIFE RESUMED ITS USUAL HUMDRUM ROUTINE after they all returned from the holiday in the south of France. Oliver went back to school, while Francesca was involved in fitting out the various branches of a well-known French fashion store investing heavily in London. As for Tina, her plan to set up her own literary agency went quiet, while Adam's novel – as novels tend to do – entered the black hole of publishers' rejections and disappeared from the consciousness of their little group. Situation normal in Jake's eyes. Which was perfectly fine as far as he was concerned. He didn't need any great excitement to inspire ideas for the writing of his lifestyle column. His editor only seemed interested in the everyday events of his life, and the everyday events of a house-husband were what she got, even though in reality Oliver was no longer the four-year-old child of the original column but five years older and in no need of a resident father watching over him during the day.

I took my son to the supermarket this morning, plonking him in the front of my trolley as I wheeled up and down the aisles. We even got into some father-son bonding where I pointed to what I wanted and he with great glee pulled the item down from the shelf. I smiled happily at other women, their own children ensconced similarly in their trolleys, as they passed me by. I could tell from their expressions that they approved of a man engaging with his son in this way, probably wondering why their own husbands weren't able to do the same. I had to admit to a feeling of contentment, perhaps even a certain smugness. Shopping, family, female approval. All was right in the world. Until Oliver started screaming that is.

Now as any parent reading this will know, a child's tantrum in a supermarket is the worst of a guardian's nightmares, akin only to a similar crying spree within the confines of an airplane cabin, or at a wedding or a funeral. The childless onlooker will glower at this aural invasion into their private self-centred space while another parent, rather than being the sympathetic ally, will turn out to be as judgemental and disapproving as a member of the Spanish Inquisition. This judging and disapproving will be even more enhanced if the parent of the offending child happens to be a man rather than a woman. The assumption in that case is that the father has in some way caused the child great pain, either through verbal or physical abuse. As a result, the otherwise disinterested shopper turns into a self-righteous informer with the consequence that after only a mere five minutes of Oliver's endless screaming despite many attempts at bribes from handy confectionery shelves, I am confronted with two members of London's finest metropolitan constabulary along with said informer – a harassed mother of her own two undisciplined young children – pointing her finger in my direction along with the accusation: 'That's him, officers. I saw him hit the child.'

The officers in question consisted of one large male of our species, breathing heavily no doubt from running to the scene of alleged paternal brutality. The other officer was a young, rather attractive blonde woman who seemed to have foregone the obvious career paths her looks may have helped promote, in favour of maintaining law and order while wearing what appeared to be a trilby hat trimmed with the familiar black and white chequered livery of our boys (should I say girls?) in blue. Both officers boasted bright yellow-green visibility jackets.

'Is that true?' the male officer asked.

'Is what true?'

'That you hit your child?'

'It depends on what you mean by hit?'

'Common assault where no injury has been sustained. Or actual bodily harm.'

'I did not assault my son,' I responded with the same conviction as a US president accused of sexual philandering.

'I would like PC Cameron to examine the child.'

'And what if I should not allow her permission to do so.'

'Then you will be preventing an officer of the law from carrying out her duties.'

I should point out that Oliver was still bawling his head off during this discussion, a distraction which seemed to find no sympathy from my accuser, the police officers or the rather large crowd of customers who had assembled around us. Above my head, CCTV cameras trained themselves in unison on what was unfolding before their lenses. PC Cameron crouched down until she was face to face with Oliver. 'Hello,' she said sweetly. 'Would you mind if I had a look at your arms?'

Oliver's response was to punch her so hard in the face that she actually fell over from the force of the blow, her flailing limbs dislodging a large bottle of Mrs Elswood's Pickled Cucumbers (other brands are available) from a nearby shelf on to the foot of my accuser, the previously mentioned mother of two children (also screaming at this point, I may add). All this kerfuffle had the miraculous effect of turning Oliver's crying binge into one of great mirth.

Now, dear reader, you are probably wondering what was the outcome of this rather amusing incident. Well, fortunately, the law of this land is such that a four-year-old child is incapable of being charged with common assault or causing actual bodily harm to a police officer, so no arrests were made. However, an ambulance had to be called to attend to the broken toe of the mother of the undisciplined children (still crying), the female police officer was left with slight bruising around her left eye while I was able to continue my shopping with a quiet and contented child riding shotgun, all allegations of child brutality forgotten in the fray.
[800 words exactly: money for old rope: result!]

The next day Jake was summoned to the office of the editor for the Sunday supplement, Estelle Robertson.

'Are you serious about this article, Jake?' she asked, furiously chewing on a tablet of nicotine gum, a habit recently adopted to substitute for the furious sucking of forty cigarettes a day.

'What do you mean?'

'Well, among other things you seem to be condoning assault on a police officer, vengeful retribution on a concerned bystander and the punishment of a four-year-old. Not to mention just a hint of sexism.'

'It's just fiction, Estelle.'

It was her turn to ask what he meant.

'I just make this stuff up,' he explained.

'I thought you were relating the true-life events of a house-husband and his toddler. That's the whole point of your fucking column. And for letting you work part-time from home.'

'Five years ago perhaps. But hadn't it occurred to you that Oliver has grown up since then?'

Estelle shook another nicotine tablet out of its box, popped it into her mouth while plucking out the already chewed one and dropping it into a bin by the side of her desk. 'I thought this was a second child.'

'I'm not going to have two children called Oliver.' He laughed when he said this but Estelle did not appear to be amused. She vigorously scratched at the side of her chin, making Jake consider that perhaps irritable dry skin was one of the side-effects of the gum.

'So your column is just bullshit stories?' she said.

Deep down, Jake felt that it would be hard to disagree but he had to defend his corner, protect his job, draw the wagons round his salary. 'Not exactly. I'm kind of recycling stories that may have actually happened with me and Oliver in the past, even though they are not happening now. So technically they are kind of true.'

'So did you kind of hit your child in the supermarket, Jake?'

'It was only a kind of slap on the back of the hand.'

Estelle looked at him steadily as if to assess the truth of what he had stated. 'I don't believe in hitting a child as a method of discipline,' she said curtly.

Jake tried to recall Estelle's own domestic situation. Divorced, two young boys, nanny during the working week, children running amok with guilty mother over the weekend. No wonder she was on forty a day, gum or cigarette, what was the difference?

'I believe reasonable force is necessary sometimes.'

'Well, I disagree strongly. It sets a bad example to the child that can lead to he or she hitting others. Or even worse, they become bullies. Set limits, reward with love and physical attention, punish by ignoring bad behaviour. There you have it, Jake. A simple recipe for good parenting. You should try putting that in your column.'

Jake mumbled some kind of agreement. It was bad enough having Estelle editing his column without her having to edit his life as well.

'That'll do for now,' she said. 'You've had your warning. Don't let it happen again.'

'Don't let what happen again?'

'Sending out the wrong message to our readers. We have moral standards to uphold. I'm pulling this piece, so you'd better hurry along and write another.'

As Jake left Estelle's office suitably chastened, he felt he could do with a cigarette himself, although he had given up five years previously and now the mere whiff of tobacco smoke made him feel nauseous. He returned to his own office, one of the few actually enclosed spaces in the building, the rest of the floor being laid out as open plan under garish neon strip-lighting in a bid to make a bunch of selfish, narcissistic, back-stabbing, lying, cheating, harassed hacks believe they were all part of one happy journalistic family. The only reason for him managing to secure the use of an actual office was because he only came in two days a week, the rest of the time the room remained empty as some kind of vacuous shrine to the post of deputy editor which no longer existed. And because of longevity, five years on the paper for Jake while all those around him had been culled, removed from the premises by force, disappeared into alcoholic or drug-induced oblivion or in one case even hastened to death. He pulled down the blinds of the interior glass walls to this cell (there was no outer window at all), he paced the small area of coffee-stained carpet. He had no idea what he could write as a substitute column. Perhaps he could just recycle one from a few years back. Certainly, no-one on the staff would notice. Readers of his earlier pieces would have moved on to different sections of the supplement as their own children had grown. Perhaps he should just chuck it all in. Perhaps this was the moment when he said 'Enough' to writing all this crap. Although he wasn't sure how Francesca would take to losing his monthly income while he toiled away at his great novel. The phone rang. Francesca. No doubt picking up telepathically this economic threat to her current standard of living.

'How's your day?' she asked.

'Pretty shit actually.'

'Oh. Want to talk about it?'

'Naw. What's up at your end?'

'I just spoke to Tina.'

'How's her brave attempt at being a literary agent getting on?'

'Pretty well by the sound of it.'

'Why? What's happened?'

'I thought I better tell you first. Get you mentally and psycho-logically prepared.'

'Just tell me, Fran.'

'She got Adam a deal.'

'Well done them. Crime really does pay.'

'So it would seem. Quite a lot actually.'

'How much?'

'She wouldn't say exactly. Well over six figures in the US. Foreign rights and translations picked up all over the place. They're going out to celebrate tonight. Tina wants to know if we'll join them. Their treat. What do you say?'

Jake put down the phone, opened the door to the main floor. 'Can I bum a cigarette off anyone?' he shouted.

For no other reason than pure masochism or perhaps it was even sadism – Jake at this point wasn't sure which, to hurt or want to be hurt were such overlapping emotions – he agreed to go out for dinner that evening to celebrate Adam's new book deal. But first, he had to very quickly write a substitute lifestyle article for the one Estelle had rejected. In the midst of all his anger towards her, he actually found it very easy to compose.

In the daily life of a house-husband, I find myself having to deal with a constant barrage of questions of varying degrees of difficulty from my young son, Oliver.

'Why can't dogs speak words?'

'Where is my lunch?'

'What keeps the sky up in the air?'

'What is water?'

'Why do I hate peas?'

'What happens if everything just stops?'

'Why are you shouting at me?'

'Why are you shouting at Mummy?'

'Can you explain the theory of relativity? (only joking about that one)

And then the real toughie.

'What do you do, Daddy?'

'I look after you, Oliver,' I reply.

'So why are you writing then?'

'I am actually writing about this conversation we are having now.'

'Is that a job?'

'Yes, it is.'

'Well, that's stupid.'

'Yes, you are right. It is stupid.'

'Why do you do it then?'

'That's a good question.'

Satisfied, Oliver chuckles to himself, then wanders off to play among his trucks.

'Why do I do it then? Why do I write this vapid lifestyle column?' Mainly because the money is good for the minimum amount of effort required. It also amazes me that people like you seem to want to read the rubbish I write. I think that is what depresses me the most. That somehow we have evolved as a society to the point where you are interested in this shit appearing in your glossy supplement every weekend, three times in your daily. Not just this shit but also associated feature articles that I commission as well as my replies to your banal letters. There is also similar shit from my colleagues. Vacuous narrations of London life as experienced by a trust fund baby. The weekly tribulations of owning a shop in rural Dorset selling only cupcakes. Reviews of seven-star holiday destinations you can never afford. So it's not only what the fuck happened to me? What the fuck happened to you? Where is your revolutionary fervour? Your ambitions? Your passion for change, for politics, for art? Your desire for quality journalism that really matters?

Every time I think my job is going to go in the next round of culls, I am stupefied to be told that survey upon survey among our readership ranks my contribution to the magazine in the higher percentiles of approval. So thanks to you, I am allowed to continue to ramble on about my fictitious four-year-old son Oliver – well, he is not fictitious in that I do have a son called Oliver – it is just that he is no longer four years old but nine – wasting my talent when what I really should be doing is writing that novel I told my wife Francesca (yes, I do actually have a wife called Francesca although she looks nothing like her caricature that *accompanies this article) from the day I first met her that I was going to write. It was what really impressed her. I always wanted to go out with a novelist, she told me just before she led me into the bedroom. Even I, dear reader, shall cease to describe what happened next.*

So why don't I do it then? Well, for a start, I have been tamed. Life has picked me up from the shelf and made me too comfortable. I have a successful wife, we have a fine son, we own an over-valued, semi-detached Victorian dwelling in south London, we have two cars, we don't worry about bills, we go on wonderful holidays, we shop at Waitrose, we will probably vote Labour in the next general election (even though as a supposedly apolitical columnist I'm not allowed to say this). What more do I want from life?

I want to write a novel. But I am fearful that I lack the talent, the discipline, the confidence, but most of all I am frightened I have nothing to write about. Oh yes, I have a lot of ideas, I have notebooks full of them, but there is nothing original in them. Write what you know is the mantra of creative writing teachers. Another is that everyone has a novel in them (but if the truth be known most are absolutely crap). So the potential writer of a great novel needs to live, he (or she) needs to experience more about life than just some middle-class suburban existence, he needs to go deeper and darker into himself, he needs to challenge himself, and he also needs to feel confident that once he has emerged from all of this down-in-the-dirt experience, he actually possesses the ability to write about it. He also needs to stop writing this stupid lifestyle column for people who have nothing better to do than to read stupid lifestyle columns. So, fuck off, Estelle, with your silly moral standards. I'm off. [800 words exactly. Result!]

Jake left a print-out of the article on Estelle's desk as he passed her office. She had already gone home, no doubt to an action-packed evening with two overactive young boys determined to take advantage of their hard-pressed, over-worked, too-tired-to-care, mother.

The recently-opened restaurant buried somewhere in the borough of Southwark was an enormous, critically well-reviewed space that occupied the ground floor of a refurbished print works, the remaining upper floors converted into expensive flats for up-and-coming city traders wanting easy access to the financial district without having to pay central London prices for the privilege. The windows were tall and heavily latticed, and another mezzanine floor level of dining space could easily have been accommodated half-way up the walls and still patrons would have felt they were in an expansive room. The brickwork remained untreated from its original state, heating pipes and ventilation shafts were left exposed, the tables were made from thick slabs of unvarnished wood, the serving staff entered and exited through swing doors covered with burnished metal riveted into place with shipbuilding precision. No fabric or soft furnishings, no colours beyond black, grey and white. Francesca called the design industrial chic. One reviewer gushed that New York warehouse vogue had finally invaded London town. Tina had been here once with clients and declared the food to be awesome. Adam had just returned bleary-eyed from a business trip to Shanghai and probably couldn't care less where he was. Jake thought the vast echoing space to be overwhelmingly noisy although there was a certain buzz about the venue that would definitely have been exciting to a younger version of himself. They ordered a bottle of champagne, two bottles of Chilean red and various platters of cheeses, cold meats and smoked fish. Once the champagne had arrived, they clinked glasses and Jake along with Francesca toasted Tina and Adam's joint effort, he in the writing of his novel, she in the selling of it. It seemed that the various advances and sales of territory and translation rights were even greater than Francesca had first suggested to Jake over the phone, for Tina announced:

'We're thinking of moving now.'

'Where to?' Francesca asked.

Tina hesitated then admitted: 'North of the river this time.'

'Oh, how could you?' Francesca complained. In London terms, north of the river to Francesca might as well be another country, and not even one in Europe. 'We'll never see you.'

'Don't be ridiculous. Highgate isn't too far away.'

Jake whistled through his teeth. 'Highgate. Jesus Christ, Adam. How much did you get for that fucking book?'

'Tina has always preferred north London,' Adam answered coyly. 'She likes being higher up. She thinks the air is cleaner.'

Jake sat back, sipped on his champagne, let the conversation inevitably expand into discussions of the property market in general, probably echoing similar conversations going on all around him at other tables. He thought of the article he had left on Estelle's desk and wondered whether he should rescue it and his career before the morning. It was during such a musing that he realised Tina was speaking to him.

'I'd love to have you too,' she said.

'What are you talking about?' He wondered sometimes whether Tina deliberately chose to come out with these possible double-entendres as a surreptitious attempt to flirt with him.

'That great novel you're always promising to write.'

'Great novels take time to mature,' he said. 'They can't just get churned out on long-haul flights.'

'What's that supposed to mean?' Adam asked.

'You know what I mean.'

'Why don't you just say it? Instead of beating around the bush like you always do.'

'Alright, alright,' Jake said. 'I know I haven't read your book yet. I'm sure it's absolutely fucking brilliant in its own right. But in the end, it's just another piece of genre fiction. The same old, same old.'

'Please don't patronise me.'

'It's not real literature. That's all I'm saying.'

This time it was Tina's turn to chime in. 'And what in your lofty opinion would you classify as real literature, Jake?'

'Something that involves time, thought and craftsmanship. Something with substance and real ideas. But most of all it should possess universality. The ability to resonate with all readers irrespective of their gender, race, class, religion, nationality. Something that touches their deepest love or fear or loss or hope or insecurity.'

Adam began a slow hand-clap. 'Bravo, bravo, my elitist, pretentious friend. Quite a speech. And is this what your novel consists of? This universality. This great work of art that hasn't even been written yet.'

'I didn't say I was going to create a great work of art. I'm too old to do that.'

Both Tina and Adam laughed, in that joint way married couples often did. Jake looked to Francesca for support but she just raised an eyebrow at him.

'Too old, Jake?' Tina said. 'You're still in your thirties.'

'Only just. But still too old. Great works of art can only be produced by the young and fearless who are also blessed with innate talent and the uncanny ability to consciously challenge the milieu in which they operate. Basically, wet-behind-the-ears iconoclasts.'

'For example?' Tina asked.

'Mozart. The Beatles. Picasso. Brando. Kerouac. Ginsberg. Dylan. The list goes on.'

'Fair enough.' Tina conceded. 'So if not a great work of art. What are you going to give me?'

'I'm working on it.'

'Does it have a title?'

'Yes.'

'Well?'

'So what is it?'

'I can't tell you.'

'What do you mean? You can't tell me. Just spit it out.'

'In my experience, anyone whoever comes up to you and tells you they have a great title for a book, will never write it.'

'Do *you* know what it is?' Tina asked, turning to Fran.

Francesca shrugged. 'First I've heard about it.'

Tina was getting irritated now. Jake could see a red flush spreading out from under the collar of her blouse, around the base of her neck. He took another sip of champagne, he liked winding Tina up in this way. For some reason, he found it exciting.

'Can you at least tell me what this book with the fucking brilliant title is all about?' she asked.

'Oh, I'm sure it will be about love. In the end, all writing is about love. The pleasure of it. The lack of it. The responsibility of it. Or the pain of it.'

'Well, you better hurry up writing this *love*ly novel of yours,' Tina warned. 'Old whities are rapidly going out of style and favour.'

'Old whities?'

'Don't you know? The industry's all about writers from the colonies and beyond these days. Africa, India, Jamaica, Bangladesh. Publishers are just drooling over these tales of hardship and oppression with a bit of colonial spice thrown in. Tales of the white, middle-class oppressors are a bit passé. So you'd better come up with something good before the coloureds take over the cotton fields.'

Jake flinched at the remark and he was sure Francesca did too. He looked over to Adam but he seemed unconcerned by his wife's comment either not having heard or pretending that he hadn't. Jake knew from Adam that Tina came from a redneck farming family from the American Midwest who owned vast tracts of land in Iowa producing corn and soybeans. He was pretty sure her family's view of the American dream didn't chime too much with that of Martin Luther King's but he assumed Tina would have shaken off some of that racist talk after she snared a job in New York, then moved across here to London.

'Well, don't worry about me,' he said, deciding to ignore Tina's lack of political correctness. 'I'm going to be working at it full time now.' He regretted the words as soon as they had exited his mouth. Champagne did tend to make him more garrulous than he would have liked. He should have waited for the red wine which had a more morose and introspective effect on him.

Unsurprisingly, Francesca butted in. 'What do you mean by that?'

If Jake had believed in God, he would have thanked Him or Her there and then for two waiters miraculously arrived to save the day, their hands full of wooden platters. But Francesca had no intention of having this conversation rescued, by divine intervention or otherwise. 'Can you just give us a minute,' she commanded. The waiting staff stepped back, their offerings of food still raised aloft, not sure what to do next. Francesca persisted. 'Jake? What's going on?'

'I resigned my job. Well, not actually resigned. I've pretty much made sure I'm going to get sacked.'

'For fuck's sake, Jake. Why?'

'Like I just said. I want to work on my novel. You know it's what I always wanted.'

'Don't you think we should have talked about this first? Before you gave up the day job.'

'Fran,' Tina said, touching her friend's arm. 'Perhaps we should let them get on with serving.'

Francesca sighed, then waved her hand at the waiters. 'I'm sorry. Go ahead.'

Jake sensed a discernible silence settle on the table as all four of them watched with great intensity the placement of the platters. Until Adam asked: 'Are you really jacking in your job?'

'I guess so. It was just how today seemed to pan out.'

'Pan out?' Francesca shrieked, her voice echoing a little louder than perhaps even she anticipated inside this vast chamber. 'Pan fucking out?' she said more softly. 'I think a decision such as this needs a little bit more time, thought and craftsmanship, don't you think? What did you do to inspire such a situation of self-unemployment?'

Jake explained.

'Well, go back now to the office and retrieve your fucking article before Estelle gets to see it,' Francesca said. And then with a less harsh tone. 'I'm not saying you shouldn't put some more time aside to devote to writing. But could you not just do this with a little bit more forethought. As well as talking to me about it?'

Jake fetched up a slither of tuna from one of the platters with his chopsticks, popped it into his mouth. It was delicious. 'No,' he said. 'There's no going back. Decision made.'

Francesca placed her napkin on the table. 'I'm sorry,' she said to both Tina and Adam. 'This was supposed to be your big night out. But I can't stay.' She scraped back her chair and Jake watched her walk away, her heels tapping out their message of resentment across the vast industrial space as she went.

'Where's that fucking red wine when you need it?' he said. 'Let's celebrate.'

NOW

FROM THE OUTSIDE, Holborn Police Station consisted of a three-level podium of brutal concrete on top of which rested a further ten floors of windowed office space. Apart from a coat of arms declaring its authority, name and purpose on its grey walls along with a blue old-fashioned Metropolitan Police lamp that reminded Jake of the classic TV programme *Dixon of Dock Green*, the building was an unadorned, functional and impersonal structure that would not have been out of place among the concert halls of the South Bank – an observation Jake tried to share with Francesca who just ignored him. They went inside ready to announce their arrival and purpose of visit with all the breathlessness, over-politeness and discomfort of two normally law-abiding middle-class citizens unused to such locations. However, instead of some kind of open reception area hosted by a benign constable, they encountered a hallway with three separate counter sections sealed off and protected by floor-to-ceiling plate-glass with automatic doors controlled from the inside. Behind the glass, police officers patiently listened to complaints while filling in forms, glancing at screens. Signs on the wall instructed the public not to knock on the glass but to wait until called. From the state of an agitated group of Japanese students clustered in a corner, a distraught teenage girl holding a screaming baby, and a young man in a hoodie prowling the linoleum, that wait could be some time. Francesca sat down on a grey plastic chair with a view of one of the occupied sealed-off reception pods. Jake hung around in front of her. Both of them were still slightly sodden from the earlier rain.

'I guess the days are gone,' he remarked, 'when you could just roll up and speak to a friendly desk sergeant.'

Francesca stared ahead, said nothing.

'Looks like we'll be here for a while,' he said.

No response.

'I'll get us something to drink. You want something?'

Again no response.

He shrugged. He knew Francesca well enough to know when she had gone into concerned mother mode, no doubt blaming him for all that had happened. He retreated back outside and over the road to a newsagent he had spotted on the way in, purchased two cans of Coke – one Diet for Francesca, a full blast of caffeine and sugar for himself. He went back into the police station, handed Francesca her drink which she took without looking up at him, then used the liquid from his own can to swig down another codeine tablet. His injured finger was throbbing and painful, the bandage stained with dried blood. He looked like he was here to report an assault.

'There you are, there you are,' brother Nick called out as he burst through the entry doors, looking as immaculate as ever in his bespoke dinner suit, white silk scarf around his neck. Even the pacing young man in his hoodie stopped in his tracks.

Francesca stood up, immediately threw her arms around him as if it were the Messiah himself who had arrived in this God-forsaken place. 'Thank goodness, you're here,' she said.

Jake could see his brother's surprised look over Francesca's shoulder. Not being the hugging type – not even with his own wife – Nick tapped Francesca gently on the back, released himself from her grasp, held off her affection at arm's length. 'Came as fast as,' he said.

'Corporate lawyer to the rescue,' Jake found himself saying. He knew the remark was unkind in the circumstances but it was such an automatic reaction to years of fraternal tension, knight in shining armour Nick coming to save the day when he, Jake, could not. 'Thanks for showing up,' he added reluctantly.

Nick nodded, a weary acknowledgement long practised from many of Jake's previous escapades. 'Not really the evening I was expecting,' he said.

'None of us were,' Francesca said.

Nick went on. 'Managed to get hold of the duty officer on the phone on my way in. Tried to push things on a bit. Oliver should be with us shortly.' He sat down, careful to hitch up his trousers at the knees before he did so, beckoned Francesca to sit back down beside him. 'Now, tell me. What's been happening here?'

'We can't get to anyone behind the glass,' Francesca said. 'All we know is that Oliver was arrested about three hours ago at the student demo.'

'Yeah, got that too,' Nick said. 'Let's wait and see what the young man has to say for himself.' Nick patted Francesca's wrist in an awkward consoling gesture. 'He just turned eighteen, didn't he?'

'About three weeks ago.'

'You realise they won't let you see him then.'

'What?'

'You're only allowed in if he's a minor.'

'But we're his parents,' Francesca protested.

'He's an adult, Fran. He's old enough to deal with these matters on his own. So says police procedure.'

'What can we do?' Jake asked.

'Nothing but wait. I'll go in when they bring him up from the cells. Do what I can. If it's looking serious, I'll call Pete Marshall. He's our crime expert. You could go off to the ceremony. I'll call you straight away with any news.'

'We'll wait,' Francesca said firmly.

'Yeah, we'll stay,' Jake added, although he could feel his phone vibrating in his pocket, no doubt from all the 'where the fuck are you?' messages flooding in from Guy. 'Did you bring the shirt?'

Nick looked up to properly take in Jake's situation for the first time. 'Jesus Christ. What happened to you?'

'An unfortunate incident with a beer can and a sushi knife.' He unbuttoned his dinner jacket to reveal the blood-stained material. 'The shirt?'

Nick held up his hands to display their emptiness. 'Completely forgot.'

Jake was aware he should be understanding. After all, here was Nick called out to a family emergency, the picking up of a dress shirt probably the last thing on his mind. And yet, he knew how efficient his brother could be, even in high-pressure situations. 'No problem,' he managed by way of response. 'I'll manage without.'

Further along the corridor, the door to one of the interview rooms opened, a police officer looked out. 'Who's for the Tully lad?'

Nick stood, pressed Francesca's shoulder as he did so. 'I'm his representation.'

The officer smiled. 'No need to dress up.'

Jake sat down on the vacated chair, undid his bowtie so he could unbutton his collar. Francesca used one foot to prise off one of her shoes, then did the same with the other. The Japanese group had gone silent, as had the baby with teenage mother, the young man in the hoodie still prowled. Jake and Francesca stared in silence at the glass of the reception pods as if it were a giant TV set they were looking at. He was finding it hard to focus, all these pills he had taken, the images of the various figures both inside and outside the glass dissolving into some colourful blur.

He also felt quite detached from the situation, a sensation no doubt inspired by the medication. He had to keep reminding himself that his son – their son – was in police custody. Perhaps there would be a custodial sentence, perhaps Oliver's whole life would now be defined by what had just happened in the last few hours. A prison record, unable to study, unable to find work, a descent into drugs and alcohol. Jesus Christ, Jake thought. He just hoped the boy had done nothing serious. He looked at his watch. Five o'clock. So much for the interviews with the broadsheets. Guy would be going ballistic. He extracted his phone from his pocket. Yes, there he was. Eleven messages already from his publisher in increasing levels of desperation and exclamation marks.

'I should phone Guy,' Jake said.

'Do what you want.'

He snatched a sideways glance. Francesca was all lip-biting and finger-wringing, her usual façade of coolness crumbling before his eyes. He put his phone back in his pocket.

'It's all your fault,' she said.

'What? My fault? What did I do?'

'All those articles you wrote about him when he was a child. They had an effect.'

'He was four-years-old. What did he know about anything?'

'He was a lot older than that by the time you finished up. And he did know. You think all the parents didn't talk to their own children about what they read in the papers? And these children would tease Oliver.'

'What's wrong with that? Not every child has a cartoon figure of himself appearing in the dailies. Probably made him a bit of a celeb.'

'In a bad way.'

'What do you mean?'

'You made him famous for helping you take the piss out of authority. For sticking it to the man, as you used to say.'

'What are you saying? That I brainwashed him into being subversive?'

'Something like that.'

'We don't even know what he's done yet.' A piece of information he was just about to find out as the door to the interview room opened and Nick stepped out. Again Francesca was off her chair to greet him as some long lost saviour. 'Well?' she asked. 'Is he OK?'

'Yes, yes, he's fine. Just a bit shook up, that's all.'

'What's the charge?' Jake asked.

'We don't know yet.'

'Is that not illegal? *Habeas corpus* and all that.'

Nick gave him an exasperated look. 'They've got 24 hours to come up with something.'

'What did he do?' Francesca asked.

'According to Ollie's statement, he was at the demo, just shouting as you do at these things. Police picked him out.'

'Just like that? At random.'

'That's what the lad said.'

For shouting?'

'Ditto.'

'What happens next?' Francesca asked.

'If indeed that's all that happened, best case scenario they'll probably just hold him for a while – you know, to show who's boss, give him a bit of a scare. They'll check out his address, any previous convictions, then let him go.'

'And worst-case scenario?

'Hard to say. For just shouting. A fine. If he was thought to be provoking any threat of violence, that might escalate things a bit.'

'Did he say what he was shouting?' Jake asked.

'I believe his words were: *Fuck you, pigs.* Repeatedly.'

'See,' Francesca said, turning to Jake. 'All your fault.'

THEN

JAKE WAS QUITE DRUNK. Next to him in the back seat of the taxi, Tina was very drunk and next to her, Adam had passed out, probably more from jet-lag rather than the amount of alcohol consumed. Jake had been arguing with Tina about who should be dropped off first only for the driver to intervene:

'I'm not taking the big bloke last,' he said, referring to the comatose Adam. And then nodding to Jake. 'You can carry him.'

'That's settled then,' Tina slurred rather smugly.

The driver drew up outside Tina and Adam's terraced two-storey house on the slowly gentrifying fringes of Putney, took one look at the steep steps to the front door and insisted on payment.

'No way I'm hanging around until you drag that sack of potatoes to bed,' he said, and drove off into the night, leaving Adam draped from Jake's shoulder while Tina struggled to raise her husband's other arm around her own shoulder. As Jake twisted his neck away from the awkwardness of his load, he caught a glimpse of the clear sky and its spangled firmament.

'Jesus, Tina,' he said. 'Look at those stars.'

'I'm not looking anywhere,' Tina said, wrestling with her husband's arm along with an attempt to prise off one of her high-heeled shoes by hopping on one leg and bending her knee back on the other. 'I've got enough going on right where I am.'

'Just get the front door. I can deal with Adam.'

Jake hauled his friend along the short pathway while Tina hobbled ahead on one shoe, the other hooked around her fingers.

'Fuck,' she said as she slipped on a step.

'You OK?'

'Hunky-dory. Where are my fucking keys?"

'In your hand.'

'Right.'

Jake had Adam in a kind of half fireman's lift as he carried him up the steps towards the front door which Tina had miraculously managed to open.

'Where to?' he said.

'Dump him on the sofa.'

Jake did as he was told, perhaps with a bit more zeal than required. Adam let out a groan as his head bounced off the arm of the settee, before settling back down again to his unconscious state. Jake stretched, felt the ache in his arms, looked around. All this effort had left him feeling remarkably sober. Tina was standing in the doorway like some stork balanced on her one high-heeled shoe, a hand against the door jamb for support.

'Where's Patrick?' he asked of her young son.

'At the bitchy witch's,' she said, waving her free arm in the general direction of the borough of Clapham where her mother-in-law stayed. 'One for the road?'

'One what?'

Tina gave him a sloppy smile. 'What d'ya think?' She let her hand slip off the door jamb, turned her back, her head twisting round over her shoulder to him as she said: 'Follow me into my lair.'

Her lair was the high-end kitchen where Jake (after a piss stop in a blindingly white-tiled downstairs loo) found Tina situated behind an Italian marble-topped counter on which sat a solitary beechwood block hosting a set of precision-forged knives (recommended by Francesca). She was pouring herself a gin into a large tumbler. 'Beer in the fridge,' she mumbled. 'Unless you want one of these.'

Jake went over to stand beside her, placed a hand over hers. 'Don't you think you've had enough?'

'That's the fucking problem, Jakey boy. I don't get enough.'

She turned to face him, hands on hips. She had managed to kick off both her shoes now, stood about six inches shorter than he. Her brown eyes looked up at him full wide, smudge stains of mascara on the lower rims and Jake wondered whether she might have sneaked in a snort of coke somewhere between him planting Adam on the sofa and turning up here in the kitchen, Tina being a bit partial to the white stuff whenever she had the opportunity. She was wearing this fabulous red dress slit quite high on the thigh and low-cut enough to reveal the mounded tops of her tanned cleavage, Tina slightly more substantial than Francesca in that department. 'Yeah,' he said although he wasn't quite sure what he meant by saying that. All he knew was that there was some kind of energy flashing between them, that perfect storm when the drink (or coke) had loosened them up, Adam was unconscious on the sofa, Patrick was with his witch of a grandmother, and Francesca had gone home in a huff. Add into the equation the resentment at his friend's mega book deal, the reckless act of getting himself fired, the fact he had always found Tina attractive especially now in a dress whose colour seemed to be spelling out danger in an irresistible kind of way. 'Yeah,' he said.

And that was that. A minute or so previously he had been concerned about her alcohol consumption, and now here he was pushing hard into her body as she pushed back at his, lips touching lightly at first, little teasing jabs, then pulling back before suddenly her mouth was all over his, tongues beginning to search, a slight moan emanating from the back of her throat that made him harden instantly. He wriggled out of his jacket and she was clawing at his shirt and he was pulling down the straps of that fabulous red dress and he knew he shouldn't be doing this, and she would be thinking the same, yet this was what they were doing, tearing off each other's clothes, buttons flying, zips catching, he picked her up and placed her on the counter, he didn't really know why he had done that, probably because he had seen the male star in a porn video do the same, pushing up Tina's dress and struggling to drag down her tights as she patted her hands along the countertop until she found the beechwood block and extracted one of the knives.

'Cut them,' she commanded, handing over this prime example of German craftsmanship.

He slashed at the seat of her tights until they slit, pulled down her knickers over the ripped nylon, then burrowed his mouth into her. She gripped the counter with both hands, threw her head back, her breath coming in short bursts, her body shuddering as she pushed down on his head between her legs, and he was tasting her moistness as she shivered herself into an orgasm. He lifted his head and she quickly pushed him away. 'Jesus Christ,' she said. 'I'd forgotten what that feels like.'

She slid off the counter, her dress still bunched above her waist, turned round, bent over and wiggled her rump at him. 'Now you can fuck me.'

'Yeah,' Jake said again, unbuckling his belt and unzipping his pants.

And so he entered her from behind with a sexual intensity he knew had been so missing from his own marriage in recent years and could only assume it had been the same for Tina. He felt so engaged physically with what was happening yet at the same time, he felt detached too, watching himself behave like some kind of deranged animal as he pumped back and forth into her before pulling out and ejaculating all over her farm-fresh, corn-fed Iowan ass. He stumbled backwards from his efforts until he came up against a corner pillar, let himself slide downwards until he was sitting on the floor. Tina turned round, picked up her knickers, reached round behind to wipe herself clean.

'What was that all about?' he said.

'Oh, Jake. I think we know perfectly well what that was all about.'

It was Oliver who woke him.

'Daddy, Daddy, Daddy.'

'Wha… ?'

'Why are you sleeping there?'

'Wha… ?'

'On the sofa, silly.'

Jake opened his eyes. His entire vision, blurred as it was, was taken up by his son's face. Oliver's spiky blonde hair darkening with every passing year – a testament to Francesca's genes slowly gaining mastery over his own. Milky teeth, childhood gaps revealing unsoiled shrimp-pink gums. Innocent eyes hovering over his father's less than innocent body. 'Yeah,' Jake groaned. 'Sofa.' He closed his eyes again.

'In all your clothes.'

'Yeah, in all my clothes.' His head hurt, his eyes hurt, his groin hurt. Radio 4 burbling away in the kitchen. The phone ringing, ringing and ringing.

'You smell too,' Oliver declared.

He probably did smell. Of what, he didn't dare think. Why wasn't someone answering the phone. 'Where's Mummy?' he asked. But Oliver was gone. He pulled the blanket over his head. He didn't want to wake up. He didn't want light or noise to creep in. He didn't want thoughts to form in his head. He didn't want to know that his life had changed irrevocably. Without doubt for the worse. Thank God, the phone had stopped ringing.

Francesca's voice. Starting off in the kitchen, becoming louder as she approached.

'… suppose I'll have to take Oliver.'

He grunted.

'Still pissed. Jesus, Jake.'

Grunt.

'Ollie,' she shouted upstairs. 'Don't forget your lunch box.' Then back at him. 'Estelle's been ringing since eight.'

Grunt.

The sound of Oliver's feet thumping down the stairs.

Francesca again. 'Lunch box.'

Radio 4 still burbling. He could imagine Francesca's vexed expression, he could almost feel her pitiless glare through the wool of the blanket. The pain in his head was almost unbearable. He needed water. He needed medication. He needed to rewind his life and let yesterday begin again. A yesterday when he had a job, his wife had a faithful husband and Adam had a loyal friend. The phone started ringing again. Francesca in retreat out the front door, their young son following. The two of them ignorant of the sins of the man on the sofa.

'Estelle,' she called back. 'Sort it out. We'll talk later.'

The front door slammed. Miraculously, the phone stopped ringing at the same time. Francesca's car pulling away. Silence. He threw off the blanket, bolted for the downstairs loo, knelt down and vomited into the toilet bowl.

Exhausted, he pushed himself upwards, knocking over a rack of magazines in the process. His head throbbed as blood pumped itself violently into his brain from his retched stomach. He stumbled into the kitchen, turned off the radio, poured himself the remainder of the coffee which he used to sluice down a couple of aspirins. He returned to lie down on the sofa, one hand cupped over his eyes against the daylight.

Adultery. When as a boy he had first heard the word, he had no idea what it meant but had assumed – quite rightly for the most part – that it was an act that could only be committed by adults. When he became an adult himself – in those days the threshold was twenty-one while now it seemed every teenager was voting, drinking and having sex at fifteen – rather than metaphorically receive the key to the door, he was given an actual metal key. A larger-than-life representation forged at his father's anvil that looked as though it could open the door to a dungeon never mind the gateway to his adulthood. Perhaps that was the unspoken parental message from Albert Tully contained in the gift. That life was some kind of darkened cell you ended up being tossed into. But Jake didn't care back then, he was in love with Francesca, body and soul. Adultery could not have been further from his mind or his loins. Yet, here he was eighteen years later, having committed the said sin for the first time with his best friend's wife.

Adultery. He could try to rationalise it. He could try to be more French, less English. An *homme* should have both a *femme* and a *maîtresse*. Or he could be more sociological about the matter. After all, monogamy was only a social norm not some moral absolute. Unless you threw the Ten Commandments into the equation. If he lived in Utah or Saudi Arabia or Gabon, he might even be criticised for having just the one wife. But he was not prepared to grant himself any of these rationales. He let out a huge groan, the physical exhalation of his enormous guilt. He rubbed his temples as he mentally re-traced his steps back to Adam and Tina's kitchen.

After their frenzied copulation, Tina seemed quite matter-of-fact about the whole thing. She tidied up her clothing, returned the tight-slashing knife to its proper place in the beechwood block, picked up her glass of gin, ambled over to the fridge. Jake remained sitting on the floor, his jeans and underpants scrunched down on his thighs, his bare buttocks cold against the Italian porcelain matte-finished tiles (also sourced by Francesca), trying to find a way to close up his shirt now that two buttons had been ripped off.

'Don't you think we should talk?' he said.

Tina hummed away as she rearranged a mosaic of post-it notes into some hierarchy of importance known only to her.

'Tina?'

'Poor Jake. Feeling guilty?'

'I don't know how I feel.'

'Well, I feel like it's time for you to leave.'

'But…'

'Now.'

He stood up, sorted out his own clothing as best he could, stopped by Tina with the intention of kissing her, hugging her, just something to acknowledge what had passed between them. This ache to act considerately towards a woman with whom he had just been intimate. Tina made no effort to reciprocate, her attention still focused on the multi-coloured notes on the fridge door. 'Go, Jake. Just go.'

To do so, he had to creep back through the lounge, past the comatose Adam on the couch. Adam snoring away happily, ignorant of the treachery that had just taken place. Adam fattened with age, his schoolboy sporting physique destroyed by deskwork and expensive lunches, his face absent of any noticeable bone structure, reminding Jake a little bit of Orson Welles – handsome in a chubby kind of way. Was Adam really his best friend? Or merely his oldest friend? Had he mistakenly assumed that their years of shared time together – at school, out on the waves, on holidays, and here in south London – represented a friendship when in fact it was a deep-seated rivalry? Perhaps all male friendships were formed and sustained thus. He looked down on Adam's sleeping form, this man who had once saved him from drowning. This man who had cruelly stolen the object of his teenage lust without even a by-your-leave. He hated to admit it but rather than feel guilt, he finally felt a sense of triumph over his cuckolded companion. Tina was right. He knew exactly what this was all about.

Outside on the front step, he looked at his watch. It was just past three. His head was remarkably clear. He decided to walk home along the side streets rather than aim for the main road to pick up a taxi. He recalled feeling quite buoyant as he strode along, as if all life was focused down onto this point alone – the clear night, a vague smattering of stars so unusual for London, the cold air in his lungs, the satisfaction of having fulfilled his masculine function. He shut out any thoughts about the conse-quences of his actions, concentrated entirely on his physical condition and his present mood. In this manner, he skipped along the pavement towards his home.

The bedroom door was shut against him. There was no 'Do Not Disturb' sign hanging from the handle but there might as well have been such were Francesca's negative vibes – even as she slept – emanating from behind the door. He picked up a blanket from the linen cupboard in the upstairs hallway, went back downstairs and slept on the sofa.

The phone was ringing again. Fucking Estelle. Going ballistic no doubt. He tried not to think about his final column. He tried not to think about Tina either. Tina in her red dress slit up at the thigh. Tina's ripped tights. Tina's white buttocks wriggling their primal invitation to him. Christ, he was giving himself an erection. The phone was still ringing. He concluded that there was no better way to stifle his arousal than to answer the damn thing.

'Jake. Jake. Is that you?'

'Yeah, Estelle. You got me.'

'You sound like shit.'

'I feel like shit.'

'What do you think you're doing?'

'I wrote it all down for you.'

'Is it a raise you're after? Is that what this is all about?'

'I can't do this stupid job anymore.'

'Jake. By noon, I need a column written, letters answered, features commissioned. I'll put your behaviour down to a mid-life wobble.'

'You're not sacking me?'

'You'll get a written warning.'

'I don't want a warning. I'm resigning.'

'What does Francesca think about all of this?'

Jake felt the bile rise again in his stomach. Surely he wasn't going to be sick again. 'I've made up my mind.'

'You didn't answer, Jake.'

'About what?'

'Francesca. She's a sensible woman. Mortgage to pay. Two cars in the driveway. Young son. Probably wants another before it's too late. Do you really want to give up the day job? Does she want you to give up the day job?'

'Francesca and I will sort it out,' he said unconvincingly.

Estelle sighed. Jake rubbed at the ache in his temples. A pause in proceedings. He knew she was re-thinking her strategy.

'I'll tell you what,' she said. 'Take the day off. Make that two days off. We'll run a *Jake Tully is Unwell* header, pull up one of your earlier pieces. No-one will notice.'

'Don't you see, Estelle? That's the whole fucking point.'

'I don't see that as the whole fucking point. The whole fucking point is that I'm paying you decent money for doing fuck-all.'

'Why not get rid of me then?'

'You know why not. Our metrics show that readers love what you do. Which means our advertisers love you too. Believe me, I don't understand it either. But there you have it. The paper is struggling as it is without me getting rid of a popular item. Do yourself a favour, Jake, think this over. Talk to your wife. Then I'd like to see your skinny arse back here in forty-eight hours.'

She hung up.

Jake stared at the receiver. This decision about his job was of little interest to him right now. Perversely, all he wanted to do was call

Tina. What was he thinking? How stupid would that be? She had more or less thrown him out of her house as soon as their sexual encounter was over. He decided instead that what he needed was a proper breakfast to settle his stomach, to absorb any residual alcohol still swishing around his veins, to soak up his guilt. After all, at the very least, he had a day-off now to think things over, two days in fact. He moved back into the kitchen, stuck a frying pan on top of the Aga, threw on a chunk of butter, followed by some rashers of bacon, a couple of Cumberland sausages. Sorted.

After breakfast, he wandered upstairs, had a quick shower, then fell asleep for a couple of hours on the reclaimed marital bed. Awoken and reasonably refreshed, he decided to go for a run. His usual route should have taken him along the Thames path, passed the fringes of Kew Gardens then on until Richmond and back again. But while that was his intended direction, he found that his feet seemed to have a different destination in mind, drawing him away from the river, along suburban leafy avenues, passed flower shops, patisseries, pavement cafes and bijoux art galleries until he ended up in front of a familiar Victorian terraced house. He knew Adam would be away networking global computer systems or whatever it was that he did while Tina worked from home, her literary agency residing in a purpose-built office shed in the back garden. He walked round to the rear lane with its colourful array of recycling bins until he reached the relevant gate which thankfully was unlocked. The lights in the shed were on and he could see Tina through the glass, busy at her computer. He knocked on the office door.

'Come,' Tina yelled.

He walked in.

She didn't seem to be surprised by his presence even though he was not the person expected. 'I thought you were the mailman,' she said.

'Do you mind?' Jake said, grabbing a chair.

'Go ahead,' she said, swivelling round to face him. 'There's coffee if you want some.' Her hair was pulled back, black-rimmed spectacles perched on her nose. She was wearing a pair of baggy tracksuit bottoms with a well-worn grey New York Yankees sweatshirt, short enough to reveal a rim of stomach flesh. Not exactly a sexy outfit but Jake felt himself stir.

'I'll stick with water.' He took a swig from the plastic bottle he carried with him when he ran.

'You look good in shorts,' she said.

'I try to keep in shape.'

'I wish Adam would do the same. He was quite fit when I married him.'

'Too many business lunches.'

'Too lazy more like it.'

'He did manage to write a book in his spare time,' Jake said, finding himself with a sudden need to defend his friend.

'I didn't mean in the writing department.' Tina leaned forward in her chair, hands on thighs. 'So what brought you here?'

'I thought we should talk.'

'That's sweet.'

'About last night.'

'You came, you saw, you conquered. Or should I say - you saw, you conquered, you came.'

'Very funny.'

'Feeling guilty?'

'It was just a one-off.'

'Whatever you say.'

'No-one else needs to know.'

'I'm not stupid.'

'I don't know what happened.'

'A mid-marriage crisis? A mid-life crisis?'

If it was a mid-life crisis for him, he wondered what it had been for her. 'That seems to be the common opinion about where my life is right now.'

'Are you still giving up the day job?'

'I'm not sure.'

'What's happened? Francesca pussy-whipping you into submission?'

'Fran does not pussy-whip me.'

'Really?'

'We just need to talk things over. That's what modern couples do.'

'What's the problem? Frightened to take a chance on your higher self? You used to be a decent writer before that stupid column took over. I remember when Adam and I first met, you were writing some pretty sharp cultural commentary back then. I'd still be interested in any novel you came up with.'

'I'll keep that in mind.'

'And we'll just forget about last night.'

'As if it never happened.'

Jake realised he too had been moving in closer to Tina as they talked. She swung in her chair, took off her glasses. She turned towards her desk, hit some kind of switch. There was a whirr behind him. The blinds were coming down. He listened as they descended, like a slow shutter on his marriage, on his life. Tina was taking off her top. Black lacy bra underneath. His erection was filling up his shorts.

'As if it never happened,' she repeated as she got down on her knees in front of him. 'And before you leave, you can take your invite to Adam's book launch. It'll save me posting it.'

Jake stopped at the fishmonger's on the way home. Fresh scallops to start, lemon sole for a mains, Häagan-Dazs *Dulce de Leche* from Waitrose to finish. A bottle of Pouilly-Fumé. All Francesca's favourites.

Jake was pleased to find that Francesca was in a surprisingly good mood when she arrived home that evening. Some big-shot client had commissioned her to come up with the interior designs for a major office block over at Canary Wharf and she was beaming. Oliver also seemed comfortably calm as they sat down for their evening meal.

'Hmmm. If I didn't know better, I'd think you were trying to seduce me,' she said, as Jake served her up a scoop of pan-fried scallops smothered with lime and coriander butter.

'Perhaps I am,' he said, pouring her a large glass of chilled Pouilly-Fumé.

'Not in front of the child.'

'I'm not a child,' Oliver protested as he dug into a bowl of spaghetti hoops. 'Are you sleeping on the sofa again tonight, Dad?'

'A wise child,' Francesca noted. 'Perhaps this conversation should go into one of your columns? That is if you're still writing one.'

'Let's leave all that until after dinner,' Jake said.

'Once you've softened me up with half a bottle of wine and some grilled sole?'

'That's the plan.'

'Well, you're not going to get off that easy.'

'Is Dad sleeping on the sofa again?' Oliver persisted.

'We'll see,' Francesca said, forking up the last of her scallops. 'We've had our invitation to Adam's book launch.'

'When is it?'

'Three weeks on Saturday. Clarendon House.'

'Not a bookshop then?'

'Some fancy-schmanzy private do, I guess.'

'That's what happens with these mega deals. Tina told me they've just exchanged contracts on their new house in Highgate.'

'When did you speak to her?'

'She called me earlier at work. Meanwhile, we could be living in a tent.'

Jake didn't take the bait. Instead, he went back into the kitchen to check on the lemon sole baking in the Aga.

Once Oliver was fed, washed, tucked-in and read to, Jake waited for Francesca to tiptoe downstairs to join him on the sofa. He had been pretending to watch the news but his mind had been all over the place as he tried to reconcile his afternoon of lust with the warmth and comfort he felt at being at home with his family. He kept zapping across the channels unable to settle. Flick, flick, flick. On the one hand, he felt remarkably fulfilled now that his sexual and familial needs were being satisfied. Only to remind himself that these needs were being met by two different women. Flick, flick, flick. And now here was Francesca – his wife, the mother of his child, his university sweetheart – wrapped up in her silk robe, skin-warm from her shower, drying off her hair with a towel as she came down the stairs. She didn't join him on the sofa as usual but took up her position on the armchair opposite. She twisted the towel turban-like around her head, picked up her unfinished glass of wine.

'So what did Estelle say?' she asked.

'She's given me forty-eight hours to think about it.'

'Not sacking you then?'

'She thinks you and I should talk things over.'

'A sensible woman. So what do you have to say for yourself?'

Jake flicked off the TV. 'I'd like to apologise. We should have talked first.'

'Hmm.' Francesca sipped on her wine. 'Apology provisionally accepted. And…?'

'I'm going to eat humble pie on this one. Beg Estelle for forgiveness, take my warning and continue as before.'

'Really? That's not the Jake Tully response I was expecting.'

'It wouldn't be fair to you. Making you take on the financial responsibility for all of this.' He waved a hand around the room to indicate the middle-class comfort in which they were enveloped. He was starting to feel a lot better now that his gesture of self-sacrifice was beginning to corrode his guilt. 'Not fair at all.'

'Well, I've been re-thinking things too.'

'Meaning?'

She waved a finger at him. 'I'm still pissed off with you for not talking to me first. But… I'm prepared to fund us so that you can take a year off to write this great novel of yours. You'd still be first in line for Ollie duty. But this new commission I've got should see us through.'

'That's very generous of you.'

'I don't want to see you having regrets for the rest of your life. And blaming me for them.'

'Not the Francesca response I was expecting.'

'Well, there you are. We continue to surprise each other. That's a good thing, don't you think?'

'Yeah, definitely. I don't know what to say.'

'I don't want you to say anything. I just want you to come over here… and seduce me.'

Jake moved off the couch towards her, his groin still drained and aching from his afternoon activities. 'Why don't you let me do all the work,' he said. 'You deserve it.'

NOW

'WHERE ARE YOU?' Giles screamed.

'I'm on my way,' Jake said.

'What's that supposed to mean?'

'I'm walking over from Holborn Police Station. Give me twenty minutes. Half-hour max.'

'Walking? Take a fucking cab for Christ sake.'

'It's rush hour. It's quicker this way.'

'You've got an interview with the Beeb in less than an hour. You must not miss that. I repeat. You must not miss that. All other media plans gone to fuck.'

'Come on, Giles. Sales are already through the roof. A few extra lines in the press aren't going to make much difference. I'm sure your sales app is *ping, ping, pinging* away as we speak.'

'The *pinging* is going just fine. It's you I'm worried about. How are things with Oliver?'

'Good of you to finally ask.'

'Come on, Jake. I've spent the last couple of hours fending off the media. Never mind the organisers. And the sponsors. There are contractual obligations to be met here. I'm covering your ass.'

'Well, since you asked, we don't know what's happening with Ollie. He's down in the nick. With my brother Nick. He's the lawyer in the family. Fran's there too. We're waiting to hear what he's been charged with. If anything.'

'What did he actually do?'

'Told some cops to fuck off.'

'Is that a criminal offence?'

'It appears so.'

'Whatever happened to freedom of speech?'

'It's a right that's being constantly eroded.'

'Well, I hope it works out OK for the lad. And you. Just be here in thirty, OK?'

'OK.'

'Promise?'

'Cross my heart. And just one more thing.'

'What's that?'

'Could you find me a dress shirt?'

'What's going on?'

'Too long a story. Just find me one.'

'How am I supposed to do that?'

'I'm sure you can get one of your minions to sort it out for me.'

Jake needed to stop. Somewhere between all that was going on at the police station with Fran and Ollie and the formalities and bullshit that awaited him at the ceremony, he needed a rest, a time to think. He needed a drink. He found a place in a quiet side street, an old-fashioned pub, the type that he didn't think existed anymore, at least not in central London. Half-light through dirty windows, unvarnished floorboards, nicotine-stained plasterwork even though smoking had been banned for years, not a TV or video-gaming machine in sight. Three old men sat at three separate tables, beer glasses at various stages of emptiness, staring ahead at nothing in particular. He hoisted himself up on to a bar stool. A young woman, far too attractive Jake thought to find herself working in a down-and-out place like this, sauntered over to him. He could imagine Fran pulling him up for that thought. 'So only ugly people are supposed to work in ugly places?' she would have challenged him with. And he would have found himself fumbling for a truthful reply that didn't land him in any more trouble.

'What would you like?' asked the barmaid whose fine features he now tried to ignore. Instead, he picked up on the Antipodean drawl, wasn't sure if it was Australian or New Zealand, decided not to comment. 'A double whisky,' he said.

'House blend do?'

'Yeah. I'm not fussy.'

She plunked a shot glass down on the counter, filled out his order in front of him. 'You OK?' she asked.

'What do you mean?'

'The hand.'

He glanced at his injured appendage, then past her to a mirrored space on the shelves between all the lined-up bottles of spirits. His wan face stared back with eyes bloodshot from the drink, the pills and lack of sleep. His collar was open, he tried to remember where he had put his bow-tie. 'Nothing serious.'

'It must have been a good party.'

'Meaning?'

'The penguin suit. The battle scars.'

He chuckled. 'The party hasn't happened yet. I'm on my way there now.'

She laughed. 'You might want to take it easy on the booze then.'

The comment irked him but he let it pass, put it down to the straight-talking culture of her particular continent. 'It's been a stressful day.'

'You want to talk about it?'

'What's this? A therapy session?'

She shrugged. 'Boredom. Not a lot happening here.'

'Well, there's a lot happening in my life.'

'Like what?'

'I'm sure to tell you.'

'That's what we bar staff are here for, didn't you know?'

'I feel like I've walked into a Charlie Bukowski novel,' he said, not expecting the cultural reference to resonate with one so young.

'You Henry Chinaski then?'

Jake held up his non-bandaged hand in appreciation of her literary knowledge. '*We don't even ask for happiness, just a little less pain.*'

'Good old Charlie.'

'He had a way with words.'

'Why don't you tell me what's causing you pain?'

He looked at her properly now. Red hair in a page boy cut, a nice little bow of a mouth, black cardigan, thin black velvet choker, her hands stretched out in front of her gripping the countertop, he was reminded of that painting by Manet, *The Bar at the Folies Bergère*. He surprised himself by making the observation out loud.

She laughed again. 'Yeah, I know the one you mean.'

He sipped on his whisky, a rough blend that burned him all the way down to his stomach. A sensation that reminded him he was terribly hungry. 'You do crisps here?'

''fraid not.'

'Peanuts.'

'Only liquid refreshment.'

'What was I saying again? Before the food requests and the girl at the Folies Bergère.'

'You were going to tell me your troubles.'

'Yeah,' he said as the whisky and the female attention began to work their magic on his tongue. 'I've got a little time I can kill.'

'And I'm listening.'

He told her about Ollie being arrested, about Fran blaming him for corrupting their child, about all the pressures of being shortlisted for a prestigious prize, about the fact he had an interview with the BBC in about forty minutes.

'So this prize? Is it like you're getting an Oscar or something?' she asked.

'An Oscar for writing, I suppose.'

'What did you write?'

He told her.

'Shit. You don't say? I loved that book.'

He tried to stop himself from looking smug. He glanced over again at the mirrored space and saw that he wasn't succeeding. 'Really? Not just saying that to make a miserable drunk happy?'

'I know it's going to sound weird, totally weird, but your words spoke for me. All my mates loved it too. God, they'll freak when I tell them I met you. Tully, right? Jake Tully.'

'The one and only.'

'Wow! This has never happened to me before.'

Jake was thinking that for a young woman of her age there was probably a lot in life that had never happened to her before. 'Perhaps I should have another drink to mark the occasion.'

She wagged a finger at him. 'I think, Mister Jake Tully, you should be on your way to pick up that award.'

'Short-listed. I've only been short-listed. But if I win, I'm going to give one of the best acceptance speeches anyone has ever heard. I'm going to… stick it to the man.'

'Sounds like you're angry and bitter.'

'I bear grudges. I'm not ashamed to say that.'

'Well, you're not going to be picking up any prizes with a bloody hand like that. Let me do something about the bandage.'

'You'd do that for me?'

'Sure can. We got a First Aid box right here. And I'm a trainee nurse when I'm not attending to the three wise men over there.'

She pottered around beneath the counter, then came round to his side with her kit and a basin of water. She even had a pair of disposable gloves. She unravelled his existing bandages, cleaned up his bloody cut, then fixed him up again with a fresh dressing, neater and tighter than before. As he watched her work, this stranger attending to his wound, wiping off the blood, moving his hand around in her own, he felt overwhelmed by a sense of… of what? Of being cared for. What a wonderful feeling that was. To be listened to. To have someone lift the troubles from your shoulders without judgement. He leaned forward and kissed the top of her forehead. It was a completely impromptu gesture, taking himself if not the poor young woman by surprise. There was nothing sexual in it. It was something deeper than that. It was an act of gratitude to make up for the ghost of a mother who had never been there for him when he needed her.

'I'm sorry,' he said. 'I didn't mean anything…too much alcohol … makes me maudlin. I apologise. Sorry, sorry, sorry.'

'No worries. No offence taken.'

'I can't thank you enough,' he said sincerely once she had finished. 'What can I do for you?'

'You can look after the counter for two minutes.'

While she was away, he could feel his mobile vibrating in his pocket. Giles, no doubt. He looked at his watch. He still had twenty minutes or so before he was due at his interview. He knocked back the rest of the whisky. The barmaid was back. She held a copy of his book.

'You just happened to have one handy?' he said.

'I live upstairs. I told you it was one of my favourites.' She handed him a pen. 'Go on, sign it.'

'Who shall I make it out to?'

'Alison. Your Australian nurse.'

He wrote her dedication with a flourish, kissed her flamboy-antly on each cheek, then left the pub ready to take on the world, Giles and the BBC. As he emerged out into the street, he half-punched the air with his newly bandaged arm. Yes, *Jake Tully Day* was definitely back on track.

THEN

CLARENDON HOUSE was a 17th-century townhouse available for private functions, situated in the elegant Albemarle back streets behind the Royal Academy and Burlington Arcade. To get there, Jake and Francesca had taken the Tube and were walking along Piccadilly past the Waterstones bookstore which had already dedicated one full window to *The Red Herring Murders* by debut author Adam Taylor. Jake would have been quite happy to skip past the frontage but Francesca pulled him back to admire the mountainous display.

'At least, they don't have a cardboard cut-out of him grinning out at us,' Jake observed.

'I believe they've got one inside.'

'Shit.'

'Only kidding.' Francesca took his arm and squeezed it. 'Have you at least finished his book?'

An advance copy had been sent to the house by Adam's publishers. 'I couldn't get past the first chapter,' Jake admitted.

'He's your best friend. You could make an effort.'

'It's just not the kind of thing I like to read.'

'Well, I think you're being terribly unfair. He writes really well. Engaging characters. Lots of twists and turns, keeps you interested right up until the last page. I'm not surprised the book's doing so well.'

'It's not even launched yet.'

'Tina says she's sold it to fifteen territories already. Lots of interest in the film rights. What are you going to tell him?'

'About what?'

'When he asks you what you thought about it?'

'Don't worry. I'll be nice.'

A couple of young women in black tailored-suits and over-eager demeanours awaited them at a table in the Clarendon House entrance hall, ticking off lists, handing out name badges while indeed a large cardboard cut-out of a smug-looking Adam holding up a copy of his book was also there to greet them. As for the real-life Adam, he was ensconced inside the function room itself, busily signing copies of his yet to be officially launched novel. Waiters wandered in and out of a crowd of about fifty people with platters of canapés, trays of orange juice and champagne. Jake grabbed a glass of the latter, strolled over to his friend who stood up mid-signing and shook his hand.

'Good to see you, my old amigo,' Adam said.

'Congratulations and all that.'

'Wasn't sure if you'd come. You know… I thought this might be beneath you.'

'Wouldn't miss it for the world.'

'Did you like the book?'

'Haven't had a chance to read the whole thing yet. But you write well, my friend. Engaging characters. Lots of twists and turns to hold my reading attention.'

'Thanks. That means a lot to me. This whole publishing thing's so bloody nerve-wracking. I should have stuck with computers. Much easier working with someone else's product.'

'You've given up the day job?'

'Yup. That makes two of us, doesn't it? Self-unemployed I call it. Has Tina spoken to you?'

'About what?'

'Dinner plans.'

'Nope.'

'No doubt she'll fill you in. I better get back to…'

'Yes, of course.'

Jake wandered back through the crowd, surprised at how few people he knew among this supposedly private function of Tina and Adam's friends and acquaintances. He noticed Tina waving him over from her stance by a Palladian pillar. He hadn't seen her since their 'rut in the hut' as she had called it. He picked up another glass of champagne on his way towards her.

'Hey,' she said.

'Hey to you.'

'Things OK?'

'Settling down nicely. And you?'

'Busy with all of this. Not much time for anything else really.'

'Crime really does pay.'

'So it would seem.' Tina sipped on her champagne. 'I spoke to Francesca. Adam and I would like the two of you to join us for dinner after this is over. Hope you don't mind being second choice but Adam's publisher and his wife had to cancel. Family crisis. It's a really nice restaurant. Close by.'

'You know me. Always up for some decent nosh.'

'There's also something else I'd like to show you.' She took him by the hand and led him off along a corridor away from the reception area, her heels clicking on the marble floors as they passed the grand library then up a white-stone spiral staircase, portraits of various notables marking their progress to the first landing.

'Look what I found,' she said, pushing open a thick oak door, switching on a light. 'Just for us.'

Jake followed Tina inside. It was some kind of private lounge with a small bar, a couple of sofas and a smattering of armchairs. She spun round in front of him, grabbed the fingers of his left hand and pushed them hard against her crotch. 'You've got ten minutes to make me come.'

The restaurant was situated within a hotel not far from Clarendon House. The dining room boasted an old-fashioned woody elegance with a modern twist thanks to the addition of some contemporary artwork along the walls. Their table was set in a corner giving them an element of privacy from the rest of the diners. Chairs upholstered in lime green and mauve – another modern touch. Adam was buzzing, his ego all pumped up and face florid from the launch. Tina and Francesca, both of them excited and slightly tipsy from too much champagne. Jake was quiet by contrast, still reeling from the quickie in the upstairs lounge over at Clarendon House. He was annoyed at himself. In the last three weeks, he had felt life had settled down after his episode with Tina in her back-garden office. He had handed in his notice but had supplied Estelle with enough copy to last her until she had found a replacement. For the sake of continuity the column would still go out under his by-line even though someone else would be writing it. *The Life and Times of a House Husband by Jake Tully* was a copyrighted title owned by the paper and as a result, his name would continue to have a journalistic career even though he himself no longer had one. He had also begun sketching out ideas for his novel, Francesca was happily busy with her new commission, they had even started to have sex again. He still loved Fran, of that he was in no doubt, and had put his previous two encounters with Tina down to a marital blip, something to get out of his system after eighteen years of marriage. He still felt guilty about what had happened but in the long run, the scratching of this particularly itch might even help towards the continuity of his relationship with Francesca until their dying days. Provided she didn't find out about it of course. But this evening's sudden relapse had shaken him, his body betraying all his previous convictions. He decided to blind himself to his failings by getting drunk. Several glasses of champagne at the launch and two large whiskies at the hotel bar before entering the restaurant.

'Have whatever you want,' Tina declared as Jake attempted to focus on the elaborate menu font detailing what was on offer. 'It's all on the publishers' dime.'

Jake decided to take advantage, going for eight oysters followed by a steak burger with half lobster. Accompanied by a side of buttered gourmet chipped potatoes sourced from a farm in Northumberland. 'Or what we ordinary punters call chips,' he slurred at the waiter in some mock south London accent. He then ordered another whisky while he was at it. He felt Francesca kick him under the table but he just shrugged back at her.

'Hey, Jake. Why don't you tell us about your new novel?' Adam asked cheerfully. 'The one with the secret title. The one that's all about love.'

'Yeah, Jake,' Tina said. 'The one that's all about love.'

Jake glanced over at Francesca who looked back at him expect- antly. 'It's all very embryonic at this stage,' he said, leaning over to extract a still-warm bread roll from a basket newly delivered to the centre of the table. He was starving. 'I'm just wondering what the best vehicle might be in which to insert the narrative.'

Adam went on. 'A vehicle for your narrative? That all sounds very literary. What are you talking about here? A bus? A tractor? A chauffeur-driven limousine?'

'Very funny.' Jake ripped the roll in two, smothered one half with butter, popped it into his mouth. Still chewing, he asked Adam: 'How about you? Another masterpiece in the works? Or is *The Red Herring Mysteries* a one-hit-wonder?'

'Murders. *The Red Herring Murders.* And yes, as it so happens there is a sequel in the works.'

'It was a two-book deal,' Tina piped in.

'Does that mean there will be a villa in the South of France as well as in Highgate?'

'Jake,' Francesca said, in that drawn-out tone that was meant to reel him in. 'Tell us about the new house, Tina.'

Jake let the conversation drift in to interior design talk. His whisky arrived, then his oysters, a combination he was starting to regret as the two items began to mix uneasily in his stomach. He was busily stuffing himself with another bread roll to soak up the combination when he heard his wife's raised voice penetrate his endeavours.

'Really, Tina,' Francesca said. 'I thought we were friends.'

'I just assumed you'd be fantastically busy,' Tina countered. 'With that Canary Wharf commission.'

Jake leaned over to Adam. 'What's all this about?' he asked.

'Tina's taken on someone else to do the interiors for the new house. I'd stay out of it if I were you.'

Jake decided to take his friend's advice as Francesca pressed on with Tina. 'I'd *always* make time for you,' she said.

Tina fiddled with her napkin. 'To be honest,' she said eventually. 'I'm not that sure you'd be a good fit.'

'What are you talking about? Part of the job of an interior designer is responding to the needs and the psyche of the client. And I know you better than anyone.'

'I've always found your taste to be a bit... a bit austere.'

'Jesus Christ! I'm sorry if I can't do American homey for you.'

Tina bit her lip. 'I would just like some colour. And patterns. I'm sorry if that's a bit maudlin for you.'

'What about a bit of loyalty to your friends?' Francesca said. 'How about throwing that into the maudlin mix.' She was getting a bit whiny now, Jake even in his increasingly drunken state could hear that.

'Loyalty?' Tina said, effortlessly shucking open an oyster with the special utensil supplied. 'I only really put up with you because of the Jake and Adam buddy-buddy thing. I always thought you were a bit stuck-up.'

'Where's all this coming from?' Francesca exclaimed.

'It's coming from the fact that I've been fucking your husband.' Tina tipped back her head as she let the ooze of shellfish slide down her throat.

'What did you say?'

'You heard.'

Francesca looked at Jake, mouth wide-open. Adam made some strange choking noise as he attempted to swallow a forkful of Atlantic prawns. Jake was still trying to understand what was going on.

'Is this true?' Fran exclaimed. 'The two of you...?'

Jake looked over to Tina who was smiling weirdly at him. He could feel the oyster/whisky mix gurgling in his belly along with all the acidic tension that was also being released. He gulped down the bile that had suddenly risen in his throat. He had no idea what to say. His emotional response to any kind of catastrophe was always delayed, a defence he had nurtured ever since he was told as a child that his mother had left and would never come back.

Francesca rose, threw her napkin down on to the table, like some kind of gauntlet challenging his fidelity, and for the second time in the last few months, she stormed off from a dinner with Tina and Adam.

Adam also stood up. 'How many years is it that you've been waiting to fuck me over? Fifteen? Twenty? You've never ever forgiven me for what's-her-name? That Canadian girl.'

'Denise.'

'Yeah, Denise. You know something, Jake? You just don't let go of stuff, do you? To think, I once saved your miserable life.'

'I think the statute of limitations ran out on that a long time ago.'

It was Adam's turn to throw down his napkin. 'Wait for me,' he called as he chased after Fran who was now at reception putting on her coat. 'I'm coming with you.'

Jake sat facing Tina. She was looking back at him as she wiped the oyster juice from her lips.

'That leaves just you and me then,' she said.

'You've gone and destroyed my marriage.'

'I think you need to take some of the blame for that.'

'What about *your* marriage?'

'Adam's being balling his secretary for the last two years. I don't think he's in a position to complain about anything.'

'And what about me?'

'Oh, I think that's a question you need to ask yourself.'

'What do you mean by that?'

'You've never really been one for much self-reflection, have you, Jake? It would be easy to say you just let your dick drag yourself into this. But no, you were fucking me to get one over on Adam. I always thought it was about his huge book deal. I'd no idea about this Denise, Denise thing. That's why you were such an easy lay. You two and your competitive buddy-buddy contest.'

* * *

Nick's office was seven floors up, off to the side of the building with a view to a similar glossy-glassy construction opposite. The offices of the more senior partners were situated at the front looking out over the concourse, the river and the London skyline. Jake had been shown in by Nicola, the young woman who had collected him from reception and introduced herself as his brother's paralegal whatever that was. Normally he would have attempted small talk, made some joke about needing to be called Nicola to work for brother Nicholas or something about para-chutes or Para-cetamol, but he wasn't in the mood. She had led him along a thick-carpeted corridor lined with leafy plants made of plastic, apologised for Nick's lateness, brought him in an exceptionally bitter coffee, then left him to wait.

Jake swivelled around in his chair, taking in the familiar trajectory of Nick's successful career and predictable life via the various certificates on the walls and the strategically placed scattering of photographs around the room. Young Nick as a member of the school rugby team, of the university rugby team, a Bronze and Silver Duke of Edinburgh Award for tutoring disadvantaged children in Lewisham, graduating LLB (Hons) from King's College London, a Master's Degree from McGill University in Montreal (when he thought he was going to marry his Canadian girlfriend Sandy whom Jake actually quite liked). Then back to London where he very quickly met and married Melanie – photo of their wedding day in a Richmond registry office suitably prominent, bride's slight bulge less so. Practising Certificate from the Law Society of England and Wales. A shelf of family pics with Melanie and their two children – Jake's nieces Jenny and Emily – at various stages of happy family with puppy-to-dog evolution and now both leggy teenagers still at school or starting university, Jake wasn't sure, he wasn't particularly close to the girls. The dog had since died. No photographs, Jake noted, including either himself with Nick or their father and mother.

'Sorry, sorry,' Nick said as he burst into his office. 'Would've have been nice to go out for lunch but too much on.'

Jake stood up to greet his brother, held out his hand, into which was thrust a brown paper bag.

'From the trolley,' Nick said. 'Prawn mayonnaise. Hope that works for you.'

Jake sat back down while Nick settled himself into his leather chair on the other side of the desk. Nick looking very blue with his bespoke midnight blue wool suit, too tight collar on his two-tone blue and white shirt, and silk sky-blue tie. Again, if Jake had been feeling in a more upbeat mood, he might have commented cruelly on his brother's cerulean display. Instead, he took a bite out of his prawn sandwich, washed it down with some cold coffee.

'I don't know why you didn't come to the house,' Nick said.

'That's because Melanie hates me. I've got enough female animosity directed towards me at the moment.'

'Mel doesn't hate you. She just doesn't like you very much. She's very fond of Fran, though I suppose that's not very helpful right now.'

'Not really.'

'I spoke to Dad.'

'What did he tell you?'

'Not very much. Just that you had come to stay.'

'Is that all?'

'You know what he's like.' Nick launched into a passable gruff imitation of their father, played out in a Yorkshire accent, even though the old man was born and bred in London: '*Not any of my bloody business.*You'd better tell me what's going on.'

'Fran's thrown me out.'

'I guessed that. What did you do this time?'

Jake swung nervously in his chair. 'I had an affair.'

Nick whistled. 'Jesus Christ. I didn't expect that.'

Jake told him about Tina. Then took another bite of wholemeal bread, prawn and too much mayonnaise while he let Nick absorb the details.

'You've really fucked up big-time, little brother. No job, no home, no wife, no best friend.'

'I don't need it explained to me.'

'What do you want me to do about it? Is Fran starting to go legal on this? You know I only do corporate these days.'

'We're a long way from that, I hope.'

'What's the current status then?'

'She doesn't want to talk to me. Doesn't want to see me. I know, I know, I've made a total mess of this. Until a few weeks ago, we'd been a happily married couple. Sure, the usual ups and downs but overall I thought we were doing OK. I just need to give her some space now. Let things calm down. I can see that. And I need to sort myself out.'

'With sex addiction therapy?'

'Not funny.'

'Staying on at Dad's then?'

'No way. I need to get away from all of this. Far away.'

'What? Like Australia?'

'Don't be ridiculous. I need to be around for Ollie. I don't want to put any stretches of water between myself and my son. Somewhere in the UK. Remote.'

'What about your morning cappuccino?'

'Fuck cappuccinos. It's nature that I need right now. Space. Peace. Time on my own. Time to reflect.'

'Anywhere in mind?'

'I wouldn't tell you anyway,' he said, even though he knew perfectly well where he was heading. 'I want to remain incognito and uncontactable. Invisible. A nobody.'

Nick swung around in his chair, began half-whistling some vague tune. Jake recognised this nervousness as a sign his brother was aware of exactly what was coming next. He decided to quickly put him out of his misery.

'I've no income and Fran's cleaned out the joint account.'

Nick still swinging, still half-whistling. 'What about plastic?'

'Anything with just my name on it is pretty much maxed out. Fran's taken the Beamer but I've still got our old Ford to run. Petrol, tax, insurance. Then all the day-to-day stuff. Rent maybe. Enough to keep me going for a couple of months.'

'How much do you want?'

'Six grand.'

Nick whistled through his teeth. 'Six grand for two months?'

'Three months then. Come on, Nick. That's peanuts for you. You probably spend that much every month on ...' Jake held up his sandwich. 'On lunch.'

Nick gave one of his smug smiles that seemed to indicate such a sum was not far from the truth.

Jake went on. 'Don't worry, I'll pay you back.'

'When you've written your best-seller?'

'That's the plan.'

Nick rolled his eyes. 'Are you sure escaping is the best way forward?'

'I've crossed a line. I know that. It's going to take a lot for me to get Fran to forgive me. But first I need to suffer. Then show her I've reformed.'

'You think you can solve all of this in three months?'

'That's what I'm hoping.'

'Six grand for three months far away from it all?'

'Yeah. A few weeks in the wilderness to achieve redemption.'

'I'll give you four. Write down your bank details and I'll send the money over. I'll expect full repayment by the end of the year.'

Jake tried not to smile. He'd only come begging for two.

With Nick's money cosy in his account, Jake called Fran's office, left a message with her PA that he was picking up Oliver. He then took the Tube over to his son's school, loitered by the gate, the only male among a crowd of chattering mothers. There were those among them who would normally speak to him, but no-one appeared to acknowledge him today. He was pretty sure Fran would not have made his affair public knowledge beyond her closest confidantes. Yet he still felt shunned as if he were carrying the scent of an unfaithful husband around with him, a spoor immediately detectable to the female olfactory system. He pretended to scroll through messages on his mobile while he waited. It was disheartening to find that now Fran was no longer in cellular contact with him, he hardly had any messages at all. He was therefore glad to have his social isolation relieved by his young son who actually seemed pleased to see him. Oliver even voluntarily took his hand as they walked back to his former marital home. The feeling of those trusting fingers clinging to his own was almost unbearable.

'You're back from your holidays,' his young son noted.

'Yes, I'm back from my holidays.'

'With Auntie Tina?'

'Mum told you that?'

Oliver seemed embarrassed. 'I heard her talking on the phone. About you going off with Auntie Tina.'

'No, I wasn't with Auntie Tina. But I'm going away on another holiday. By myself.'

'Why?'

'Because I need a rest.'

'But you have no job?'

'She told you that too?'

'Deffo.'

'Deffo?'

'Definitely, Dad. Keep up.'

'Yeah. OK. It's just that I'm tired.'

'How can you be tired if you're not working?'

'I just am.'

'How long are you going on holiday for?'

'I don't know. Two or three months.'

'Where are you going?'

'It's a secret.'

'Like a secret mission?'

'Yeah.'

'Like a spy?'

'Something like that.'

'Does Mum know?'

'No. It's a secret even from her. But don't worry. We'll still be in touch. I'll call you every day.'

'Even if it puts your life in danger?'

'Yeah. Even if it puts my life in danger.'

'I'll give you a special ringtone then. So I know it's you.'

'Good idea. Deffo.'

Jake stopped on the pavement outside his own gate. His house already felt hostile to him. After so many bleak years with his father after his mother's death, he had moved on to this lovely nest Francesca had created for them both. And now he had betrayed his home, a place he dearly loved. Oliver let go his hand, raced up the path to the front door, let himself in. 'Dad's back,' he shouted before he ran upstairs. Jake walked up to the open door. Fran was already lurking behind it.

'I told you not to pick him up,' she hissed through the gap. 'We don't want to see or talk to you. Go away.'

'I just need to get a few things.'

'What things?'

'Clothes and stuff.'

'Email me a list. We'll leave them in a box outside for you.'

'I need them now.'

'We don't want you in the house.'

'Will you please stop doing that.'

'What?'

'Saying "we" when you mean "I"'.

'We will not.'

'Dad's going on holiday again,' Oliver shouted from the top of the stairs.

'Is that true?' Fran asked.

'Can we talk about this?'

'No.'

'I need things to go away with.'

'You'll just need to buy them then.'

The door closed slowly on his face. He could hear Oliver's plaintive voice in the background. 'I wanted to say goodbye.'

Not to be outmanoeuvred, Jake walked down to the bottom of his street, then round to the lane that ran along behind his row of houses until he came to his own tall wooden gate at the rear of his garden. He tried the handle just in case but it was locked. Fortunately, it was rubbish collection day, his first bit of luck for ages, so there were a couple of solid green bins lined up outside, giving him enough of a height lift to get up and over the wall. He clambered up on top of one of them. But the lid wasn't as solid as he'd given it credit for, it crumpled under his weight and his left leg went right through into a mass of tins and plastic, the edge of an open can ripping right through his jeans and into his calf. He stifled his yell, pulled out his bleeding appendage and jumped back down to the ground to properly examine his wound. It wasn't as bad as he thought, the denim taking care of most of the slice but it was still a decent cut, mostly into flesh rather than veins. It was the loss of the expensive jeans that bothered him the most. He ripped off some of the hanging denim, and with the help of a handkerchief, he managed to make himself a decent tourniquet. He then set about his task again, this time ensuring that he stood astride the tougher hard plastic edges of the bin. He hoisted himself up and over the wall, then slid down the other side. The fact that his jeans were already ruined meant he didn't need to be as careful as he might have been among the mud and the plants. He found the key under its usual brick and let himself into the shed, still with enough daylight left for him to rummage around inside without having to figure out the torch app on his phone. In one of the large storage bins, he found his wetsuit. Against the wall, his old surf board. With a handy pair of stepladders, he was up and over the wall again with his haul. What other passengers on the London Underground made of him with his ripped jeans, his gashed leg, his muddy shoes, wetsuit and surfboard, he didn't care. He had what he needed for his journey.

The next day he packed up his old Ford with all his belongings, which weren't much such were the diminished possessions of an exiled cuckold. He finished off by strapping his surfboard onto the roof rack then went indoors to say goodbye to his father.

Albert Tully seemed unperturbed by the hastiness or rationale behind his decision to leave, never having shown any willingness to engage much with the situation that had brought his son to come to stay with him in the first place. He was standing by the sink, washing up the cup and saucer from his morning tea.

'That's me, Dad.'

'Off surfing then?'

'It's not like that.'

'Nice work if you can get it.'

'I just need some time on my own.'

His father grunted then waved a tea towel at him. 'You should be facing up to your responsibilities. Not running away from them. Where would this country be if that had been the attitude in my day?' Albert Tully had a habit of bringing any mention of place or activity back to time spent in the army. 'Better times those were.'

'Better times, Dad? You were at war.'

'Camaraderie, son. Loyalty. Discipline. Responsibility. It's all gone now. You wouldn't understand. Where are you off to?'

'Out west.'

'Well, if it's good surf you're after, I'd say Pembrokeshire would be your best bet.'

'What would you know about good surf?'

'I was in and out of it down there. We'd been sent to a place called Saundersfoot, along with the Yanks. Hardly a village it was. If you're passing through, you could pick up a souvenir for me. A postcard or one of these teaspoons with the local crest on it. I never bothered with anything myself when I was there. Too busy getting my feet wet coming off the LCAs.'

'LCAs?'

His father looked at him with a slight disgust. 'Landing Craft, Assault. Platoon ferries between ship and shore. That's what we were down there training for. D–Day. Just remember the bloody spoon.'

NOW

JAKE COULD MAKE OUT GUY from across the courtyard, standing under a Gothic archway, mobile clamped to his ear in the classic pose of the modern era. Guy in his dinner suit, a trim tube of a man, not one ounce of fat, any extra meat being immediately burned off by nervous anxiety and incessant movement. As soon as Guy saw him, the phone was instantly abandoned, making Jake think that his publisher had been using it as a social prop rather than for any actual communication. 'Where the fuck you been? You told me thirty minutes.'

'I got waylaid.'

Guy let out an exasperated sigh, not that dissimilar to those often expressed by brother Nick. He then lit up the dead-end of a half-smoked cigarette with one of those old-fashioned Zippo petrol lighters. 'I mean, look at you, Jake.'

'What?'

'Your hand. And where's your bow tie? You look like shit. And is that blood on your shirt?'

Jake made to button up his jacket. 'I asked you to get me a new one.'

'What do you think I am? Your butler, your bantam, your slave. I'm your fucking publisher, for Chrissake.' Guy took a drag on his cigarette, then tossed it out into the courtyard. 'I've got one of my PAs on it. She's doing her best. We're not exactly in a retail part of town.'

'OK, so where's Sylvia for my big interview?'

Guy waved a hand at him in desperation. 'There's something else to attend to first.'

'Like what?'

'The police are here to see you.'

'That was quick. Have they released Ollie?'

'They wouldn't tell me shit.'

Jake turned round. It was her smell that first alerted him. A perfume he had never forgotten. A scent that went from his nostrils straight to his brain then down to his groin as the memory of her followed her scent. She was wearing a fashionable mid-length trench coat, loosely belted so he could see the red dress underneath. Her favourite colour. That was Tina. Always flashing designer. Always flashing danger.

'Hey, Jake,' she called out. 'Long time, no… whatever.'

'Jesus, Tina. What are you doing here?'

'My job, Jake. One of my clients is sitting right there with you on the shortlist.'

'Oh, right. Who?'

'Thanda Masuka.'

'Yeah, Thanda,' said Jake, giving Tina a thumbs up, although he wasn't sure why. He hadn't really warmed to Thanda's tale of oppression, abuse and survival in Zimbabwe. 'I didn't realise she was part of your stable. Fabulous book.'

'Sure.' Tina looked at him knowingly, then at Guy. 'You got lucky,' she said. 'Jake always promised me his one great novel.'

'You wouldn't take it when I offered,' Jake protested.

'If I recall correctly,' Tina countered. 'You weren't willing to meet my conditions.'

Guy looked up from the pinging on his phone. 'Writers are such fickle creatures, aren't they?'

'You can say that again,' she said, waving them both off. And then to Jake. 'Let's catch up later,' she added in that tone of hers, as suggestive as it was mundane. 'It's been too long.'

Guy watched her as she went, looked set to make some comment but realised he probably should have more important things on his mind. 'Yeah, Jake. The police. You'd better see what they want.'

'Where are they?'

'There's a side room over there. And here, you'd better have a couple of these.' Guy passed him a packet of mints.

Guy led him along a short corridor, opened a door, beckoned him to enter first. It was an odd room, Jake thought, the kind of space that couldn't make up its mind what it wanted to be. All round the walls wooden panelling to shoulder height, some giant portraits of civic dignitaries in their robes, tall latticed windows, a chandelier, a set of grey filing cabinets, more files in red plastic boxes on the floor, a Formica-topped table at which were seated two police officers – one male, the other female. The man was flicking through his mobile while the woman was watching a video on her iPad.

The male officer looked up. He had plain, no-nonsense features, the kind of florid face Jake would describe as rural, a man who bid for horses at auction with no time or patience for urban bullshit. 'Tully,' the officer said. It was a statement rather than a question.

'Yeah,' Jake said, feeling the need to respond anyway.

The officer put down his phone. 'I'm PC Brogan. This here is PC Ritchie.'

Jake wasn't sure what he should do. PC Ritchie hadn't even looked up when introduced, Brogan didn't seem in any hurry either to disclose any information. Guy had come up behind him and they both just stood there waiting.

'Is Oliver OK?' he asked eventually.

'Who's Oliver?' Brogan asked.

'My son.'

'What's your son got to do with anything?' Even PC Ritchie looked up querulously at this remark. Hers was a face that might have been quite pleasing if she hadn't been a policewoman, Jake thought. Eyes deadened, mouth down-turned, features hardened into a cynical scowl by having to witness the constant frailties of human nature.

'I thought that's what you're here about.'

Brogan looked at Ritchie then back to Jake. 'Your son?'

'He's been arrested. Down at Holborn.'

'Naw, we're Wood Street,' Brogan said, looking slightly relieved. 'Something else entirely.'

'Could we get on with this,' Guy said. 'We've got places to be.'

Ritchie stood up. Jake thought she seemed too small to be a police officer. Did height restrictions still apply to members of Her Majesty's constabulary these days? He wasn't sure. What he was sure about was that Guy's remarks would do nothing more than slow down these two representatives of law and order even further.

'There's been a complaint against you,' she said.

'What? Who's made a complaint?'

'A certain Mister Brian Sproule.'

'I don't know anyone by that name.'

'Well, it seems you two met earlier this afternoon.'

'Like I said. Never heard of the man.'

Ritchie went on. 'Assault. Damage to personal property.'

'What?'

'That's the complaint, Mister Tully.'

'Don't know what you're talking about. Whatever it is, I'm not your man.'

'You'd better have a look at this then.' She picked up her iPad, tapped the screen, then turned it round to face him. 'The wonders of modern technology,' she said. 'Certainly makes our job easier.'

Jake followed the images on the screen, the picture was a bit jumpy and the falling rain hadn't helped but it was clear what he was watching. His earlier encounter with the university lecturer in Covent Garden. His partner must have switched to video on her phone after she had taken the photograph of them together. The conversation wasn't particularly clear, he could just make out a few words here and there but it was obvious that his relationship with said Brian Sproule was deteriorating rapidly until he pushed the man. Jake wasn't sure if it was because of the shaking of the phone or a certain blurriness caused by the falling rain but his blow to Sproule's chest came across as much heavier than he remembered. It actually looked more like a punch than a push. And then there was the crushing of the man's spectacles underfoot. It appeared to be a much more deliberate action than the accidental damage he recalled. Francesca had also now appeared into view, her obvious expression of shock at what he had done. The video then followed their backs as they retreated further down the street. Like two escaping criminals. It didn't look good.

Jake held up his hands. 'Caught red-handed,' he said.

Neither police officer seemed amused. 'What did Mister Sproule say to you to cause you to assault him?' Ritchie asked.

'I didn't assault him,' Jake protested. 'It was merely a push. A robust push, perhaps. But I didn't assault him.'

'I think that is for us to decide. What did he say?'

'He didn't like my book.'

'You assaulted him because he didn't like your book,' Ritchie said incredulously. 'That's a bit… how can I say?… Thin-skinned of you. I thought all you writers were used to rejection and criticism.'

'I know it looks and sounds bad,' Jake conceded. 'But Sproule was a lot more irritating than the video makes out.'

'So you think it is OK to assault someone for being irritating? And then causing malicious damage to his personal property?'

Before Jake could respond, Guy piped in. 'Where did you get this video?'

It was Brogan who replied this time. 'YouTube. Sproule posted it on YouTube.'

'Can I see?' Guy asked, before peering over Jake's shoulder to have a look. 'Twelve hundred views already. That's absolutely brilliant.' In some kind of recognition of what he had just said, Guy's phone pinged a couple of times.

Jake couldn't help himself. 'For fuck's sake, Guy. Can you just stop obsessing about sales figures for a moment and focus on what's going on here?' Then back to his female accuser. 'You were saying, Officer Ritchie?'

'Assault is a serious offence.'

'Alleged assault.'

'Really?' Ritchie said, with a glance to Jake and then to the image of the broken spectacles now frozen on her screen.

'We'll pay for the damage to the glasses,' Guy offered. 'Surely that will settle it.'

'Financial compensation is a civil matter,' Brogan informed them, taking up his part of this police double-act. 'We're here on the criminal aspect.'

'So what do you do with him now?' Guy asked. 'Arrest him? It was only a push. He's due right now on national TV.'

'And then what?' Ritchie asked.

Guy laid out the evening's schedule. 'I mean he's one of the centrepieces of the event.'

Ritchie and Brogan exchanged glances. 'I suppose we can invite you in for a voluntary interview for later on this evening. So you can properly give your side of the story. After all, it seems your movements will be recorded on TV until then. Shall we say 9.45 pm at Wood Street, Mr Tully?'

'Does he need a lawyer?' Guy asked.

'Only if he thinks he's guilty,' Brogan replied.

THEN

SPIKY POINT. Jake breathed in deep as he gazed down from the clifftop towards the murky waters, feeling relieved that an on-shore wind was turning the ocean into a churning, unrideable mush. He wasn't ready yet, either physically or psychologically to get out there into this kind of surf. The cut in his left leg from its foray into the recycling bin was worse than he'd thought and the last time he'd been out in the waves was back in the summer at Cap-Ferret when he had a wife, a family and a best friend. And even then, those French waves were pretty benign compared to what Spiky Point had to offer.

As he turned to walk back to his car, he noticed a hand-written sign saying 'Caravan to Rent'. A burst of nostalgia washed over him for when he and Adam used to come out here on their surfing trips, first with his parents, then later to rent a caravan or a cheap room for a week or so while they conquered the waves. He looked beyond the gate in the fence, along a stony track, to the distant outline of the caravan standing in a dip just back from the headland. He undid the latch and walked the track, a hundred yards or so over to the vehicle. The caravan was a decent size, was in reasonable shape, a bit of rust here and there, he kicked one of the tyres for no other reason than that was something his father would do. He could see there was a connection to a gas cylinder, a couple of solar panels on the roof but other than that the caravan was situated too remotely to be linked up to the grid. It sat in a dip so there wasn't a direct view of the ocean but it also meant the on-shore wind skimmed over the top. Jake kicked one of the tyres again. 'Perfect,' he said. He walked back out to the sign, tried the mobile number given. No signal. He'd drive out to the farm, name and directions also supplied.

The farmer's name was Morgan. Jake had no idea if that was the man's first or last name but it was the only piece of information offered. Morgan had a spouse somewhere in the house but she was only referred to as 'the Missus' and never appeared for the conversation. Nor was Jake let in across the threshold even though it was drizzling outside. He and Morgan just stood there in the wet discussing their business. The farmer was a middle-aged man with a good head of tight grey-white curls, a couple of tiny chick feathers caught in amongst them. Ruddy face, a checked shirt, rolled-up sleeves, broad arms folded against his potential tenant. The let of the caravan was offered at £70 per week.

'You used to this kind of living?' Morgan asked.

'Back in the day, I'd come out here surfing with a friend. We rented a caravan then too.'

Morgan scratched his head, picking out one of the feathers which he stared at, then tossed aside. 'I've fiddled around a bit with some solar panels. But basically, at this time of year, there's no electrics. Unless you want to run stuff off your motor.'

'That'll be fine. Gas lamps and candles will do. I've got a laptop I can charge off the car.'

'The toilet's a "bucket and chuck it" set-up so you'll need to bury your own shit. Usually fills up every three or four days on average. You'll see a spade marking a ditch for the purpose. There's a cabinet heater run off LPG so be careful to keep a window open. I don't want to be burying any suffocated bodies alongside your shit.' Morgan chuckled at his own remark then went on with his well-worn *spiel*. 'The gas will also give you a cooker and some hot water. You might get some off the solar but I wouldn't depend on it. There's a sink but the shower doesn't work. If you want one of those, you can come up to the house. I've rigged up a shower room in an outhouse out back, key on the lintel. You can bring up the bedding once a week and the Missus will change it for you. You can bring your £70 at the same time, cash in advance. Food and petrol in the village, I'm sure you know that since you've been down here before. Decent pub too. We can let you have some eggs and milk if you want. Mobile reception's patchy but you might pick up a bit of Wi-fi close to the house if you're lucky. To be honest, it's rare to have anybody stay for so long this time of year. It's usually just two or three days for a bit of surf if at all. What are your plans?'

'I'm here to start work on a novel.'

'I don't read novels,' Morgan said emphatically. 'Non-fiction is my bag. But the Missus loves them. Devours them so she does. Always has two or three on the go. A real literary type she is.'

'What kind of things does she like?'

'The American classics, I guess. Steinbeck, James… Hemingway. You write stuff like that and she'll read it.'

'I wish,' was all Jake could say.

'You'll have plenty of peace and quiet for that. There's nothing to do out here but to surf and read books. Or to write them for that matter.' He passed over the keys and went back in out of the rain.

Jake drove back out to properly inspect the caravan. It was cosier and better appointed than he anticipated. Cooking range was modern, good set of dishes and pots, nicely upholstered banquettes, decent sized cool box, clean bedding on a shelf, some left-over tins and condiments in the food cupboard. He made a list of things he needed. He liked what he was doing, organising his survival, keeping himself busy, keeping his mind off other things.

He drove the five miles out to the village on one of those scary, narrow Cornish roads hemmed in by tall hedges, full of blind bends and motorists who thought they could still control a vehicle after a meal with six pints and two bottles of wine. He picked up the rent from a cash machine, checked out the menu in the pub, stocked up on supplies from the village store, got some petrol and a bag of ice from the garage, paid off Morgan and was back in the caravan before dusk.

A vase of fresh flowers had been left on the fold-out table. A welcoming touch. Probably due to the literary type Missus, he didn't have Morgan pegged as a soft furnishings kind of guy. He unpacked his shopping, lit up a gas lamp, boiled up some tinned soup, made some tuna and cucumber sandwiches, opened a can of beer and a packet of crisps, sat back in his dining/bedding area. 'Cheers, you lonesome bastard,' he said as he looked around at his new set-up. 'Home sweet fucking home.'

He pulled open the floral-print curtains and peered out at a darkening sky filling up with stars. If he could just maintain concentration on the present, he felt he could keep himself reasonably sane and productive here. Away from the noise, the lights, the frantic energy of London that made it impossible to totally relax in that city. Why hadn't he done this more often? Why hadn't he and Fran and Oliver done this more often? How easy it had been to get stuck in the rut of one's own life. To lose the passion for adventure. To lose the passion for his wife.

He finished off his supper and decided to call his son. Five minutes later, he was outside the caravan with his phone, staggering around in the drizzle and the dark, the tiny lit-up unit raised to the sky like some kind of technological totem that kept flashing out the same response. No signal. No signal. No signal. How was he going to manage without network coverage? Without broadband?

The weather was good to him the following few days – dry, sunny, not too cold and he worked himself into a pleasant routine. He'd get up early morning, wander over to the cliff edge to check out the surf. If the waves were half-decent, he'd squeeze into his wetsuit which was always a struggle given the weight he'd gained since he'd bought it. He'd then pick his way down the half-sandy, half-stony path to the bay to the east of Spiky Point. This inlet was more sheltered than its westward counterpart and broke across a sandy bottom rather than on Spiky's more treacherous reef. It was a good wave to practise on, getting out the back was relatively easy and the height was never more than five feet. Such benign conditions attracted a lot of attention, especially from tourists, grommets and bodyboarders buzzing in and out of the waves with little respect for oldies like himself, bobbing around like a tea-bag in the line-up for waves. But as the muscle memory from his younger days came back to him, he soon began to assert himself and caught some decent rides, with the added benefit of the salt water acting quick to heal up the gash in his leg. After his morning work-out, he'd fix himself some brunch, fire up his laptop and get to work on his novel.

He had brought along six moleskin notebooks filled over the years with sketches of ideas, short stories that could be first chapters, random phrases of wisdom from self-help books, overheard sentences of clever dialogue, scribbled down fragments of dreams. He also had his one overriding theme, based on that profound memory of what his mother and *The Little Prince* had tried to teach him. The responsibility of love. Ironically, not a quality he could attach to himself given his recent behaviour. All he needed now was to find a structure, an array of characters, a narrative thread with which to bind his theme. He picked through his notebooks, typing into his laptop the ideas which he considered relevant. There was no need to worry at this stage. He was merely assembling a piping bag of thoughts that hopefully he would be able to squeeze out as words on a page.

Come the evening, he'd drive into the village, have a drink while he used the pub Wi-fi to catch up on mail (nothing from Fran – what did he expect?), check out Amazon to see how Adam's book was doing (#42 in *Crime, Thrillers and Mystery* and still climbing – shit!), scan the news and examine the next day's surf report. He'd then phone his son.

'Are you still on a secret mission?' Oliver asked.

'You could say that.'

'I'm under the duvet so Mum can't hear.'

'That's a good lad. How was school?'

'Boring. Can I get a smartphone?'

'A basic model is all you need right now. So we can keep in touch with you.'

'All my friends have one.'

'That doesn't mean you need to have one too.'

'Yes, it does.'

'Why?'

'For the sake of preserving my self-esteem within my peer group.'

'Jesus, Oliver. Where did you learn to talk like that?'

'I checked it out on the Internet. On my friend's smartphone.'

'What does Mum say?'

Silence.

'Oliver. What does she say?'

'Mum doesn't know you're a spy. How can I help you if I don't have a smartphone?'

'Actually, we spies prefer basic phones. We call them burners. You should check that out on the Internet.'

Silence.

'Oliver?'

'Why can't you come home?'

'I told you. I'm on a secret mission.'

'That's not what Mum says.'

'What does Mum say?'

'That you are a bad boy.'

'So how was school?'

'I told you. Boring.'

After the nightly call, he alternated between eating at the pub with its welcoming fire or making something back in the caravan with his gas heater stifling the place out. By the end of the week, he was feeling fitter and had made a decent start on his book. He analysed the following day's weather, checked out the weather reports. Surf was up. He was ready to hit Spiky Point.

He made himself a decent breakfast of fried eggs and sausages, let the food digest a bit, eased on his wetsuit and a pair of rubber bootees, made his way down to the beach. He walked over to the tide-line, sat down on the damp sand, gazed out at the ocean. The sky was dark, the water was bleak, the rain was coming down but there was a good off-shore wind holding the waves up to a daunting six to seven feet, the break was right to left running across the whole width of the bay with decent top to bottom barrels. He had hoped there might be some other surfers out there for company given the forecast of a decent swell so he was surprised to find he was on his own. It seemed modern-day young wave-riders had jobs to go to midweek. He could feel the tightness in the pit of his stomach, that mixture of excitement and fear as he watched the waves crash to the ocean floor before lapping up in front of him, as if to taunt him. He was nearly forty-years-old, for Christ sake. What was he doing pitting his body against the strength of Mother Nature in a test like this? He let his hand drift around to his back where he could still feel the shallow indent below his shoulder-blade left by Spiky all those years ago.

He shoved himself up off the sand, picked up his board, walked to the edge of the beach, then across the rocks about fifty metres or so to the dropping-in spot. From there, he counted the seconds between each wave, figuring that once he had launched into the water, he would need about ten good paddling strokes to reach and then get under the following wave before the suck from the previous one dragged him back into the rocks. He took three deep breaths, let the first wave break at his feet, then launched himself into the water. He paddled as fast as he could, feeling the strain and stretch in his shoulders and forearms as he battled the swell. One stroke, two, three, four, five, six, seven, gasp, eight, nine, the next wave was on him, gulp for breath, he went under and through. He was out the back into calm waters. All smiles. Phase one over.

He straddled his board, felt the power of the ocean as it swelled beneath him before it crashed onto the reef ahead. His heart was yammering, he was still gulping for breath but at least he had time to regroup, properly take in his surroundings. The water was colder than he had anticipated, his teeth were chattering and he could have done with another couple of millimetre thickness to his suit. He would take just the one wave, hoping it would be the perfect one and he would survive the reef with body intact.

He positioned his board like a lance, ready to swivel for take-off. It was like sitting in the growling body of a beast, bobbing in the bloat and ebb of its stomach, watching the dark walls of the waves build up behind him in the bleak light. He let a couple of good ones pass, waiting for his courage to overtake his fear, he needed to get it just right or he would be slammed down on the reef again but with no-one to rescue him this time. And here it came. The swell building and building, he could feel the suck back of energy beneath him that would push up the walls of the approaching wave, the power behind him as he turned, pushed his board forward and paddled with good strong strokes. The wave picked him up, he swivelled into the face of it and sprang to his feet all at the same time. He was in the perfect position, the power of the water breaking behind him pushing his board along the sheer liquid surface that stood up to his side and in front of him. And then he was into the barrel, crouching down on his board through a tunnel of water, the tubing wave all around him, immersed in an envelope of silence for what seemed like forever but was only for split seconds, poised exquisitely within a state of pure joy and perfect harmony with Nature, before he was spat out the other side, still on the face, still ahead of the break, totally in control, performing a couple of nice little turns, before the power of the wave receded and he allowed himself to drop down and off his board into calmer waters. He had done it. He had fucking done it. He punched the air then slid back on the board again, paddled towards the shore. His whole body was tingling, he could feel his face stretched apart by the breadth of his smile, he was ecstatic. His only regret was not being able to share this moment with Adam.

At the top of the cliff, he collected the plastic bag containing his car keys, his bank card and his mobile phone from its hiding place underneath some gorse bushes. He was cold and wet but he couldn't remember the last time he'd felt this exhilarated as he jogged his way along the path to the caravan. Even the rain had passed, making way for some rare autumn sunshine. He'd get out of his suit quick, drive up to the farm for a hot shower, then a pub lunch in the village to celebrate. As he fumbled for the key with his cold fingers, he realised he'd left the caravan unlocked. Yet he was sure he hadn't. He pushed open the door. The place had been trashed. Cushions, bedding, clothing everywhere. He quickly went to his hiding places. His laptop and wallet were gone. His good leather jacket too. He cursed himself for not locking his stuff in the car boot. All his previous exhilaration and high energy drained out of him. He'd lost everything now. His wife, his best friend, his job, his writing, his money. The joy of what he had achieved this morning disappeared in an instant. He pressed on his mobile. No fucking signal. Shivering and wet he collapsed into a miserable curled-up heap on the floor.

'Is this how a writer spends his days?'

Like some kind of beached whale, Jake looked up from his foetal position within the pool of sea-water. The accent was unmistakably American. His gaze took in the green Wellies, the long skinny legs in slim fit jeans, black polo sweater, hands laden with sheets, blonde hair chopped to the shoulders. The late morning sun framed her in the doorway, it was difficult for him to properly make out her facial features in the blinding light. She brought with her the smell of a just-smoked cigarette, a sprinkle of ash on her dark sweater as evidence.

'Who are you?' he groaned.

'Angie. Angie Morgan. This is my trailer.'

Jake hauled himself half-way off the floor, then fell back into a sitting position on one of the banquettes, now devoid of any cushions, caught between feeling angry and embarrassed by the intrusion. 'I got broken into,' he said in case she assumed this was always how he looked after things as a tenant.

'I got that. Lose anything valuable?'

'Laptop. Wallet. Good leather jacket.'

She moved into the caravan. He could see her face now. No make-up, pale, weather-beaten skin, eyes more grey than blue, wide generous mouth. Those vertical lines above her upper lip serving as some kind of barcode testament both to her age and her smoking habit.

'Hard to know who'd do such a thing,' she said. 'We don't get much passing trade through these parts.' She spoke slowly in a throaty drawl, as if nothing could faze her. Even a break-in on her property. Jake watched as she stacked the fresh linen on a shelf, began to pick up a few items here and there. Cushions.

Table mats. One of those snow domes he'd been using as a paperweight. 'If you need to cancel cards, I can take you back to the house,' she said. 'Cellphone reception is pretty patchy around here.'

'I had my debit card with me. Force of habit.'

'Lucky for you then. Cash?'

'Nothing much. It's the laptop that bothers me. It was an ancient thing but I'd got a few thousand words of new stuff on it.'

'Backed up?'

'Naw.'

She wagged a scolding finger at him. 'Careless. You got insurance?'

He shook his head.

'We got none either for this place. Security's never been an issue out here.' She held out a towel to him. 'Why don't you get out of that wetsuit. I'll make ourselves some tea. I keep some herbal here. Cheer you up.'

She closed off the curtain that separated the living/bedroom space from the rest of the caravan. While she busied herself in the kitchen area, he peeled off his suit, quickly got dressed.

'Decent?' she asked.

'Yeah.'

She pulled open the curtain, handed him in a mug. She then came in herself, sorted out some cushions for the banquette, sat down opposite him at the table with her own mug. She clawed back a strand of hair from over her eyes, blew on to the tea. 'Chamomile. It has calming properties.'

'So they say.'

'Want to call the cops?'

'No point. What could they do?'

Angie shrugged her thin shoulders. 'Not a lot in my experience.'

She pulled back one of the window curtains, closed her eyes.

He watched as she turned her cheek to the warmth of the sunshine, a slight moan as the rays caught and bathed her skin. He felt as if he were intruding on an intimate moment and looked away. A small painting hung on the wall just above her head, he'd not paid any attention to it before – a portrait of a young woman. The similarity to Angie suddenly struck him. She opened her eyes, smiled at him as if she knew he had been making the comparison.

'My ex did that,' she said.

'He's certainly captured your likeness.'

'Yeah. My lovely younger self. He did a lot of portraits of me back then. I was his muse. He said I helped him capture the pain inside himself. I didn't know whether to take that as a compliment or not.'

'So he was a proper artist then?'

'Actually, he was a musician. Lead singer in a rock'n roll band. But he was all-round creative. Words, music, paint, wood, stone. You know these backstage riders where rock stars ask for booze and hookers and only the red M&Ms? My guy just wanted a supply of paints and brushes. That kind of made him hard to resist. After all, I was just an innocent kid from Reno, Nevada. The divorce capital of the world. You'd have thought that would have taught me a thing or two about relationships.'

'Is that where you met?'

'Back then I had a talent for the piano but I didn't want to end up in one of those Nevada casino lounges playing Andy Willlams classics to sad, old gamblers. So I took myself and my electronic keyboard off to New York and that's where I met rock star guy. Take my advice. Don't go marrying someone who writes music. Their songs will haunt you for the rest of your life.'

'Would I know him?'

'For sure, yes.'

'So who was it?'

'Can't tell you.'

'Why not?'

'Then all the talk would be about him. When I was wanting to tell you about my current husband Mike and the paintings. You see, Mike wouldn't have any of them in the house. Clean slate, he insisted, couldn't blame him for that really, there were some nudie ones after all. He sold the whole Goddamn lot. Which was a bit odd as it meant he was quite happy to have strangers looking at me naked even if he couldn't. Made more sense if he'd burnt them. Never could understand men. Anyway, they're all gone now. The paintings and the men. Although Mike's still hanging in there, God bless him. He doesn't know I've still got this one portrait left.'

She sipped on her tea as if to let him dwell on a much younger image of herself as a rock chick. Or as a naked model. Or merely to give him time to absorb all this information. She'd been yattering on like some nervous schoolgirl, he wondered if she might be on speed or coke or this was just the way she was. She reached across the table to the vase of flowers that had somehow remained intact amid all the chaos. 'Hellebores,' she said, touching one of the pink petals. Her fingers were long and bony, a couple of them nicotine stained. No wedding ring, he noticed. 'Promise of spring,' she added wistfully, drumming her fingers on the table, probably aching for a fag. 'Back in Nevada, all we had was sagebrush.'

'How come you ended up here in Cornwall?'

'I was on the road with rock star guy and London was where we split. And there I stayed. Apart from six weeks when I was over in Reno getting myself a quickie divorce. I guess my hometown was good for something. Then years later I met Mike. And we came down here. He's a very practical guy. Good with his hands. That's what a woman needs in her later years, don't you think?' She went back to sorting out the flowers in the vase. 'He told me you're writing a novel. How's that going?'

'Slow and painful. Until it got stolen.'

'Will you be able to re-write what you've lost?'

'Probably not worth it. It was pretty crap anyway.'

'Can I ask what it's about?'

'Not yet.'

'Hey, I just told you my life story. Doesn't a gal deserve something in return?'

'I didn't realise we were doing a trade-off.'

'I don't get much chance to make intelligent conversation these days. And I do love reading.'

'Is that how you pass the time down here?'

'I like to paint too. And to meditate. That's the trick, isn't it?'

'What do you mean?'

'The ability to be with yourself.'

'What happens if you don't like yourself?'

'Well, that's something you'll need to sort out.' She touched the back of his hand as she rose from the banquette. 'I'd better go and get a padlock for your door. I don't want you feeling all insecure now.'

With Angie gone, Jake dumped the chamomile down the sink, poured himself a whisky instead, some gut-rotting stuff he'd bought a couple of days ago at the village store not known for its collection of fine malts. What he really wanted to do was to call Francesca. Instead, he washed down the inclination with the Scotch then went for a walk along the clifftops. He grabbed a bite of lunch and a couple of pints at a local pub, hung around until it was time for Oliver to be out of school. Back at the caravan, he found a padlock and key on the kitchen table then stepped outside with his mobile, wandered around with it stretched to the sky until he got a signal.

'Hey, young man. What's happening?'

'Mum isn't happy with you.'

'I know that.'

'She wants to know where you are.'

'What do you tell her?'

'I tell her I don't know where you are.'

'Which is true.'

'You're beside the sea.'

'How do you know that?'

'I can hear the waves. And the seagulls.'

'You'd make a good spy.'

'Thank you. Can I have a smartphone then?'

'What does Mum say?'

Silence. And then: 'You owe me big time, Dad.'

'What's that supposed to mean?'

'For all the pain you've caused.'

This time, it was Jake's turn to be silent. 'I'll buy you a smart-phone for Christmas. How about that?'

'Christmas is ages away.'

'For your birthday then.'

'You're coming home for my birthday?'

'I promise.'

He hoped it was a promise he could keep. Oliver's birthday was in less than two months.

NOW

JAKE SAT IN FRONT OF THE MIRROR in the ornate Gents bathroom, now temporarily converted into a dressing room for the television guests. The formidable Sylvia no doubt had her private green room suite somewhere else in this impressive medieval building. He looked like shit, a fact that he had conveyed to Gerald his make-up artist and one which had not been contradicted. He had succeeded, however, in locating his bow tie in the top pocket of his jacket although Gerald was not impressed by the state of his shirt.

'It's a pity we're OB,' he said, trying to rub out the staining with some magic liquid. 'I've got a wardrobe full of shirts back at base.'

'OB?'

'Outside Broadcast. I'm assuming the blood's your own.'

'Unfortunately, it is.'

'I'm glad to hear that. I'd hate to hear Sylvia'd gone missing.'

Jake laughed even as he tried to ignore the ghoulish appearance in his own face reflected back at him. He had managed to pluck a glass of whisky from a passing waiter back in the corridor, a refreshment he had used to knock back a codeine tablet and a Lorazepam. The cocktail had done the trick in that he was feeling less anxious and free of the throbbing pain in his hand. However, all blood appeared to have drained from his face to pool into his eyes, and he was feeling decidedly light-headed. *Jake Tully Day* was losing its shine.

'Can you do something with all of this?' he asked Gerald, passing his unbandaged arm over and around his face and head.

Gerald laughed. 'I'm a make-up artist not a bloody magician. But I've seen worse.' He produced a little phial, got Jake to hold his head back so he could squeeze the drops into his eyes. 'There. That'll get rid of the Dracula look. Hair and skin I can sort. Toothpaste for the breath. And make sure you gargle. Sylvia's nose doubles as a breathalyser. I'll get someone to bring you a coffee.'

The *ping ping* of a nearby mobile phone alerted Jake to the presence of his publisher.

'Hah,' Guy said. 'More hits. That YouTube video is going viral.'

'That's because you're sharing the shit out of it.'

'You judge me too harshly.' And then with a sudden concerned tone. 'You OK, man? You don't look too healthy.'

'Don't worry. Gerald here is working his magic.'

'Can he make you stop slurring your words?'

'I'm fine, Guy. It's been a tough day. Haven't you noticed?'

'Doesn't mean you need to drink and drug yourself to the eyeballs.'

'My eyeballs are absolutely fine now, thanks to my pal Gerald. And don't worry. I always come good for you.'

'I hope so. Because Sylvia is not feeling kindly disposed towards you. You've upset her scheduling.'

'I take it I'm last on.'

'She's just finishing up now with that Thanda woman. You're on next.'

As if on cue, a female production assistant put her head around the door. 'On in ten, Mr Tully,' she said.

'Ten seconds?'

'Minutes.'

'Thank Christ for that.'

Gerald quickly powdered Jake's face, tried to work away the dark shadows under his eyes. 'You're sweating.'

'It's probably the drugs.'

'I'll apply a mattifier then.'

'Whatever it takes, Gerald my man.'

Guy rubbed his hands together. 'So, Jake. This is pretty straightforward. It is not a confrontation. It's just about telling Sylvia and two million viewers what your marvellous book is all about. She loves it, by the way.'

'She told you that?'

Guy held up his hands. 'I heard a rumour.'

'Just stick to the plot. I'm not in the mood for your bullshit.'

'OK, she's probably just skimmed it. But as far as the big prize is concerned, I imagine the judges have already made their decision so no need to try to sway them. I doubt they will be watching anyway, locked away as they are in a dungeon somewhere. Have you prepared a speech in case you actually win this damn thing?'

Jake patted his jacket where the Decca List nestled in his inside breast pocket. 'Typewritten on two A4 sheets, double-spaced, short and sweet.'

'You're not going to say anything stupid?'

'My eloquent words of wisdom shall be like pearls before swine.'

'That's what I like to hear. After all, this is all about good PR. Raising the profile of both yourself and the book. So behave yourself. Got it?'

'I got it. But you should know that Sylvia and I have got previous.'

'What's that supposed to mean?'

'It's not the first time she's interviewed me.'

'I don't need to hear this.'

'It was a long time ago. I doubt she'll remember. She must have done hundreds of these programmes.'

'Why was she interviewing you?'

'It was back in my journalism days when I was writing that lifestyle column. The house-husband thing. About the role of men in contemporary parenthood. It wasn't even just me she was interviewing. It was a panel discussion. The Minister for Equalities, if there still is such a person, was there. As well as a professor of something. And someone who had written a book on the subject. Sylvia wouldn't remember.'

'She wouldn't remember what?'

Gerald was tackling his hair now. Such a nice feeling to have someone massage your scalp like that then brush away, brush away.

'Jake. She wouldn't remember what?'

'I got into a bit of an argument with the Minister. I wish I could remember her name. She lost her seat in the following election which I was delighted about.'

The production assistant again. 'We're ready for you now, Mr Tully.'

'Just a last-minute tweaking,' said Gerald.

A waiter entered. 'Someone order coffee?'

'I'll have that,' Jake said, seizing the espresso cup and downing it in one.

'She wouldn't remember what, Jake?'

'I think I was a bit drunk. I stood up to argue with the Minister, moved around a bit, fell off the stage. Sylvia wasn't happy. The audience thought it was hilarious. At least it wasn't live TV.' His mobile started buzzing.

'Phones off on-air, Mr Tully,' scolded the production assistant as she tried to usher him out the door.

He looked at the screen. Francesca.

'Someone died?' asked the assistant.

'I hope not.'

'Then we have to go.'

'Ah, the notorious Mr Tully,' Sylvia said as they almost collided in the corridor. The illustrious presenter was wearing black pants tucked inside calf-high black leather boots, a black military-style jacket with a high collar, silver epaulettes and silver buttons down the front and on the cuffs. Properly dressed for battle, Jake thought.

'We meet again,' she said.

'You remember?'

'You fell off the stage. That's not an easy thing to forget.'

'I guess not.'

'Your hand? Not another fall, I hope.'

'A momentary lapse with a sushi knife.'

'Well, I brandish no knives. And you'll be pleased to know that we are on level ground this time.'

'You have no idea how much that pleases me.'

'Shall we go in then. We're running late.'

The room was not that much different from the one in which he had been interviewed by the police. Wood-panelling up to head height, parquet flooring, some giant paintings of unknown dignitaries on the walls and a massive marble fireplace in front of which had been placed two red velvet-covered chairs face-to-face, a small table in between. He had noticed that this kind of *mise en scène* seemed to be the norm these days – two people talking in front of the obligatory fireplace, must be the sense of cosiness about it. The rest of the space was filled with arc lamps, cameras and the technicians that made up a typical OB unit.

'It'll just be a wee fireside chat,' Sylvia said, a make-up artist at her side powdering her forehead. 'I loved the book, by the way.'

'I bet you say that to all the short-listees.'

Through the fuzziness of his brain, he was trying to consider whether 'shortlistee' was actually a word when he tripped over one of a number of cables snaked across the floor. Normally, he would have had both arms outstretched to break his fall, but with one hand already out of commission, he landed rather awkwardly on the rolled-out equipment. The make-up artist and production assistant rushed forward and hauled him to his feet.

'No damage done,' he said, brushing himself down, only to find that somehow he had managed to rip a hole in the knee of his dinner suit.

Sylvia looked at him with barely disguised disgust. 'There's no time to fix that. We'll just make sure we shoot from the waist up,' she said. 'Now sit.'

Jake did as he was told. Crossed one leg over the tear and let his bandaged arm hang loosely below the seat of the chair. A technician came over, fixed him with a lapel mike then instructed him to put the small wired-up transmitter into his jacket inside pocket.

'Say something,' the technician told him.

Normally, Jake would have uttered what everyone else did in the exact same situation and said: 'One, two, three, testing. One, two, three testing.' But whether it was the drugs or the booze or Sylvia's authoritarian presence, he found himself singing the first few bars of the anthem of Liverpool Football Club: *You'll Never Walk Alone*. He had no idea why he had chosen this particular refrain. He had never been to Liverpool, didn't support Liverpool FC and didn't even like football. Somewhere from the back, behind the blinding lamps, a voice shouted back: 'Right on.' The technician gave him the thumbs up and left him to the mercy of Sylvia, who was now seated across from him, similarly miked up. His mouth felt remarkably dry, his tongue thick with some kind of metallic taste from all the pills. He leaned forward, filled up a glass with water from a carafe, noticed thankfully that his hand was not shaking, fitted the lip of the glass between his lips and the mike, knocked the whole thing back in one gulp.

'Aaaagh,' he said, now that he was suitably refreshed. The

sound reverberated through the mike and around the room. Sylvia gave him one of her steely looks. A technician shouted. 'On in five.'

'No time for prep, Jake,' she said. 'I hope you're ready'

Jake held up his unbandaged hand. 'Ready when you are,' he said.

'Just remember we're live this time.'

'Good evening again,' Sylvia said into camera with that Edinburgh burr of hers that oozed schoolmarm authority. Even Jake who was slipping down slightly in his chair, sat up and took notice. 'We come eventually to the last of tonight's short-listed candidates for this most prestigious of prizes. Jake Tully. For his debut novel *The Responsibility of Love*. Are we forever responsible for those that we have allowed to fall in love with us? That is the underlying theme of this book. It is a theme I seem to recall from my childhood reading. From *The Little Prince*.'

Jake squinted back at her. The television lights were blinding. And the heat. He just wanted to rip off his bow tie, open up his collar. 'I do acknowledge that book as an inspiration,' he said, hoarsely, feeling the sweat prickle on his forehead under Gerald's thickly applied mattifier. He leaned forward, picked up his glass from off the table. 'But my novel is also based on something my mother once told me.' He took a sip of water and continued. 'I was about to be six years old...' And he began to relate the story of how as a child he attempted to pick up the teddy bear in the toy shop. Very quickly, he found himself warming to his task, the whisky and various drugs putting him in an expansive mood. He knew it was a good anecdote, one that always drew in his audiences. He felt that even Sylvia was moved, that her posture towards him was also softening slightly, until she asked:

'So, tell me, Jake. Have you always been responsible for those you have tamed?'

Jake stared back at her, cleared his throat. It was not the kind of question he was expecting. Something so personal right up front. 'I thought we were here to talk about my book.'

'I think you're savvy enough to know how the publishing world works these days.' She turned her face to camera in some kind of collusion with her audience. 'Readers are just as interested in you as they are in the book.'

'I think they are also savvy enough to know that when an interviewer tackles someone *ad hominem* it is usually because they haven't read their work. Or at least just skimmed it.'

Jake saw Sylvia visibly shudder. It was his turn now to face the camera with a conspiratorial smile to the invisible viewers.

'I can assure you I have read all the books on the shortlist,' Sylvia said, her voice pitching higher than usual. 'Perhaps you could answer the question. After all, you just regaled us quite engagingly about a story from your childhood. I would have thought the floodgates were now open, so to speak, on personal reflection.'

'That's the whole bloody problem.'

'What do you mean?'

'There was a time when readers didn't give a damn about the writers. Who knew what Proust was like? Or Flaubert? Or Austen? Or Golding? Or Bellow? Or Saint-Exupéry. Who were these people? Were they tall or short? Clean-shaven or bald? Did they vote Labour or Tory? Were they wife-beaters, husband-beaters, drug takers, devil worshippers? Were they responsible for those they had tamed? Readers used to be only interested in what they were reading. Now we writers have to go out there and promote ourselves like some kind of performing seals. Radio. Festivals. Bookshops. Libraries. Television.' Forgetting his bandaged limb, he spread out his arms to include the situation in which he found himself. 'Yes, television.' He turned to face camera again. 'You. Yes, you out there in audience viewing land. You want to know our opinions. You want to hear our confessions. You want to pry into our lives. But we're the last people who want to do this kind of stuff. That's why we're writers and not...' He was going to say TV personalities. '... actors...' He paused, took a breath. That felt good, he thought. He wriggled himself straight and faced Sylvia again who stared back at him, mouth open in astonishment. She also shook herself into a kind of attention.

'You sound very bitter about the world you work in,' she said.

'You're damn right I am. It's got to the stage now publishers would rather promote a writer than the book. So bring on the celebrities. Bring on the comedians, TV presenters, models, politicians and your royal in-laws. Roll up, roll up. People think that just because they can use a pen or a keyboard, they can write.'

'You know what they say. Everyone has a book in them.'

'That's very true. But that doesn't mean that they are any good. You've written a novel, Sylvia. You know what it's like.'

'I'm not sure what you're implying.' Sylvia shook her silver epaulettes at him. 'Can we just get back to the matter at hand. I was asking you whether you consider yourself as someone who is always responsible for those you have tamed.'

'And I was telling you that I would rather talk to you about my novel.'

Sylvia touched a finger to her earpiece and scowled. Jake guessed she was receiving some unwanted instruction from her frantic producers tucked away amidst polystyrene coffee cups and burger wrappers in a broadcasting truck parked outside the building. He tilted his head to the side and smiled at her in what he imagined was his most charming manner. She didn't smile back but instead said: 'I guess what I am asking then is... how much of this novel is autobiographical?'

Jake picked up his glass again, took another sip of water. 'Aren't all novels autobiographical? Aren't we as writers just expressing some kind of loss? A deeply hidden trauma? Some unresolved childhood slight? Some deep yearning for innocence. It's all about that Rosebud moment, isn't it? But dressing it up and disguising it in a fictional narrative vehicle.'

'I don't know if we can say that about all novels.'

'What about yours then?'

'An historical novel about a witch in Jacobite Scotland?'

'Exactly.'

Sylvia smiled into camera. 'I think you might be trying to avoid the issue here.'

'What issue? I forget what we were talking about.'

'Whether your novel is really about you?'

Jake could see himself in one of the monitors. He was splayed out low across his chair. His jacket was open so that it showed the blood-stained flap of his shirt that had escaped the waistband of his trousers which in themselves were torn at the knee. One hand was bandaged, the other clasped a glass of water that was spilling its contents on to the floor. He was a mess.

'What do you think?' he said as he looked out to camera and smiled to the two million or so viewers. Or at least, he hoped it was a smile for at this point it felt that through the accumulation of drugs and alcohol, he had lost control of his facial muscles. 'Do I look like someone who is responsible for anything? Or anybody?'

The production assistant was signalling for Sylvia to wind it up by slicing her finger across her throat. Jake could see Guy standing there as well, performing a similar action. And Francesca had turned up too, standing with her arms folded and an appalled look on her face.

Sylvia played with her earpiece again and said: 'I'm afraid we don't have time to find out what I think. We're going to take a break now for the News. We'll be back on air in ninety minutes when the guests have had their dinner and we settle down to the business end of the evening. Until then...Good evening from all of us here in this wonderful building in the City of London.'

Jake unclipped his microphone.

'Jesus Christ, Jake. What the fuck was that all about?'

'What?'

'That was absolutely appalling. I didn't think you could top your falling off the stage performance. But this fucking car crash of an interview will be playing on YouTube for the rest of my bloody career.'

'That should make my publisher happy.'

'I don't appreciate your glibness. Or your aggressive tone.'

'You were being too personal.'

'That's what interviewers do.'

'I was here to talk about my book. Not to attend some confessional.'

'Well, I wish you good luck. And if you actually go on to win this thing, maybe you can try expressing your bitterness in your speech. Or will you try to be gracious and kind?'

'I think I'll go with the bitterness angle.'

'It seems you've got another platform for that. I believe you're going to be on the News as well.'

THEN

AFTER THE DAY OF THE BREAK-IN, it rained. For three days. Solid. Normally, when the skies opened and threw down a burst of rain like this, it would stop, exhausted, after a few minutes. But this rain had limitless stamina, it just went on and on at the same pace forever. Jake lay back on the banquette and listened. He was quite surprised by the resilience of the caravan to this watery onslaught. Not a leak anywhere. Just this incessant drumming on the roof, the lash of downpour against the windows, the ground sucking up the moisture until large pools and channels began to form around the vehicle like a protective moat. He liked this feeling of being trapped by the elements. He couldn't go anywhere and he had no desire to go anywhere anyway. He possessed enough supplies to see him through. He had a bottle of cheap whisky, a six-pack of beer in the cool box, half a cooked chicken, tins of soup and beans, a packet of ground coffee. His computer was gone, his mobile was devoid of charge and signal, his leather jacket had probably been sold off by some drifter with a drug habit to feed. This was it. The end. No wife, no best friend, no job, no novel, no cash. Just a solitary, thin plastic card that would give him access to a line of credit supplied by his brother if he could be bothered getting up out of his lethargy, stomp across a muddy field and drive through a sheet of rain to the nearest ATM. And even then, he felt that each banknote retrieved would represent a symbolic monetary victory for brother Nick (and everyone else for that matter). At night, with the rain still pouring down, he dressed up in all his clothes against the cold, and shivered under the blankets. Even with all this empty time on his hands, he hadn't written a word. He viewed his suffering as some sort of penance, a purging of his soul before he could prostrate himself before the goddess Francesca again and beg for forgiveness. Then just as the whisky bottle slipped towards near emptiness and the six-pack became a no-pack, the rain stopped. All was quiet. The sun came out, the birds came out. He came out. He opened the door of the caravan and breathed in the cool, washed air. He caught himself humming. He was aware that allowing random sounds to emerge like this was merely an expression of some deep feeling buried within his subconscious. A kind of vocal Rorschach test. His humming had combined to form a familiar tune. A Rolling Stones song. A golden oldie. *Angie.*

A few hours later, she walked by. He was sitting by the window with a pencil and notepad, trying to find a new way in to his book. He decided that the theft of his laptop had been a sign, an admonition from the gods of decent literature that what he had written so far had simply not been good enough. But nothing fresh was emerging. He couldn't even tell himself he had writer's block. For the use of the word 'block' suggested that there was some kind of flow to stop. The only flow he had was the humming of the same tune he hadn't been able to get out of his head all day. And suddenly there she was. As if his constant musical mantra had summoned her up. She wore a black beret, a black, belted raincoat, the same Wellington boots, striding purposefully across the field on those long legs of hers. Underarm she was carrying what looked like a portable easel and paint box while she had some other gear strapped to her back. She had a tricky ascent to make on the grassy hillock to lead to the top of the dunes, especially as the surface was slippery and wet from the rain. His first inclination was to go out and help her but he decided to let her be. Once she had made it to the top, she set out her equipment – easel and canvas, paint box and a small fold-up stool. She sat down, stretched out her legs, lit up a cigarette and stared out to sea, as if she were an old mariner content to wait the hours until the ships appeared on the horizon. He wondered whether she knew that he was watching her, that this was all some kind of performance for him. Apart from the occasional movement of hand to mouth with her cigarette, she stayed still. He tried to imagine the look on her craggy, once beautiful face, formerly the inspiration for her famous musician lover and now the weathered witness to a long-time smoking habit. Those grey blue eyes that seemed to reflect a certain hurt, a certain loneliness, a certain dissatisfaction with what her life had become. He was surprised at this feeling of empathy he seemed to have for her, no doubt a totally deluded one, as she and Mike were probably enjoying an ideal existence down here in remote Cornwall. Perhaps he was merely projecting his own misery on to her. He picked up his pencil, flipped open his notebook and he found himself starting to write. Something in his observation of her was inspiring him. Yet what was emerging on to the page was an entirely different character and narrative than the one he imagined was playing itself out in front of him.

Even by the most benign and generous of standards, Max was not a handsome man. His bulging, frog-like eyes crowded either side of a flat, boneless nose. There was his almost non-existent chin. The blubbery lips that glistened with nervous spittle. Straight, greasy hair that no amount of expensive conditioner could flatter. A physical repulsiveness that, reflected back at him by observers, caused his shoulders to hunch, his chest to cave inwards, his thin body to stoop, his whole being to shrink in readiness for the next insult or look of revulsion that was sure to come.

It was a great pity that even the kindest of people would hardly ever venture beyond this veneer of distaste for if they did, if they actually talked to him, they would make the most wondrous of discoveries. That Max had a beautiful voice. Not a singing voice but a speaking voice. A deep yet soft, gentle, well-mannered, soothing, charming tone. A wooing voice. A voice that could pontificate on even the most boring of subjects and still enchant an audience. With one's eyes closed, it was possible to believe that it was the most gorgeous of men who was speaking.

Max was an only child of elderly parents who had both passed away when he was still in his early twenties, leaving him a decent sum. He continued to live in their spacious Victorian brownstone apartment, the one he had been born in. He lived a secluded existence, he had no friends and the idea that he might attract a girlfriend was fanciful and remote. He was resigned to a life without love, sexual pleasure or companionship. But that did not mean he could not enjoy other worldly aspects of his presence on this planet. He loved music, he loved books, his inheritance allowed him to indulge in fine food and expensive wines. He arranged to have most of his essentials delivered where possible so that he hardly ever needed to go out. Why should he? When all that would happen was to be laughed and stared at.

His apartment boasted a south-west facing balcony, just broad and long enough for a small table and chair, with a view out on to a park, a rare half-block of green space in this part of the city. It was on this balcony that he sat reading, drinking wine and nibbling on expensive delicacies when the weather was clement. Being located in an apartment building, there was a neighbouring balcony, but it had never been used, as the occupant for as long as he could remember was an elderly widow confined to a wheelchair. It was therefore with some surprise that one day as he was outside reading, a young woman should emerge on the adjacent balcony and introduce herself as his new neighbour.

'I thought that…' Max stuttered. 'I thought that Mrs…'

'I believe she passed away a few months ago,' the young woman told him. 'I am the new tenant. Catherine. Catherine Vance.'

Jake put down his pencil. His wrist ached. He hadn't written this much for years, especially by hand. He flicked back through his notebook. Where had all this come from? An hour or so ago, he had known nothing about Max or Catherine. He looked out of the window. Angie was still there. She was working now, painting or sketching on her canvas. The sky was darkening yet she continued in her task. Defiant. He picked up his pencil again.

'And you are?'

'Ah yes, I'm sorry… Max.'

'Pleased to meet you, Max. I just wanted to let you know that I am a piano teacher. Pupils will come to my home for lessons. I sincerely hope I shall not disturb you.'

'I like music,' was all that Max could muster in response.

Catherine was not a beautiful woman but not an unattractive one either. She was petite with dark wavy hair that she wore unstyled, the kind of hair that Max felt demanded to be tied up with ribbons. She was neat and precise, all her movements performed with short, sharp gestures. Catherine liked everything to be in its proper order. Like notes on a piano score.

From next door, Max could hear Catherine's pupils stumbling over their assignments, especially the beginners, of course. He quite liked these faulty, repetitive sequences, possibly because they reminded him of his own imperfections. He had compassion for these students. And his tolerance was often rewarded by the occasional gifted student, or even Catherine, who would play for herself later in the evenings. As he sat on the balcony, reading his book, sipping on his wine, nibbling on his cashew nuts, he looked across at the park opposite while Catherine played her Debussy, always Debussy, and thought that a life such as his, devoid of the usual social and physical intimacies, could have its pleasant moments as well. This rare moment of positivity was further rewarded when Catherine stepped out on to her balcony with her own glass of wine. She kept many plants on her little patio, so there was no room for a table, just a chair. She sat down and said as she often did:

'I hope my students don't disturb you.'

'Not at all,' he replied. And that would usually be the end of their interchange as he would then be compelled to retreat inside. But feeling somewhat buoyant this evening, no doubt egged on by the uplifting qualities of a rather pleasant Grand Cru Beaujolais, he added: 'I actually enjoy their efforts. It gives me hope.'

'Oh. In what way?'

'That playing the piano is still relevant.'

'It has been for hundreds of years.'

'But these days there are so many other distractions.'

'I know what you mean.'

And so the conversation continued. The sun went down and despite the sudden chill, neither of them decided to leave or even to go inside to fetch a jacket or a cardigan. She was mesmerised by his voice, of course, and he was seduced by the fact that another person, one of the opposite sex even, did not seem repulsed by his looks or his company.

Jake looked out of the window. Spots of rain had fallen on the glass, Angie was packing up her equipment. Again, he could have gone out to help her, even taken her an umbrella, the rain was coming slightly heavier now. But he wanted to keep that distance, he didn't want to break the spell. Instead he waited until she had gone past the caravan and down the path to her pick-up truck. He then drove to the nearest town and searched out a store that sold re-conditioned laptops.

The routine continued the next day. Angie appeared in the late morning. This time she wore a long woollen calf-length cardigan and some kind of odd hat with earflaps. He watched yet again as she traipsed up the grassy side of the dune until she reached the top, set out her equipment, sat down on her little stool and stared out to the horizon. What was his fascination with this woman? He felt he could just sit here by his window and watch her for hours. Was this what famous rock star ex-husband meant when he said she helped him capture the pain inside himself? Whatever the reason, it made him want to write. He took out his laptop and began to type, quicker this time, his fingers over the keys far faster than anything he could write by hand:

Max and Catherine. They started to spend more time together, on those summer evenings, after she had finished up with her students. He found space for another chair on his balcony and she would step over the low dividing railing and there they would sit, weather permitting.

'Will you read to me?' she asked him one evening.

'Why would you want me to do that?'

'You have a beautiful speaking voice.'

'Really?'

'No-one has ever told you that?'

Max shook his head. 'My mother used to. But I never believed her.'

'Why wouldn't you?'

'I just thought she was saying it to make me feel better.'

'Oh, Max,' she scolded.

He smiled sheepishly. He loved it when she used his name like that.

She went on: 'Your voice… it's so… what's the word? Mellifluous. Yes, that's it. You could be one of those people that do voice-overs for advertisements. Or promoting the latest films. Or speaking the news.'

'That's very nice of you to say so.'

'I'm not just being nice, Max. I honestly think so. As a fact.' She stamped her foot on the metal balcony floor. A childish gesture, he thought, that endeared her to him even more.

'Well, thank you,' he said. 'I shall accept the compliment. And what would you like me to read to you?'

It started off with Tolstoy, after that they alternated with their choices, mostly the classics. He introduced her to Orwell. She came back at him with Woolf. He countered with Kafka. And after that she went all American on him with James and Steinbeck and Hemingway. Then, on a particularly warm and pleasant evening, she said to him:

'Let's go over to the park.'

'The park?'

'Yes, why do we need to sit in this cramped little space when we can stretch out over there? I'll find us some fruit and snacks. You can bring the wine.'

'Yes, I can do that. Bring the wine. Of course.'

He managed to find an old picnic basket of his parents which they packed with glasses, a bottle of his finest Burgundy, a small jar of caviar. Catherine contributed cheese and olives and crackers and pears.

'A moveable feast,' she declared.

For Max, this was a huge adventure. To go out in public like this. With a woman. He carried the hamper. She brought her book of choice. Madame Bovary. Together they emerged from the elevator, then crossed the road and entered through the wrought iron gates. They decided they would head for the far side where there were benches, trees for shade and beds of seasonal flowers. As they moved towards their destination, he felt her body close to his and she took his arm in hers. The feeling of exhilaration, of sheer joy, that passed through him at that moment was overwhelming. He actually felt his heart leap. It was a sensation that he always thought was exaggerated in novels – his heart leapt to her touch – but now he realised that such a thing could exist. His heart soared. It beat that little bit faster. His skin tingled. His footstep was lighter. He could feel the weight and heft of her arm on his. He started to hum. When they reached their destination, they found a bench in a shady bower. He commented on the vibrant colour of the geraniums, she on the lovely pink blooms on the butterfly bushes. She had let go of his arm but he felt that she was sitting closer to him than perhaps ordinary decorum allowed. He realised he was shaking with delight. He read to her. Madame Bovary. How appropriate. A woman in charge of her own destiny. A woman willing to take risks. A woman who didn't care what others thought of her. He was transported. He was in ecstasy. He took her hand. She didn't pull away. He had never held a woman's hand before. The skin was cold, even though the day was warm. So soft to the touch. He could feel himself become aroused, even though he didn't *want to think of this moment as sexual but as sensual, as loving. He put down the book. She was staring out towards the broad avenue that led to the heart of their city. That dainty little face with those dark waves that he wanted to tie with ribbons. He still held her hand. He couldn't help himself, some instinct propelled him forward, to overcome his fears, a lifetime of being rejected, mocked and humiliated. He leaned his face in towards hers.*

'I love you,' he said as he kissed her on the side of the mouth.

She jumped. Her body actually lifted up an inch or two off the bench. She began screaming. He wasn't even sure if she was saying actual words. There was just this high-pitched shriek. She was up on her feet now, pushing him away. And just as before his heart had leapt with joy, it was now shrivelling and shrinking and hardening against the pain. Now he could hear the words she was saying: 'What did you think was going on here? Did you honestly believe I would want to kiss someone like you? I was just being nice. Can't a girl just be nice to you without you wanting to take advantage of her? Get away. Get away from me. You disgust me.'

Later that summer's evening, Max threw himself off his balcony. Not so much as threw, but by just allowing his body to fold and collapse, he dropped over the railing, all reason for loving and living having drained out of him so that there was nothing left to hold him up. With a glass of fine wine in hand. Catherine heard the scream of a passer-by above her piano playing. Debussy. Always Debussy. The last wondrous and exquisite sounds Max ever heard. She rushed to the balcony. She saw the splayed and twisted body lying on the pavement below, blood and wine pooling vermillion on the concrete. It was her turn to scream.

A knock on the caravan door. He snapped down the laptop lid and went to open it. Angie stood back off the step, scrunching a cigarette into the mud with the toe of her Wellington boot. The woollen hat with ear flaps had been discarded and he was surprised to see that most of her face was covered in white paint, her eyes bordered by a thick black mascara. She looked like an actor in a kabuki play.

'What's with the Marcel Marceau look?' he asked.

'I got bored with the canvas. So I decided to paint my skin. Do I scare you?'

'Not at all.'

'Can I come in then?'

He opened the door wider. She eased off her boots, left them by the side of the steps along with her painting gear and a covered canvas.

'You got something to drink?' she asked.

'I've still got those herbals.'

'I was hoping for something stronger.'

'I can offer you a few fingers of rot-gut whisky.'

She gave that phlegmy throaty laugh of hers. 'My gut's pretty rotten these days. A little more won't do any damage.'

She stretched out on one of the banquettes, her limbs all loose and floppy in the manner of the mime artist she presented herself as. She was wearing a pair of colourful striped socks, a hole in the big toe of one which she wiggled at herself in amusement. He poured her out a glass of cheap Scotch, handed it over. She took a gulp, its coarseness not seeming to faze her. He served one for himself and sat down on the banquette opposite.

'How's the great English novel?' she asked.

'I've started on something completely different. I think it's much better than the stuff I lost.'

She raised her glass to him. 'Glad to hear your sojourn in my cosy little trailer is working for you.'

'It's a beginning.'

'New beginnings are the hardest.'

'You can say that again.' He glimpsed up at her portrait on the wall. 'I was thinking of you being the muse for rock star guy...'

'...just so you know I wasn't like his paid model or anything. And he wasn't painting me as a means of getting into my pants.'

'Tell me what it was then?'

She knocked back the rest of the whisky, held out her glass to him. 'Fill me up first, cowboy.'

Jake duly obliged with what was left in the bottle and once he had settled back down again, she said in her lazy drawl: 'I was his inspiration. Gala to his Dali. Edie Sedgwick to his Andy Warhol. I was the representative of his feminine side. I don't mean like some kind of fertility symbol, given that I am not exactly a gal toting child-bearing hips. The opposite, in fact. I was his ingénue. His innocent. It was like it gave me some kind of power over him. A yin-yang tension. Which in turn inspired his male side to want to be creative. In a wild, frenzied kind of way. It was amazing to watch. A bit of a privilege really. But…' Angie snapped her fingers. '…as soon as we split, the painting stopped and the music got worse. All the critics say those few years were his best period, that time we had together. No kids, mind you. We didn't have any of those. His creativity didn't stretch to that. Do you have any?'

'Just the one. A boy.'

'And the mother?'

'I don't want to talk about her.'

'You won't talk about your writing. You won't talk about your marriage. And yet you want to know all about me. Play fair, Jake. Look at me. I am the lady in the mask. A keeper of secrets. I could be your muse too. I love books. And I've got myself my own writer in residence trapped down here in my little trailer. Confess something. Tell me what your book is all about?'

'It's about the responsibility of love. Whether we are forever responsible for those we have tamed.'

'Ha! The responsibility of love.' She laid her head back so she could see her own portrait. 'I don't think I should be responsible for someone else's feelings. That's their problem if they fall in love with me. Why should it be mine?'

'What about if you have enticed them, deliberately made them fall in love with you?'

She pointed a finger at him. 'This is all about you, isn't it?'

'No, it's not.'

'You can disguise your story as much as you want, Jake, but in the end, it's always about you. That's what rock star guy taught me. You just have to look at that painting up there. That's not about me, it's all about him. And his ingénue fantasies.'

'What I've written couldn't be further away from who I am. For a start, the main character is a woman.'

Angie put down her glass and got up from the banquette. 'Let me show you something.'

She opened the caravan door and brought in her canvas in its case. She unzipped the cover and took out the painting, the one presumably he had seen her working on for the last couple of days.

'See,' she said.

He looked at her work. The canvas was painted entirely in black.

NOW

As soon as Jake was off-camera, Guy grabbed him.

'We have to talk.'

'I need to speak to Francesca first.'

'She went outside to take a call from your brother.'

Guy led him to the side of the room, the *ping ping* of his phone accompanying their passage across the cables and wires splayed across the floor.

'You're going to be on the national news.'

'So Sylvia said.'

'Apparently the Beeb are sending over reinforcements to cover the event.'

'What's the big deal? It's just a literary prize.'

'Jesus, Jake. You. You're the fucking big deal. The media got hold of the YouTube clip. And now this.'

'I don't understand what "this" is?'

'This interview with Sylvia.'

'I thought she was out of order.'

'Sylvia? You. You were out of order. You were all over the place. You were half-way slid down your chair, limbs splayed out like a bloody octopus. Your dinner suit is torn at the knee, your shirt is covered in blood, your hand is all bandaged up. How much have you had to drink? How many painkillers?'

'I thought I was being quite lucid...'

'And now you're on the national news. When is a novelist ever on the fucking national news? This is absolutely brilliant. Absolutely brilliant. They're going to use you as click-bait to promote the prize-giving on BBC2. Even if you don't win this thing, your profile's going through the roof.'

'How do you know all of this?'

'Can't you see? Just take a look around.'

Jake did take a look around. Cameras, lighting, TV monitors, sound engineer, a couple of production assistants pouring over laptops. 'So?'

'Live feeds from all over the fucking planet, Jake. The outside broadcast truck in the street is rocking. Producers making instant decisions on what's hot and what's not.'

'I still don't get it.'

'You're hot right now, Jakey boy. Fucking boiling. If you'd just given birth to a royal baby, out of wedlock, on board the Titanic, you couldn't be hotter.'

'Because?'

Guy counted off the reasons on his fingers: 'One: the video of you assaulting a fan.'

'Allegedly assaulting a fan.'

'OK, allegedly assaulting a fan. It's Twittering all over the place. There's a meme, a GIF. *Writer strikes back. Shit hits the fan. One-star review. Kerpow!* Two: this car crash interview you just did on live TV.'

'I thought it went rather well.'

Guy gave him a blank look. 'Three: the fact your son has been arrested.'

'Wait a minute. How do they know Oliver was arrested?'

'Someone must have leaked it to the press.'

'Who would have leaked it to the press?'

'Don't look at me.'

'I am looking at you.'

'It could have been a whole bunch of people. The police for a start. Let's not get into this now.'

'Is that not confidential information?'

'Who am I? Clarence fucking Darrow?'

'Who's Clarence Darrow?'

'Forget it. Oliver's fair game, I'm afraid. Unless he's a minor. He isn't, is he?'

'Not according to the criminal justice system.'

'Nothing much we can do then.' Guy went back to his finger counting. 'And four....'

'There's more?'

'Yeah, this whole thing is moving fast. It's hard to keep up...'

If Jake was in any doubt about the veracity of his publisher's claim, the sound engineer from the TV crew shouted over: 'Hey, Guy. Looks like your man's up in a mo if you want to come over.' He pointed to a monitor that Sylvia and a couple of production assistants were crowding around. 'I've got the news coming in on a live feed.'

'Let's have a look at this,' Guy said. 'Come on.'

Jake tucked in his shirt with his unbandaged hand as he watched Guy wander over. He wasn't really in the mood to see himself on national television. He was actually feeling quite light-headed. Food. That's what he could do with right now. He was absolutely starving. When was the last time he had eaten? Had he even eaten at all today? Don't they have some kind of finger food at these events? Mushroom vol-au-vents? Mini burgers? Christ, he could kill for a mini burger right now. Two mini burgers. Four mini burgers. Four? Guy had four things to tell him. Yes, Guy, what was the fourth? Guy was waving him to come over. As was Sylvia. All this frantic signalling. He found it hard to resist. As were the plates of sandwiches for the TV crew.

Jake huddled in, peered over the backs of heads towards the screen. He recognised the news presenter – the Welsh guy with the soothing calm-in-a-crisis, somebody-famous-just-died, voice – but he could only catch the occasional word from where he was standing. Pictures of a royal baby, the Duke and

Duchess, then back to the presenter. He went to grab one of the sandwiches – egg mayonnaise with cress, that would do – when he saw a photograph of himself flash up on the monitor. He actually had to take a step back such was his surprise at viewing his blown-up face like that. An old profile shot. Quite a flattering one, he thought. A headshot from his journalism days. It must be ten years old. He looked back to the sandwich plate. Shit! Someone had taken it. Back to the Welsh presenter. Then the video clip of his now seemingly infamous street encounter with Brian. Back to the presenter. A clip from the interview with Sylvia. He indeed looked a mess. Although he couldn't make out what he was saying. Something about Proust. Why had he been talking about Proust? He had never even read anything by him. Then a cut to an interview with some young woman. Who was this person? What was she saying about him? She did look familiar. He could just make out the caption on the screen. Oh God yes, the Australian barmaid at the something Arms. How did they even get hold of her? It could only have been an hour or so since he had been there. What was she saying? It couldn't be anything derogatory surely? She had been really nice to him. Bandaged up his hand. She was holding up a copy of his book. Guy would love that. He probably paid her to do it. What the hell was she saying? *And then he kissed me.* That was it. No explanation. Back to the presenter who gave some kind of wry, knowing smile then signed off for the evening. Guy turned to him, put up a hand with four fingers raised and mouthed: 'Number Four.' Sylvia was also saying something to him.

'I hope when this debacle is over, you'll give me an exclusive,' she said. 'Win or lose, I think you owe me.'

'I owe you for what?'

'For screwing up my fucking interview.'

At which point, Francesca turned up at his side.

'Thank God, you're here,' Jake said. 'What's happening with Oliver?'

Francesca took a deep breath, calmed herself. 'They still haven't charged him with anything. Nick's going to hang around until they do or they don't. He'll call me with any news. I felt you might need me more than Oliver.'

'What made you think that?'

'Guy called me.'

'Good old Guy. Well, I'm glad you're here.'

She turned her attention to the little ensemble clustered around the TV monitor. 'What's going on?'

Sylvia looked up from the screen. 'I have to get ready for round two,' she said, punching Jake lightly on the shoulder as she passed. And then to Francesca: 'I'm sorry to hear about your son.'

'What did you hear?'

'That he's been arrested.'

'How do you know that?'

Sylvia shrugged and left, leaving Francesca to divert her question to Jake.

'Speak to my publisher,' Jake said, searching around for the sandwich plate.

'Guy?' Francesca said.

Guy pointed to one of the monitors. 'It was on the news.'

'How the fuck was it on the news?'

Jake couldn't find the sandwiches but he did manage to locate a pack of crisps. Salt and vinegar. His favourite flavour. As he struggled to open the packet with his teeth and one undamaged hand, Guy explained to Francesca what had happened.

She was almost in tears now. 'I don't trust you, Guy. There are real people involved in all of this. And one of them is my son. Life isn't just about book sales, you know.' As if to counter her claim, Guy's phone let off a series of *ping ping* sounds. She grunted in disgust. 'I need to talk to Jake. Alone. Now.'

Guy held his hands up in silent acquiescence. 'Dinner is about to be served. I'll see you at our table.'

Jake was tempted to go too. The crisp packaging was totally unmanageable. He was still feeling light-headed. And he was shaking now. Or being shook. Francesca had grabbed the lapels of his dinner jacket and was moving him backwards and forwards on the balls of his feet.

'Look at me, Jake. Look at me. I need you to focus.'

'I'm hungry.'

'We'll eat in a minute. Please, focus.'

He looked at her. Her face appeared quite blurry, close up to him like this. He blinked. And blinked again. He could definitely do with dinner now. Or another painkiller. His hand was beginning to throb again. She was still quite blurry. Francesca.

'Are you still angry with me?' he asked.

'About what?'

'About everything.'

'What is wrong with you, Jake? I've never ever seen you like this before. So out of control. Will you please tell me what is going on? Please.'

Jake managed to bring her into focus. He stared back at those dark brown, pleading, teared-up eyes. And he found himself having a moment of extreme and exquisite clarity. He realised that she knew more about him than he did. This must happen eventually in every relationship, he thought. The insight that comes from loving someone for so long. Francesca could see into the parts of him he even kept hidden from himself. 'I don't know, Fran. I just don't know.'

She stepped back, still holding on to his lapels, which was just as well, Jake thought, as he felt he might topple over. She gave out a deep sigh of resignation. 'We need to get you cleaned up. And sobered up. Christ, we've got a dinner and a ceremony to get through.'

She held out her hand and he took it gratefully.

As he was escorted through to the dining room, another thought came into his head.

'Fran. There's something you should know.'
'What's that?'
'Tina is here.'

THEN

AFTER THE INTERLUDE with her painted face and the black canvas, Jake found himself avoiding Angie. Or that she was avoiding him. Perhaps she had been too intimate, too revealing to him. On the days the weather was pleasant, he would see her up on the ridge with her paints and easel. He left her alone and she did not drop by. Sometimes their vehicles would pass on the narrow Cornish roads and they would give each other restrained nods. When he went up to the house every other day for a shower, he would time it for when he knew she wouldn't be there. On one such occasion when he was towel-dried and ready to go back to the caravan, he saw Mike waiting for him at the back door to the farmhouse. He held a shotgun, guitar-like across his stomach.

'Don't worry, Hemingway,' Mike said, laughing. 'For the rabbits.'

'I don't see many bunnies around here.'

'Just cleaning it when I saw you. I'd like a word.'

'I'm not behind on the rent, am I?'

'It's about the missus.'

'Yeah?'

'I know she's been to visit.'

'A couple of times.' And then as if he felt the need to defend himself, he added. 'That's all.'

'She seems to have a weird effect on you artsy people.'

'I wouldn't know.'

'Her first husband...'

'The rock star?'

'She tell you about him?'

'Not in any detail.'

'He used to write songs about her. Miserable, depressing stuff. And paint her portraits. All the fucking time. He's long dead now. Killed himself.'

'Because of her?"

'Because of her.'

'And your point is?'

'I don't want to see her appearing in any of your books.'

'Are you worried I might end up killing myself?'

He jerked the shotgun slightly. It was a subtle movement but threatening nevertheless. 'I'm being serious.'

'I have no plans to use her.'

'That's what they all say at the beginning. But then she has a way of getting under their skin.'

'Like I said, I have no plans for any Angie cameos.'

'Well, just make sure it stays that way. *Capisce,* Hemingway?'

'*Capisce.*'

'Oliver. It's Dad.'

'I know. Your name comes up on my phone.'

'How are you?'

'I'm getting old.'

'I know. You're going to be ten soon.'

'It feels like such a burden.'

'When did you start to talk like this?'

'Like what?'

'Like an adult.'

'I don't know, Dad. These are just the words that come out.'

'I feel like I'm talking to a kid in a Woody Allen movie.'

'Woody's not a kid. He's a sheriff.'

'I don't get it.'

'Woody. The sheriff in *Toy Story*.'

'Why are we talking about *Toy Story*?'

'I don't know. You started it. Are you OK?'

'I'm fine.'

'Do you have a job?'

'I'm writing.'

'Am I in it?'

'It's not like before.'

'Is it funny?'

'It's a novel.'

'Can't novels be funny?'

'They can be. But this one isn't. It would be good if it was but it's just what comes out.'

'Like my words?'

'Yeah. Like your words.'

'Mum wants to talk to you.'

'She does?'

'Deffo. She said that when you come on the phone, I've to pass you over. Hold on.'

Jake waited. And listened. He could hear Oliver calling her. And then Fran in the background. Oh, how he had missed that voice. He could feel himself tense up, his heart clattering away. It was as if he were to talk to her for the first time. Back at that party in his student flat. With her hair all tied up and he wanting to kiss the back of her neck. 'Who are you?' That's what she had asked him. As relevant a question now as it was then.

'Hey,' she said.

'Hey back,' he said, trying to keep upbeat, trying to stop his voice from cracking.

'Before we start, these are the parameters of this conversation,' she said. 'We are here to talk about Oliver's birthday. Nothing more. Got it?'

'I got it.'

'Good. It's your son's birthday next week…'

'You think I don't know that?'

'Who knows what prioritises your thoughts these days.'

'You think just because I've been away for a couple of months I've forgotten my son's birthday. What do you think of me?'

'What you seem to have immediately forgotten, Jake, are the parameters. What I think of you at this point is irrelevant to this conversation. We are here to talk about Oliver's birthday party.'

'He's having a party?'

'Yes, he's having a party. We've invited about sixteen of his friends, mainly from school, a couple from the neighbours. The parents are coming too. An afternoon tea for about thirty bodies. We're also having a magician.'

'Bouncy castle?'

'I hate bouncy castles.'

'I know you do. I was trying to lighten the mood.'

'Parameters, Jake. Parameters.'

'The party sounds like a lot of work.'

'It is a lot of work.'

'I could help you with that.'

'We don't want you to.'

'Will you stop saying that.'

'What?'

'We instead of I.'

'I do mean we.'

Jake bit back his anger. 'It would be a fatherly thing to do. To help with the party.'

'And it would be a furious wifely thing to say … that you're not invited.'

'Oh, come on. You can't do this to me.'

'It is what I am doing.'

'I have a right to be there for him on his birthday.'

'You probably have. And I'm not denying you that right.

I agree that we should try to uphold some kind of parental normality for the sake of our son and the day of his birth. I'm just saying that you're not invited to the party. It's too public for me, Jake. I don't want our marital situation to be on display to friends and neighbours. I don't want people observing us. I couldn't bear that. I'll be much better on my own. So I suggest therefore you come round earlier. Let's say around eleven. For brunch. And leave before the guests arrive. You can give him his present then. If you don't forget to get him one that is.'

'Of course, I won't forg…'

But he was talking to an empty line.

He was on his way back to the caravan from a morning's surf when the pick-up truck passed him on the road, stopped, waited for him to catch up. The window rolled down letting out a cloud of smoke. Angie.

'Chuck the board in the back,' she said. 'I'll give you a ride to the trailer.'

'I'm still pretty wet.'

'No worries. I've got a doggie towel for over the seat.'

He did what he was told, then got in beside her. The cabin stank of cigarette smoke and wet hound. She had on a thick woollen sweater, a pair of shorts and sheepskin boots.

'You been avoiding me,' she drawled as she slammed the vehicle into first and drove off.

He wasn't sure if it was a statement or a question. 'I was thinking the same about you.'

'Was it my painted face? Or did Mike put you off? With his old shotgun routine?'

'He made his point.'

'He's a jealous guy. Intensely so. But he wouldn't hurt a fly.'

'He was getting ready to kill rabbits.'

'You know what I mean.'

'Not sure if I do.'

'He's got this thing where he thinks every guy I come across wants to fuck me.'

Jake had enough experience to know that this was one of those dangerous lose–lose statements that women often put out there. As he had learned with Francesca, when a woman used the word 'fuck' in whatever context, the other person (usually a male) was teetering on the edge of a conversational minefield. In this particular case, he could either agree with Angie that every man wanted to sleep with her (and therefore by implication, so did he) or he could disagree with her statement which would then be an insult to her sexual attractiveness. He decided therefore to take the prudent route and asked:

'You got a cigarette?'

'Didn't know you smoked,' she said.

'Just the occasional one.'

She wriggled a bit in her seat, pulled a packet out of her shorts pocket. 'Help yourself.'

Which he did and lit up. Unfortunately, his diversionary tactic did not get him off the hook.

'He says it's because I was married to a rock star,' she said, continuing on her theme, crunching through the gears as she did so for which she apologised. 'Never can get used to these manual shifts,' she muttered. 'Now where was I? Oh yes, Mike and his theory that men can say *I fucked the lady who was married to*.... Bob Dylan, Robert Plant, David Bowie, fill in the blank. Same with the whole naked muse model thing. *I fucked the lady up there in that portrait in the gallery, in the museum, in the cafe, wherever.* But I think it's because he watches too much porn. You know. MILFs. Moms I'd Like to Fuck. He thinks I'm one of those. Not that I'm a mother or anything.'

Jake opened the window on his side, blew out his inhaled smoke, decided yet again not to take the bait.

'How about your kid?' Angie asked. 'How old is he?'

'He'll be ten next week.'

'I got a nephew that age. Sweet. Just before they get bratty.'

'He's having a party.'

'That'll be fun for you.'

'I'm not invited.'

She turned to look at him. 'Well, there you go,' was all she said.

The conversation went quiet after that as they bounced along the rutted path that led up to the caravan. Angie drove up alongside, snapped up the handbrake. She pulled down the sun visor, checked herself out in the mirror, did that thing women did by running her tongue over her teeth. 'Going to ask me in then?'

'I don't have any more rot-gut whisky.'

'I got some good coke.'

He looked over at her. Fingers of both hands drumming on the steering wheel, eyes all glazed up and popping, wriggling her bare thighs in her seat. She was probably all coked-up now even though it was not yet noon. He thought her conversation had been a bit manic. He flicked his cigarette butt out the window. There was no doubt Angie was still a very attractive woman. A self-defined MILF. And he had to confess his body was not entirely immune to her suggestion. Or to those naked legs close beside him.

'What do you say?' she asked, still drumming away. 'Don't you want to hang out with your muse?'

Jake half-opened his door. 'I'm going to pass, Angie. I've got a novel to write.'

It was time to move on. He packed up the Ford, strapped the surfboard on top. He clicked shut the padlock on the caravan door, stepped back from the vehicle, tried to give his temporary home a bit of credit. Apart from the break-in, it had served him well. He had enjoyed getting back into surfing, he was feeling fitter and healthier than in years, he had finally started to write his novel. He had retreated into his cave and was now prepared to come out again. Whether the world or Francesca was ready for him remained to be seen.

He drove up to the farmhouse. Perhaps Mike had a telescope trained on the caravan or his car had broken through some kind of security system along the road, but there he was, standing at the front door, waiting for him. Although thankfully this time without a rifle.

'Leaving us already, Hemingway?'

'I need to get back to London.'

'Finished the novel then?'

'A decent chunk of a first draft.'

'I take it Angie does not appear.'

'You have my word on that.'

'Don't worry, I'll be checking out the bookshops in months to come.

Jake Tully, author. I won't forget.'

'That's one sale I can rely on then.'

'I wouldn't be so flippant about it, Hemingway. I don't take kindly to you artist types exploiting my missus. Songs, portraits, novels. It feels very intrusive. And I don't like to be intruded upon.'

'Well, say goodbye to her for me.'

'I'll let her know you've gone,' Mike said as he closed the farmhouse door.

Jake drove on to the village, filled up with petrol, decided to have lunch at the local pub before the long drive to London. Fish and chips, a pint and a chance to log in to some decent Wi-Fi. He checked his email first. Just the usual crap, except there was a message from Francesca. If he was expecting some emotional plea telling him all was forgiven, he was very much mistaken. She had merely sent him a brief schedule confirming his attendance at Oliver's birthday celebrations.

11.00am: Brunch with Francesca, Oliver and Grandpa Albert

11.30am: Present giving

12.30pm: Departure*

*Please note that Grandpa Albert can stay for the party

He knocked back most of his pint, and would have ordered a whisky chaser had it not been for the fact that he needed to get back in his car and drive for five hours. Instead, he checked out Amazon to see how Adam's book was doing (#197 in *Crime, Thrillers and Mystery*). Good. It was starting to slide down the rankings. He then Googled Adam proper. It seemed he had events scheduled for Harrogate, Stirling and Dublin, then he was going on a short US tour of the East Coast. After that, he checked out Tina's literary agency website to see if she was still keeping Adam on as a client. Yes, he was still there. Perhaps the cost of the new house in Highgate was a marital and professional glue that their respective infidelities weren't going to disrupt.

Just as he finished his browsing, his lunch arrived. The person who brought it introduced himself as Ben, the manager of the establishment. A young, stockbroker type who had probably bought this old-fashioned pub with a view to turning it around with craft beers and a fancy menu. Jake's fish was served on an ersatz laminated page from the Times newspaper, his chips came in a pewter tumbler alongside a miniature plastic bottle that sprayed vinegar.

'I'm usually back of house,' Ben said. 'But we're short-staffed today.'

Jake picked up his knife and fork, waited for Ben to leave. But Ben wanted to chat. It turned out that Ben wasn't a stockbroker type at all but a born-and-bred local whose family had owned the place for years.

'I understand you've been staying out at the Morgans,' Ben said.

'I was renting their caravan for a couple of months.'

'How did that work out for you?'

'Pretty good. I got to surf, I got to write.'

'Did you get to meet Angie?'

'Hard not to. It was her caravan.'

'Did you get the painted face, "I was a muse to my ex who was a rock star" story. "But I can't tell you his name."'

'Sure did.'

'You realise it's all made up.'

'You're kidding.'

'I kid you not. Dead rock star husband never existed. She and Mike Morgan have been together for as long as I can remember … sorry, I should let you get on with your lunch.'

'No, no. I can eat, talk and listen at the same time.' To prove the point, he dug into his fish and took a mouthful. 'She's not some gal from Reno, Nevada then.'

Ben took a seat. 'Her father was military. Stationed with the US Air Force during the war, stayed on after and married a Cornish lass. I'm not sure where he was from. Could've been Reno for all I know.'

'So what's the deal then?'

'I believe they say the role-playing spices up their marriage. They didn't have any kids and it gets pretty lonely out there. So they make up these fantasy lives. Might be some drugs involved too. You're not the first resident of their caravan to be part of their little game.'

Jake sat back, not knowing whether to be amused or angry. 'Well, what do you know? I wasn't the only one making up stuff out there.'

NOW

JAKE WAITED WHILE FRANCESCA scanned the noticeboard at the entrance to the ornate dining room, ascertained the relevant seating arrangements and set off purposefully in the direction of their allotted table. He found it hard to keep up. Several people stopped him en route, most of whom he didn't know. They shook his hand, kissed his cheek, made various comments about his book, about the interview, about the video. It was hot, very hot, there was too much noise and he was starving.

A tall, burly, bald-headed bruiser of a man, stinking of some very expensive cologne, stood up in front of him, grasped his hand, shoved a business card into his top pocket. 'Give me a call tomorrow,' the man said, his American accent somehow adding a daunting element to both the scent and the request. 'Guy's too puny for you, Jake. You need a heavyweight. With clout. Both sides of the pond. Call me.'

Then a rather elegant black woman in a rather elegant black dress rose gracefully out of her chair like a twisting wisp of smoke and accosted him. 'I wish you luck, Jake. We are all winners here tonight.'

It took him a few seconds to realise who it was. Thanda Masuka, another of the short-listees if there was such a word. 'And we are all losers too,' he said for want of a response. As Francesca dragged him away, he wasn't sure if what he had said was profoundly witty or profoundly stupid. He also noticed that Tina was standing there beside Thanda in her fiery-flame trademark dress. Still with a slit up the side. He wondered if she had worn it on purpose. A reminder of that red rag to his libido even after all those years.

Again he weaved through a barrage of handshakes and cheek kissing until he reached their table. Guy was there already, standing up to greet him. He introduced Jake to his partner for the evening. Arush. From Kolkata. Which Jake seemed to recall was the city formerly known as Calcutta, it was hard to keep up these days, especially in his present mental state. Arush was a dapper young man with thick blue-black hair, long delicate fingers and the most immaculate grey suit. In the event that Jake might actually win this prize – it was still *Jake Tully Day* after all – he thought he might invest some of his winnings in such a bespoke item of clothing. He wanted to ask Arush who his tailor was but Guy was already ushering him on with the introductions. Two empty spaces beside Arush reserved for brother Nick and wife Melanie if she deigned to come and then:

'The tradition at this event,' Guy said, '... is for the organisers to assign a literary reviewer to the table of each publisher of a shortlisted book. In this case, we have the pleasure of hosting Arabella Danes... and this is her partner... Lance.'

Jake knew exactly who Arabella was. A sour but highly erudite veteran critic who was well-known for thinking her reviews were better written than her subject matter. Which they often were. Lance appeared to be about twenty years her junior, boasted thick slick-backed blond hair and pink-scrubbed handsome Aryan features that radiated all the intensity of a graduate of the Hitler youth. Without standing up, Arabella held out her hand in the way a minor female royal might do, expecting it to be kissed. Jake shook it more firmly than he intended. 'You loathed my book,' he said.

'Loathed is a rather strong word.'

'Hated then.'

'That's better,' she said, smiling. 'I actually preferred your writing in that life-style column way back in the Stone Age.'

Jake smiled back but before he had a chance to exchange greetings with Lance (who had stood up to stiff attention) he was interrupted by a young man sporting a lapel badge with the name of the evening's sponsors embossed on it. 'Excuse me, Mr Tully. But we need you in the Berkeley Suite. Photographs. Everyone is waiting.'

The Berkeley Suite was a reception room set up with a small stage and several banner backdrops displaying the logos of the BBC and the evening's sponsor. Standing on the stage in a five-person formation that seemed to be lined-up specifically against him were the other short-listed candidates. Jake would probably declare publicly that he had not really taken any interest in his competitors – 'happy just to make the shortlist,' was his mantra. Followed by: 'Winner's just down to sheer luck.' But in reality he had read all of his rivals' novels as well as followed their progress closely ever since the list had been announced. Amazon rankings, public appearances, reviews, position of said novels in bookshop windows and on shelves, any reports of rights sales to overseas territories or even movie deals. So when Giovanni (just call me Gio) Ventura, the extraordinarily handsome photographer had said to him: 'And have you met any of your fellow authors?', Jake might have been telling the truth when he answered in the negative (apart from the brief encounter with Thanda in the dining hall), but he knew exactly who they were:

Thanda Masuka: Debut writer, born in Rhodesia on 10th November 1965, the day before her country's prime minister, Ian Smith, declared independence unilaterally from Britain and became the nation now known as Zimbabwe. Unsurprisingly, her novel *Landlocked* (like the country) tells the story of a young woman born in Rhodesia but growing up in Zimbabwe striving to find her own independence away from the influence of cruel and domineering men. *Landlocked,* often referred to as the *Midnight's Children* of Zimbabwe, had already picked up several prestigious literary prizes in Africa, movie rights had been sold to Hollywood with the actor Thandie Newton, herself the daughter of a princess of the Bantu people, also of Zimbabwe, reported to have been slated for the lead. Thanda acquired British citizenship in 1992 and currently lives in London.

Shona Murray: at 31, the youngest of the group but already with three successful published novels under her belt. Based in Stornoway on the Isle of Lewis, *Salt and Guts* is an historical novel set in the early 20th century telling of the prohibited love between two herring girls working in the fishing industry. Renowned for its sexually explicit content, *Salt and Guts* is considered an outsider in this evening's proceedings although domestic sales have been the highest among the shortlisted novels. BBC Scotland are considering a TV serialisation of the book.

Vernon Harper: at 70, the oldest of the ensemble. An irascible New Yorker, he wears an eye-patch courtesy of a war wound (helicopter pilot, Vietnam, 1972. Awarded the Purple Heart). A previous winner of this evening's prize albeit back in 1979 for his highly acclaimed novel *Tet*, he has enjoyed an end-of-career comeback with his latest tome (649 pages) entitled *O, Jackie*. In his current offering, Harper imagines an historical twist, following the path the United States might have taken had Jackie Kennedy assumed the presidency after the assassination of her husband, JFK.

Mary Strauss: another literary heavyweight, Strauss has been nominated for this prize three times but never won. Born in

Cornwall in the early 1950s, she is known for being something of a recluse. She refuses to make any public appearances in promotion of her books and the only reason she has turned up tonight is apparently because she felt her previous failures were somehow due to her non-appearance at these ceremonies. Her latest novel, her ninth, is entitled *China Duck,* a love story set in Daxing at the little-known court of Emperor Wen at the end of the 6th Century. *China Duck* has been hailed as a 'triumph of the imagination', especially as Strauss has hardly set foot out of Cornwall, never mind out of the country to China. Sales are reported to be poor though.

Wayne Kassova: the son of Slovakian immigrants, Wayne is considered to be one of the new angry brigade of writers highly influenced by the Slovenian philosopher Slavoj Zizek. Kassova's novel *Saint Shit!* is considered to be a controversial choice, the judges having been accused of merely trying to look 'cool' by placing it on the shortlist. Indecipherable in places, profane and hugely scatological in others, *Saint Shit!* has been hailed both as 'a masterpiece' and as 'a sainted piece of shit.' It has huge appeal to a younger demographic and is to be released shortly as a video game although how it will transfer from page to multi-player graphics, only Zizek knows. Sales are through the roof, second only to Murray's *Salt and Guts.*

Jake screwed up his eyes, trying hard to focus on his fellow nominees in the glare of the arc lamps set up for the shoot. Gio was fussing around him, speaking terribly fast. He could see one-eyed Vernon Harper up there on the stage, tapping the boards impatiently with his cane. All five of them were holding copies of their own book, and a copy of his book was handed to him also. He placed it under his arm as he grabbed a glass of champagne from a nearby table with his unbandaged hand. 'Cheers, everyone,' he said, toasting the line-up on stage and downing the flute in one. 'Here's to demographics and the political *zeitgeist*.'

He immediately regretted having said this (even though Wayne Kassova had given him a thumbs-up) but he couldn't help himself. He believed that while the longlist was a sincere and honest attempt to whittle down the huge number of entries on the basis of quality, the shortlist was a different matter altogether. He was convinced that other issues came into play, even if they might be subconscious and the panel would never admit to them in their deepest darkest nights or under pain of death. 'Do we have the right gender balance? What about ethnic minorities? Debut writers v seasoned veterans? The large publishing houses v the small indies? Do we have an American candidate to make sure that huge market is paying attention? Jake knew from the line-up of this current crop that this jury had pretty much ticked all of the boxes. Except for one rogue choice. What the hell was he doing here?

He shuffled up to the stage with Gio in solicitous attendance.

'We've been waiting twenty minutes,' snarled Vernon, brandishing his cane to include the other nominees.

Jake felt like saying: 'And you've been waiting nearly forty years since your last big hit,' but this time he decided to hold his tongue. Instead, he nodded courteously towards Wayne, Thanda, Mary and Shona as he tried to listen to Gio's commands.

'I think we'll have you right at the end, Jake. Tucked in beside Mary. And now if everyone could just turn to me with their book covers facing out. Ah, Jake. I wonder if you would mind turning your body to the side slightly, it's the bandage. And that hole in your *pantaloni*. Yes, still with the book facing towards me. Can you manage that? Good. Now just hold still. A half-smile, please. A Mona Lisa smile. A little less of a grin, Mr Harper. Hold…and…'

Jake was finding it difficult to keep his balance. He was still feeling light-headed from the lack of food, the quick knock-back of the champagne hadn't helped. Neither was the difficulty of holding this position with his body facing inwards towards Mary Strauss while he faced out towards the photographer with his one free hand trying to keep the book flat and straight.

'Flash!'

The light blinded.

And Jake fainted.

THEN

'DID YOU BRING ME BACK ONE OF THOSE SPOONS?' Albert Tully asked.

'I was nowhere near your Normandy-landing rehearsal place,' Jake said, as he laid out the two fish suppers on the dining room table.

'I thought you said you were going surfing in Wales.'

'I was in Cornwall.'

'I thought you said Wales.'

'I think maybe it's time for you to have your hearing tested.'

'My hearing's just fine.'

'Well, you're not listening then.'

'You want me to listen too?'

As if to prove his point, his father leaned over from his high-backed chair, flicked a switch on the tape deck. Debussy. Albert Tully's favourite composer. The eloquent sounds lapped from the delicate touch of fingers on a piano keyboard to the appreciative ears of a man who had hammered metal all his life. His father sighed at the irony of it all, picked up his knife and fork, and proceeded to tackle a large portion of fried haddock.

'I wasn't just surfing, Dad. I was writing as well.'

'That column for that paper?' Albert Tully's political sensibilities would not allow him to state the name of the broadsheet Jake had sold his soul to.

'I quit that months ago.'

'Fran told me you were fired.'

'So you do listen then?'

His father paused a chip-laden fork on its way to his mouth, seemed to be about to say something, but thought against it and let his fork continue on its journey. 'What are you writing then?' he asked through a mouthful of fried potato.

'A novel.'

'Will it support your family?'

'I'm not sure I've got a family to support.'

'Once you've lost someone's trust, you can never reclaim it.'

'Thanks, Dad. That's not very supportive.'

'It's the truth. You might get back together, but it will never be the same.'

'When did you become such an authority on relationships?'

'From living this long,' his father said with a Buddha-like serenity. 'So what did you get Ollie for his birthday?'

'A smartphone.'

'Does Fran know?'

'I think I can decide what is best for my son.'

'I hope it's the latest model.'

'Dad. I'm virtually broke. I've done the best I could.'

'You know how kids want the latest in everything.'

'How do you know what a boy wants? You bought me a dog I didn't want.'

'It was a rescue dog.'

'It was me who needed rescuing, Dad.'

'From what?'

'I'd just lost my mother, for God's sake.'

'I thought I was giving you something else to love.'

It was Jake's turn to pause in the consumption of his meal. He glanced across at his father who looked away. Debussy's *La Mer* filled the gap.

'What did you get him then?' Jake asked eventually.

'A model ship. One of those build-it-yourself kits.'

'Don't tell me. A Normandy landing-craft.'

'Why would I get him something like that? It's a pirate galleon.'

'I didn't know he liked ships.'

'When I take him to the pond in that park near your house, he'll sit watching those remote-controlled ones for hours.'

'You take Oliver to the park?'

'Who else is going to do it?'

This was the greatest feeling of all, Jake thought. That unconditional love of a young boy for his father. Oliver had rushed towards him, screaming, 'Dad, Dad,' then hugged him around the waist. Jake just stood there basking in the soothing balm of it all, having felt until this point like a stranger in his own house. This was a love that didn't judge or blame. At least not until Oliver was old enough to discover that his father had betrayed his mother, causing the break-up of his parents' marriage, thereby forever making Oliver lose trust in the possibility of sustaining a lasting relationship, resulting in years of expensive but useless therapy and a life of eternal loneliness.

'So…?' Francesca's voice.

Jake opened his eyes. Yes, Francesca. With a smile. A parental one not a spousal one. Francesca. The woman formerly known as his loving wife. Francesca still appearing beautiful but with a look of pain in her eyes that probably only he could detect, for he had been the cause. ('See there, just at the very corner of the iris, that loss of sparkle, that little area of dullness, that was me. I did that.') Oliver removed his grasp and moved on to his grandfather. Jake held out his hands. 'What is it to be?' he asked her. 'A kiss? A hug?'

'A peck on the cheek will be acceptable. Parameters. Remember.'

'Ah yes, parameters.' He did as instructed, held her by the shoulders and leaned forward to touch her skin with his lips. He was trembling. Francesca felt as cold as ice.

'You just missed Nick and Melanie,' she said. 'They can't come later so they popped in early to give Oliver his present.'

'Look what they got me,' Oliver said, pulling an iPhone out of the bib pocket of his dungarees. 'It's the brandest newest,' he said, waving the supreme model, so sleek and shiny, compared to Jake's meagre re-conditioned offering. 'I can be the bestest spy now,' Oliver whispered to him.

'Well?' Francesca asked. 'And what did your father get for you?'

'Yes, Dad. What's in the big bag?'

What was in his holdall was nothing apart from a birthday card and his own slither of a now redundant present. The rest of the space was reserved for some of his clothes, books and papers he had hoped to pick up on this visit.

'*Mea culpa*, Fran,' Albert Tully said, stepping into the conversation with hands raised in surrender. 'I told Jake I'd be in for the delivery yesterday afternoon. Sod's Law. I was only out for an hour and that's when they came.' As he spoke, he magically pulled a coin from behind his grandson's ear, the same stupid trick Jake had enjoyed as a child and that still held a fascination for the following generation.

Jake watched as Francesca screwed up her mouth, let her head bob up and down as she scrutinised his saviour of a father and then him, in search of the truth. Albert Tully meanwhile unclenched his hands to show to Oliver's amazement that a fist-concealed sweet had now miraculously disappeared.

'I'm going to pick it up from the Post Office later,' Jake said. 'I've got the little notecard thing they put through the letter-box.'

Jake could see that Francesca was considering asking him to produce the said notecard as Exhibit A in evidence but let it drop. Oliver, meanwhile, no longer mesmerised by his grandfather's antics, asked:

'Can you tell me what it is?'

'It's a secret,' Jake said, which was true as he had no idea what to get him now.

Oliver shook himself to attention, placed his hands on his hips and said in what Jake thought was a rather adult demeanour.

'Don't worry, Dad. I like it better to get your present tomorrow. It'll be like having two birthdays.'

Jake followed Francesca through the lounge – trestle tables set out with paper cloths, plastic plates and cutlery, waiting for the arrival of the caterers; balloons and streamers; *Happy 10th Birthday, Oliver* banner, goodie bags for guests. He was a gift-less gate-crasher at his own child's party. Into the kitchen where Fran had prepared a tasty brunch of eggs Florentine, Cumberland sausage, hash browns and toast which Albert Tully piled on his plate and returned to the living room to watch TV. Oliver was wired on excitement and sugar which was just as well as he needed all his energy to be the conduit for all the conversation that flowed at the table. Jake tried to engage Fran directly but she was having none of it.

'Ask your father where he's been for the last two months?'

'Ask your father if he enjoyed his holidays?'

'Ask your father if he's found himself an actual job?'

'Ask your father how Auntie Tina is?'

Until eventually even Oliver was forced to say in that increasingly mature way of his: 'Mum. Dad isn't invisible. Ask him yourself. He's sitting just there.'

'I've started writing,' Jake told her.

'I don't know why you think that might be important.'

'I realise you've lost faith in me. That I'm some kind of wastrel. But I'm trying. I'm really trying.'

'Wastrel might not be top of the list of why I've lost faith in you. But parameters, Jake. Parameters.'

'Fran. We really need to talk.'

'You might need to talk. But I don't. And I would prefer if we didn't do this in front of the boy.'

'That's what I'm trying to suggest. Can't we meet up in some place of neutrality for a chat?'

'Like Switzerland?

'You know what I mean. Away from here.'

'What does 'neutrality 'mean?' Oliver asked, looking up briefly from tapping away on his iPhone.

'It doesn't matter, honey,' Francesca said.

'Fran,' Jake pleaded.

'Don't you have to go to the Post Office? I have a party to organise.'

Jake stood up, grabbed his hold-all. 'I need to pick up some things.'

His presence in what had once been a joint share of the marital bedroom and adjoining *en suite* was now reduced to one closet of the built-in wardrobe. All those years of fucking and plucking and pissing and shitting and shaving and reading and talking and laughing and loving had been eradicated. It was as if he had been airbrushed out of his own home's (and Francesca's) history. Or at least packed away into this little side cupboard. It all seemed so final. So irreversible. While he had felt that the situation was still salvageable, that a reconciliation was still possible even if, as his father had not refrained from pointing out, that it would never be the same as before. He opened up his hold-all and half-heartedly packed away some of his shirts off their hangars. He noticed that Fran had even stashed away the family albums. He was frightened to look inside in case his face had been cut out of the photographs.

Back downstairs in the hallway, he hugged Oliver for as long as his son's patience allowed, promised that he would return the following day with his present. He had already decided what he would get him. One of those fancy kites with some cool graphics on the fabric. A brilliant idea, he thought, that had struck him within the midst of his misery up in the bedroom. A simple, ecologically-friendly, non-digital, eminently sociable, outward-looking gift that allowed father and son to share quality time together in the park staring up at a cloudless sky on glorious summer days.

He kissed Francesca on the cheek, mouthed a silent gratitude to his father for his earlier timely intervention and left before the other guests were due to arrive with hold-all swung over his shoulder like some homeless vagabond (which in many ways he was). The front door closed behind him, he walked down the garden path, out of the gate, turned left, passed the family BMW Francesca had now claimed as a down payment towards his infidelity, and clambered into his own beat-up Ford via the passenger seat (driver-side door-handle inoperable). As he checked his mirrors before pulling out, he saw a familiar car coming down the street, drawing in behind the Beamer. He scrunched down in the driver's seat, praying Adam wouldn't recognise his car (fortunately he'd taken his surfboard down off the roof rack earlier in the day), adjusted his mirrors slightly and watched. Adam got out of his Range Rover, moved around to the kerb, opened up a rear door and extracted a top-of-the-range bodyboard, still in its polythene wrapper. He zapped the vehicle locked and turned to the garden gate with the present under-arm. Jake gave his passenger wing-mirror an electronic tweak in order to properly follow his progress. As Adam turned to close the gate, giving Jake a full-frontal view, he realised his old friend was wearing his stolen leather jacket.

What he should have done was drive to the nearest station and taken the Tube into the city to find Oliver his kite. After that, he should have gone back to his father's house, fired up his laptop and got on with writing his novel. Instead he found himself driving the leafy streets of this part of south London with only one thought and one direction in mind. Adam was wearing his jacket. Could he have been mistaken?

Not a chance. He knew that piece of sculpted leather as if it were his own skin. He had been responsible for each buff, scuff and crease. How had Adam known where he had disappeared to? Now that he thought about it, it couldn't have been that hard. On going out to the back lane to retrieve the bins, Francesca would have probably noticed his muddy footprints leading to the shed. The absence of the surfboard and wetsuit would be obvious, she would have then alerted Adam who would know immediately that Cornwall would be his destination, most likely somewhere around Spiky Point. It wouldn't have been difficult to ask around the village if there were any strangers staying around these parts. And voila! Jake was hiding out at the mad Morgans' caravan. Adam might have even watched him surfing Spiky. After all, that was the day he was broken into. Jake supposed he was lucky Adam hadn't slashed his car tyres at the same time or found his stash of keys and debit card. Did Francesca know what he had done? She surely would have recognised the jacket as well. Although perhaps Adam was wearing it for the first time to Oliver's party on the chance he'd bump into him. A clever little move, a subtle reproof, Jake had to concede that. Not that he cared now that he had arrived outside his old friend's residence wondering whether Tina would be home and alone on this Saturday afternoon.

He thought about checking out the rear of the house to see if she was working in the office in the garden, the scene of their so-called 'rut in the hut'. But no, he would walk straight up the path to the front door. After all, that was what Adam had done, wearing his favourite jacket. He placed his hand on the handle of the gate. He took a couple of deeper breaths to regain his composure from his angry drive over. And in the small space that he had momentarily given himself to calm, a more rational part of his brain took over. What was he doing? Why was he letting himself be led by his anger, a need for revenge? It was Francesca he wanted, not Tina. It was his marriage that he needed to save. It was a novel that he wanted to write. He lifted his hand from the latch, turned around, drove to the nearest Tube station and headed into the city.

NOW

WHEN JAKE CAME TO, he felt a sharp coldness pressing on his forehead. Faces were hovering above him like bobbing balloons – Francesca dabbing him with a compress, Guy peering in and out, yabbering away on his mobile. A dark-skinned face he didn't immediately recognise. Ah yes, Guy's lover. Arush. Wearing that beautiful suit.

'Everything's fine,' this Arush said. 'You just fainted.'

'He needs to eat,' Francesca added.

'That and the fact that he's been losing blood,' Arush noted.

'Blood?' Jake asked.

'Yes, your hand,' Arush said. 'I should re-dress that for you.'

'You can do that?'

'Arush's a doctor,' Guy told him. 'The St John Ambulance guys are here too.'

'So let's get you sitting up,' Arush said, gently lifting upwards with hands to his neck and back. 'I've got the first aid kit.'

Jake looked around. He was sitting on some kind of platform. The photo session. He remembered that.

'Nothing broken,' Arush confirmed.

'Which is more than I can say for Mary Strauss,' Guy added.

Jake was confused. 'Mary Strauss? What happened to her?'

'You collapsed on top of her. She cushioned your fall but then she toppled off the stage. Suspected broken arm. She's already been carted off to the hospital.'

Francesca stopped applying the compress, handed him a glass of water. He gulped it down.

'It's ironic,' Guy said. 'She always refused to come to these ceremonies in the past. And when she does…anyway, at least the photographer got some shots in before it all went pear-shaped.'

'Can we not talk about this right now,' Francesca scolded.

Arush intervened. 'I'm just going to get you to stand. Slowly now.' With a hand under his armpit, he helped raise Jake to his feet.

'It's OK,' Jake said. 'I'm fine.'

'Are you sure?' Francesca asked.

'Yeah. I just need to eat something. Let's go back to the dinner.'

'Not until I've had a look at that hand of yours,' Arush said. 'Now, let's have you sitting on that chair over there.'

Jake did as he was told and sat back down. Arush unpeeled the dressing that had been applied by his kiss-and-tell Australian barmaid. 'That's a deep cut,' he said. 'It should really be stitched.'

'I'll take him straight to A&E once this evening's over,' Francesca said.

'Actually, he's due at Wood Street Police Station after this,' Guy told her.

'What are you talking about?'

'I forget to tell you,' Jake said. 'Remember that guy I pushed in Covent Garden. He's accusing me of assault. The police need to see me.'

Jake watched as Francesca's mouth contorted into various shapes, emitting weird sounds as she struggled to find the words to match her exasperation. 'Oh, for God's sake,' she said eventually. 'I don't think I can take any more of this.'

'Can we just sort out this dressing first,' Arush said, jacket off and equipped with a roll of bandages, gauze and a pair of scissors.

'Needle and thread coming through.' It was Gerald the make-up artist, his utensils held aloft.

'I think we should leave the stitching to the hospital,' Guy said.

Gerald looked confused. 'I'm here to fix his trousers.'

Jake was feeling much better now. He'd just polished off a plate of leek and potato soup along with a basket of assorted bread and could feel the nourishment coursing through his veins, dislodging his light-headedness, filling his brain with witty conversation. Arush had given him a couple of painkillers which was also helping the situation. Several well-wishers had already approached, many with the same comment regarding the unfortunate incident with Mary Strauss: 'Well, that's one way of getting rid of the opposition.' He laughed good-naturedly despite the underlay of guilt. He would have loved a glass of wine but opted for mineral water in an effort to appease Francesca who sat stiff and silent beside him, cutting up his roast beef and vegetables, and drinking rather a lot of wine herself. Otherwise, order around the table had been restored. Guy was back in position, sharing some video clip on his mobile with Arush (no doubt another YouTube visit to Jake's alleged assault incident). There was no news from Nick who was still at the police station while it seemed that sister-in-law Melanie would not be making an appearance (as was so often the case). Hitler Youth graduate Lance was twisting and kissing the palm of critic Arabella's hand while she forked a piece of halibut towards her mouth with the other. But before the flaky flesh reached her lips, drawn thin and cruel from years of literary snarking, she said:

'So, Jake. Taking yourself out of the equation, who do you fancy to win tonight?'

Jake waited until Francesca had moved his plate with the cut-up food in front of him, then speared a piece of beef with his one good appendage in a sort of one-handed sparring gesture towards his questioner. 'I'd probably go with Thanda Masuka and *Landlocked*.'

'Hmm. I thought it was all a bit too typical of the genre.'

'What do you mean by that?'

'We boorish British exploiting the people and resources of Africa. A metaphor for racial inequality. Imperialism. Colonialism. Yawn, yawn, yawn.'

'So taking Jake, and obviously Thanda, out of the equation, Arabella,' Guy said. 'Who would you put your money on?'

'I thought Wayne Kassova's *Saint Shit!* was brilliant,' she said. 'So original. So vital. So refreshing. But I doubt if the jury will agree. It's all a bit too *avant garde* for them.'

'I thought it was a piece of shit,' Francesca said, noticeably slurring her words. 'Pretentious crap.'

Arabella ignored her and went on: 'And you know something, Jake. I didn't hate your book. I just wish male writers like you – and that old misogynistic git Vernon – would stop appropriating the female voice. I'm sure you've got plenty of good male material of your own without having to pretend you know what lurks inside a woman's mind.'

'I'll go along with you there,' said Francesca. 'Jake hasn't got a clue about the female psyche.'

Arabella dipped her glass of wine towards Francesca in a gesture of female solidarity and then went on to say: 'I wouldn't even mind if you won, Jake. If your interview with Sylvia was anything to go by, I'm sure a Jake Tully acceptance speech would be rather entertaining.'

'I am told the world, the BBC and the Twittersphere awaits,' Jake added, feeling desperate now for a glass of wine.

Arabella retrieved her hand from her slobbering beau and applauded mockingly. 'I shall look forward to it. Not that you'll win, of course.'

'You know something, Arabella,' Jake said. 'Next time around, I'm coming back as a tennis player.'

'What are you talking about?'

'Ah yes, the famous Roger Federer theory of life,' Francesca interjected.

Jake went on. 'All this subjective jury stuff. Political correctness. The current *zeitgeist*. Reviews by critics who think they know better. Just hit the ball over the net, get it between the lines and beyond your opponent. And voila! You win.' As if to demonstrate his point, Jake stood up and took a swipe across the table with his good arm, knocking over Francesca's (fortunately empty) glass in the process. 'I think I shall go to the loo,' he announced.

Jake raised a glass to himself in the toilet mirror, a tumbler of Scotch he had grabbed from the bar as he stumbled en route to the Gents. He looked awful. Where was that make-up artist Gerald when he needed him? His eyes were blood-shot, his complexion ashen, his hair was all over the place. He ran some cold water out of the tap, splashed his face. That was better. He returned to contemplating his features. He had a little bit of a buzz on now what with the whisky, the painkillers and whatever else he had consumed during the day. So many things to distract him that he had almost forgotten what this day was all about. *Jake Tully Day*. This was it. This was his moment. He left his tumbler on the glass shelf and retreated into one of the cubicles. It was one of those old Victorian units with the elevated cistern and the chain with the wooden handle. He stood there urinating for what seemed like ages. He couldn't remember stopping for a piss all day, his bladder must have been full to the brim made up almost entirely of alcohol with a dash of leek and potato soup. He zipped himself up, pulled the chain with a certain aplomb, washed his hands, retrieved his tumbler of Scotch and exited into the hallway. Waiting for him against the opposite wall, resplendent in her red dress slit up at the thigh was Tina.

'So, here we are, Jake,' she said.

'Yes, here we are.'

'Who would have thought that after all that has happened, we would both end up here? Together. At this pivotal moment in our lives.'

'On Jake Tully Day.'

'Is that how you see this then? As your day. I wouldn't bet on that. Though I'm surprised to see you here with Francesca. I thought you two were over long ago.'

'She's here to lend support.'

'I always thought she was a bit up herself.'

'I'd rather you not talk about the mother of my child like that.'

'You're still a free man then?'

'Are we ever free from those we have tamed?'

'Jesus Christ, Jake. You sound like your novel.'

'What about you then? Are you a free woman?'

'Why? Would you like to tame me?'

THEN

Jake rarely looked up to the sky. When had he last gazed up at the clouds or the stars? Or the tops of buildings, especially in London where much of the best architecture lay in the turrets, the cornices, the finials and the canted bay windows of its upper structures. But he was looking up at the sky now. Because up there in the blue yonder flew a delta kite with the picture of a dragon emblazoned on the fabric. While down here on the ground – on a grass-covered hill on Hampstead Heath to be precise – he lay side-by-side with his son Oliver who maintained an umbilical connection to the soaring and swooping fabric by virtue of an extraordinary length of nylon string.

'This is so cool, Dad.'

'Yeah. Really cool.'

The weather had been kind to them this spring. This was the third time now that Jake had been able to take Oliver up to north London to fly his birthday present on the heath. He picked at the salt and vinegar crisps from the bag that lay split open between them, took a sip from a can of lager. He felt like a real father. 'Yeah. Really cool.'

'It's like the beginning of an episode of the Simpsons,' Oliver said.

'What?'

'The fluffy clouds and the blue sky.'

Such was the tragedy of the post-modern world, Jake thought, when the main reference point for celestial beauty was the title sequence for an American cartoon series. 'Yeah, I get it.'

'*Cumulus humilis.*'

'What?'

'Those cloud shapes.'

'How do you know that?'

'That's what school's for.'

'Is that what they teach ten-year-olds these days?'

'We need to start young with the environment… if we're going to save the planet and right the wrongs of previous generations.'

'That's a very mature thought.'

'Ten's the new twelve, Dad. Didn't you know?' Oliver jumped up quickly to tighten the string as the kite began to sag on the line. Then once he'd wrestled the dragon back into his control, he bent down, picked up his can of Coke, took a swig and asked: 'When are you going to come live with us again?'

'As soon as your mother and I can sort things out.' He was beginning to feel a bit more positive about the situation with Francesca. Each time he'd been at the house to pick up or deliver back Oliver, their conversation had lengthened slightly. He felt their relationship was improving one sentence at a time.

'Is it still because of you going off on holiday with Aunt Tina?'

'Is that what your mother said?'

'Sort of.'

'Well, that's sort of the reason.'

'She doesn't come round anymore.' He toggled the winder and high up in the sky the kite responded. 'Pity. I liked her.'

'Does Uncle Adam come around?'

'Yeah, quite a bit.'

'With Patrick?'

'Naw. We fell out. Big time.'

'Really? You were such good friends.'

'Relationships change, Dad.'

'I suppose they do.'

'It's a matter of trust.'

'Your mother teach you that?'

'Grandpa Albert actually. Hey, you know Uncle Adam's got a leather jacket just like yours.'

'Yeah.'

'He gave me a bodyboard for my birthday. Top of the range.'

'Not much use in London though.'

'He's taking us all down to Cornwall for the summer. If me and Patrick patch things up that is. I can use it then.'

Jake finished off his can of lager. It seemed that the number of sentences between himself and Francesca would need to be increased.

'Dad?'

'Yes.'

'Your turn to take the controls.'

Jake stood up and took possession of the winder as he tried to absorb the news of Adam's increased intrusion into his family. He kept his eye on the kite, let it drop then hauled it in so it would catch the air and lift again. There was something soothing about keeping his attention on the azure vault above, removing him from his troubles on planet earth.

'Do you have a job now?' Oliver asked.

'I'm writing a book.'

'Is that a job?'

'It's a vocation.'

'It's a holiday then.'

'That's a "vacation". A vocation is like a noble profession. A calling.'

'Do you get any money from it?'

'No.'

'Is that what makes it a noble vocation?'

'I suppose so.'

'So how do you live then?'

'Good question.'

'I've got my birthday money. You can have that.'

'That's very kind of you, but I'll manage,' he said, feeling himself tearing up at his son's offer. He took another sip of lager, turned his attention back to the kite as it began to sink in the dying breeze.

Oliver went quiet for a while then asked. 'What is your book about?'

'It's about taking responsibility for those you have allowed to fall in love with you.'

Oliver whistled through his teeth. 'Wow, Dad. That's pretty heavy stuff.'

'We need to talk,' Jake said, on returning Oliver from his kite-flying expedition.

'Parameters, Jake,' Francesca said. 'Parameters.'

'I don't want to talk about us. I want to talk about Oliver.'

'OK, then.'

'Can you at least let me in?'

Francesca folded her arms, turned her back on him, retreated into the kitchen, where she took up her position on a high stool by the central island. 'Just don't expect refreshments,' she said.

Jake eased himself onto a stool opposite. 'What happened with Oliver and Patrick? They used to be such good friends.'

'They fell out over a girl.'

'What? At their age?'

'Kids are so precocious these days. Haven't you noticed?'

'Maybe I should write a column about it.'

'Don't you dare.'

'And what's this about Adam taking you all down to Cornwall?'

'Parameters, Jake.'

'To hell with parameters. This is about my family.'

'Maybe you should have thought about that before you slept with Tina.'

Jake inhaled deeply. 'OK. Let me put it another way. I'm concerned that Adam might be trying to replace me in Oliver's life. What with bodyboards and stuff.'

Francesca appeared to soften slightly. 'Given the Oliver and Patrick situation, Cornwall might not be happening. Anyway, don't you mean you're concerned Adam is trying to replace you in my life?'

'Well, is he?'

'Adam's been very supportive during this difficult time for me. And I've supported him.'

'I don't see why he needs support. He was quite happily having an affair with his secretary. And he's been paid a fortune for a crappy crime novel.'

'Two crappy crime novels.'

'OK, two then.'

'Which you haven't read.'

'Which I haven't read.'

'You don't get it, do you?'

'What don't I get?'

'How much you hurt him. For betraying your friendship.'

'I betrayed our friendship? That bastard betrayed our friendship a long time ago.'

'We're going back to the Canadian Lolita era, are we?'

'What if I am? It happened at a hugely formative time in my life. You can't just unforget these things. And if we're talking about childish revenge here, he's the one who trashed my caravan. He took my laptop. He stole my fucking leather jacket.'

She laughed. It took him by surprise. It was the first time she'd done that in his company for months. 'Yeah, I noticed he was wearing it at Oliver's party.'

'I don't think it's funny.'

'He did it because he loves you, Jake.'

'So what?'

'And you did it because you love him.'

'What are you saying? My feelings for Adam were so profound, I was prepared to sacrifice our marriage to get revenge?'

'That's a reasonable way of putting it.'

'Can you please stop all this Freudian shit? All I want to know is if there's anything going on between the two of you.'

'And all I want right now is that you should be a good father.'

Jake went back to his own father to find Albert Tully sitting in his kitchen with his other son. Nick was wedged uncomfortably behind the small Formica-topped table, kitted out in his fancy mohair suit, silk tie and hand-made shoes.

'Come for your money?' Jake said.

'I came to see our father.'

Albert Tully grunted, picked up his paper. 'I'm going to watch the news,' he said.

Jake filled up the kettle, helped himself to a chocolate digestive out of the biscuit jar. 'How's life in the fast lane?' he asked.

'It pays the bills.'

Given that Nick had a shopaholic for a wife, one daughter at university, one at a private school, a house in north London and one in south-west France, a pedigree dog that cost more than the average car and a brother who was homeless and destitute, Jake appreciated that these bills might be quite hefty. 'Crime pays then.'

'You know very well I'm corporate.'

'Same thing.'

'Oh, for fuck's sake, Jake. Don't be so self-righteous.'

'It was just a joke,' Jake said, enjoying his feeling of smugness at getting Nick all riled up. It was the kind of remark their father would have made too. Nick had begun his legal career with aspirations for doing good in the world, bringing justice to the down-trodden, campaigning for the rights of human beings who had none. In the end, he had just gone for the money.

Nick unbuttoned his shirt collar, loosened his tie. 'There's something I need to talk to you about.'

'If it's about the money I owe you, you'll just have to wait.'

'It is about money.' Nick got up, went over to close the door that led to their father and the TV. 'I've got a proposal I'd like you to consider.'

Jake dunked his teabag in his mug. 'I'm all ears.'

Nick fiddled with one of his diamond-encrusted cufflinks. 'Dad's not getting younger.'

'None of us are.'

'Can you just lay off the smart-ass comments and listen to me for a moment.'

'Go on.'

'He's what… eighty-three now. Nearly eighty-four. How many good years has he got left? Three? Six? Twelve if he's very lucky.'

'He could live until he's a hundred. What's your point?'

'Just hear me out. This here is a fine property. Not the house. The house is a dilapidated piece of shit.'

'It's the family home.'

'It was fine in its time.'

'Jesus, Nick. I'd have thought you'd have a bit more sentimentality about the place. After all, it's about the only connection we have left to Mum.'

Nick went back to fiddling with his cufflink. 'If anyone has connections to this place because of Mum, it's me. You were only six when she died.'

'I've still got memories.'

'You were always fighting with her. Tantrums. Screaming. Do you remember that? Kicking out at her. I remember you scratched her once so bad across the cheek we had to tell Dad the cat did it. Otherwise he'd have spanked your little arse off.'

'I remember her for other reasons.'

'Well, Dad hasn't invested in this wonderfully happy, happy, Disney family home of yours for years. It's falling apart. But the land. This is a good half-acre in a highly desirable area with a great view of the city. So...'

'So what?'

'Well, it's been my dream...well, Melanie's and my dream... to retire and build our own home.'

'You're going to retire? You're not even fifty.'

'I'm not ready to retire. I can't afford it. But when I do, I'd like to knock down this house and build something on the land. So what I'm suggesting, Jake, in a way that I hope you will think is fair and beneficial to both of us given our current situations... is that I buy out your share in this house. Now.'

'I don't get it. You want to pay me off and make Dad homeless?'

'Don't be ridiculous. What I'm suggesting is this. Let's say this property is worth what....? Four hundred thousand? Don't worry, we can get a proper independent valuation if we decide to go ahead. So your share is half that at two hundred. Well, I'm offering to buy you out now in six annual instalments of twenty-five thousand each.'

'That's only a hundred and fifty thousand.'

'As you said, Dad could live until he's a hundred. That's seventeen years away. House prices could also go down. This London boom isn't going to last forever. I'm offering you a guaranteed income right now of twenty-five grand a year for the next six years in exchange for your share in the house. That's more than the average London wage. Net not gross. And I'll even write off what you already owe me. That'll give you six years to write your great novel, establish a literary career while keeping up Oliver's child support with the minimum of financial worries. And I get this house and land when Dad dies, whenever that is.'

'What happens if he goes in the next couple of years?'

'That's a risk you'll have to take. As do I, if he lives until he's a hundred.'

'You're wanting us to gamble on our father's life expectancy?'

'I was thinking more in terms of me helping you out of a financial jam right now. While I get to build the house of my dreams at some later date.'

'I'm going to have to think about this.'

'Take your time.'

'You'll pay for an independent valuation?'

'I can do that.'

'You'll write off the four grand I owe you?'

'I'll do that too.'

'And you want to give me twenty-five grand a year over six years.'

'That's what I'm offering.'

'Make it thirty grand over five years and I'll take it.'

Nick reached into his pocket, pulled out his phone, tapped away at his calculator app before looking up and saying: 'You gotta deal.'

Jake shook his brother's hand. 'Why do I feel like Essau?'

'What?'

'When he gave away his birthright to Jacob for a mess of pottage.'

'What the fuck's pottage?'

'Some kind of Biblical stew, I guess.'

'This is a business deal, Jake. Let's not get all religious about it.'

NOW

IT WAS A STAND-OFF.

Jake leaned against the wood-panelled wall, his one good hand grasped around a glass of whisky. His trousers were stitched up at the knee (albeit a fine example of invisible mending by make-up guy Gerard) and the flap of his blood-stained shirt hung out from the waistband of his dinner suit. On the opposite side of the thick-carpeted corridor, Tina also stood with her back against the wall, fingers pulling slightly on the top of the slit on her dress so that it rode further up her tanned leg. Or her tan stocking, it was hard for him to tell. Her hips were pushed out towards him in an almost obscene gesture. Jake had consumed too many pills and too much alcohol throughout the day but his head felt remarkably clear at this point. It was a clarity that made him realise Tina was drunk or high or both.

'Aren't you excited?' she slurred.

He wasn't sure what he should be excited about. He enquired accordingly.

'About now,' she said.

Again he wasn't sure to what she was referring. This was the trouble when trying to communicate with drunks or stoners, he thought, as he put down his whisky glass on a convenient side table adorned with a leafy plant of some considerable height and girth.

'About this.' She raised both her arms wide, palms flat, in a kind of expansive shrug. 'You and me, Jake. Look how far we've come. You've been shortlisted for a major fucking prize. And so have I. Or at least one of my writers has. A writer whom I may add that I've dragged through the whole fucking process from start to finish. Jesus, I so edited the shit out of that book I might as well have written it myself. What do you say, Jake? Shouldn't we celebrate?'

'Nobody's won anything yet. Although I believe your client Thanda has a good chance.'

Tina looked at her wristwatch, moving it back and forward in front of her eyes as she tried to focus. 'We've got thirty minutes of dinner until we're back on air with the speeches. Let's fuck. There must be an empty cubicle in there behind you.'

'I can't believe you're even suggesting this.'

'I can't help myself. I find myself hopelessly attracted to you at this moment.' She moved across the corridor, grabbed his wrist above the bandage, tried to pull him towards the door of the Gents. 'What's wrong? Have you lost your mojo?'

'Stop this.'

'You know you want to.' Her hand slipped from his wrist to his groin where she discovered that despite his verbal resistance, his body had different aspirations. She gave a little cat purr of satisfaction. 'See. I know you want it.'

'You can never take "no" for an answer.'

'I don't hear you saying "no"'.

He moved Tina's hand away from the front of his already beleaguered trousers. 'I have more important things to do,' he said. He picked up his whisky, knocked back the rest of the contents, dumped the glass in the plant pot and strode off down the corridor, thinking this must have been how Jesus felt having foregone his last temptation.

He opened the heavy door to the dining room and as he readjusted his eyes to the blaze of the chandeliers and the arc lamps on the TV gantry, he realised that standing there, waiting for him was his brother Nick. And beside Nick, stood his son Oliver.

'Dad.' Oliver flung his arms around his neck, then stepped back to look at him. 'Christ, you look like shit.'

'It's not been a great day.'

'That makes two of us.'

Jake took a good look at his son. He hadn't seen him in weeks and he seemed to have evolved considerably in that time. Was he taller? Did members of the male species still grow at the age of eighteen? He thought he was looking at a much more mature Oliver yet a younger version of himself. Then Oliver's face partly morphed into Francesca's before moving on to display some of his own father's features. He blinked himself back into focus and asked: 'So what happened?'

'Uncle Nick here got it sorted.' Oliver patted his uncle on the back. 'Justice prevailed.'

Nick shrugged. 'Nothing to sort in the end. They just wanted to hold him a few hours to give him a bit of a fright. You know, to express their gratitude for Oliver here calling them "fucking pigs".'

'It was a peaceful protest, Dad. Heavy-handed police tactics were not required.'

Nick continued. 'No charges brought. So I thought I'd drag my ex-con of a nephew along with me to cheer on his father. My plus-one since Melanie can't make it. I assume there isn't a dress code for guests.'

Oliver was kitted out in the usual student garb – an olive T-shirt with a black, defiant fist and the words *Youth for Truth* emblazoned on the front, torn jeans and battered trainers. Jake also noticed the tattoo, the lower section of it sneaking out below his son's T-shirt sleeve, some elaborate design with the words *Youth for Truth* lettered underneath. Normally, he would have said something but now was not the occasion. Let Francesca deal with the consequences of a time-limited motto inked on their son's skin for life. And considering his own blood-stained shirt, patched trousers and blotched face, Jake didn't think he was in a position to judge. 'Does your mother know you're here?' he asked.

'I've seen her already.'

'Why don't you go back and join her?' Nick said. 'I need to have words with your father.'

Oliver did what he was told while Jake let Nick usher him back into the corridor from which he had just emerged.

'I've got something for you,' Nick said, holding up a plastic bag.

'What?'

'Take a look.'

Jake opened the bag. Inside was a brand-new dress shirt, still in its cellophane wrapper. Whether it was the drugs, the drink or the whole heightened emotion of the day, he did something he had never done before. He stepped forward and hugged his brother.

Nick broke away from the embrace, scratched his head and sighed. 'OK, fine. Come on, let's get you sorted.'

Jake followed Nick down the empty corridor, Tina having disappeared to who knows where. Then back into the Gents where he quickly stripped off his jacket and shirt. Nick unwrapped the packaging from the new one, then helped him get his arm through the sleeve, do up the buttons, tie up his bow.

'That's a bit more respectable,' Nick said.

Jake looked at himself in the mirror, spat on his fingers and patted some hair back into place. Mutton dressed as lamb, he thought. But at least *Jake Tully Day* was back on track. There was even a bottle of up-market *eau de toilette* on the sink. He used an elbow on the pump to get a squirt on his free hand, dabbed some on his cheeks and neck. When he glanced back in the mirror, he saw his brother standing behind him.

'Mum loved books,' Nick said. 'She always had a stack on her bedside table. Her leaning tower of Pisa she called it. She read to us all the time. Every night, without fail. Even when she wasn't well.'

'She used to do all the different voices.'

'She could be quite funny really.'

'It's hard to remember that about her.'

'She'd have been really proud of you.' Nick's voice went all quivery at this point. 'And I know we've had our ups and downs over the years. But I just wanted to tell you that win or lose, I'm really proud of you too. For all the success you've had with this book.'

Jake gazed at his brother's reflection. At that shiny, smooth-shaven, blue-eyed, immaculately dressed, not-a-hair-out-of-place big brother of his. Who had just managed to express the most affection towards him that Jake could ever recall. 'Yeah, thanks. I appreciate that.'

Nick patted him gingerly on the shoulders. 'I might even get to reading it one of these days.'

Back at the dinner table, Jake was feeling all aglow. His fresh appearance had been greatly complimented upon and he was particularly enjoying his *bombe glacé* of mango ice cream coated in chocolate. Oliver had taken over his place beside Francesca, leaving him to squeeze in between his son and the indomitable Arabella who unlike Francesca did not place a hand over his glass every time he tried to pour himself some wine. This was what this part of *Jake Tully Day* was all about. These precious moments suspended between knowing and not knowing if he had won. Between wondering whether he was going to deliver his Decca List or being left merely to consider what might have been. Between success and well, not success.

'What's it like being a writer's muse?' Arabella asked Francesca from across the table as she speared a pink *petit four* with a toothpick.

Francesca paused in the delivery of her own piece of *bombe glacé* to her mouth. 'I don't know what you are talking about.'

'Jake's book. What was her name again? The piano teacher creature. Catherine. I get the sense she resembles you, Francesca.'

'She looks nothing like me.'

'I wasn't thinking physically. I meant character-wise.' Arabella let her fingers dance in the air. 'Her essence.'

It was not often Jake saw Francesca flustered in moments that did not involve the welfare of their only child. All those years of dealing with wealthy, entitled and demanding clients had forced her to create a kind of professional Buddha-like carapace that allowed offending comments to pass her by. But it appeared Arabella's observation had managed to pierce that armour for a red flush of anger rose on her neck and around the yoke of her shoulders. However, before she had a chance to respond, it was Guy's doctor-lover Arush who yet again came to the rescue.

'So where *do* you get your ideas from, Jake?' Arush asked. 'I mean all that Reno divorce stuff, for example. I found that to be really interesting. I guess you had to do a lot of research. Did you travel over there?'

'I've never been to Reno in my life,' Jake said. 'I just made it all up. Isn't that what writers do, Arabella?'

THEN

JAKE PRINTED OFF WHAT HE HAD ALREADY WRITTEN. Despite having to use up an over-priced ink cartridge, he just wanted to feel his manuscript in his hands, get a sense of its heft, make it more real than just a series of keystrokes on an electronic page. He wanted to hold it, smell it, weigh up its depth. Where had it all come from?

Fragments. That's what his novel was. Pieces of his life he had plundered from here and there, and then elaborated upon to form some kind of fictional narrative. But what had made him choose this fragment and not that fragment? This memory and not that memory? What was his personal psychological magnet that had sucked up these iron filings of a story from his subconscious? Was it the death of his mother? Was it the break-up of his marriage? Was it his relationship with his father? Was it because of his sense of failure? Was it because he had not been true to himself?

Yet somehow he believed his novel already existed and that really all he was doing now was writing and re-writing and re-writing until he could arrive at the perfect version of his story in its sublimest form. He was like an archaeologist brushing away the dust from a hieroglyphic tablet buried deep within a tomb rather than a writer creating something new. That was what he had to do now, that was his purpose in life.

This interior version of himself that was so much better than the exterior version he manifested to the world. This is what would prove to Francesca that he was still worthy of her. That despite his infidelity, she should take him back.

As brother Nick had predicted, the valuation of the family home came in at four hundred thousand, making Jake's bought-out share worth one hundred and fifty thousand, which translated into an annual income of thirty grand net over the next five years. Now this might have been a decent wage for a single man with a novel to write and half a child to support living anywhere else in the United Kingdom, but for someone trying to survive in London at the height of the property boom this sum was a mere pittance. He sold his car and rented a studio flat in Peckham that was not much bigger than a broom cupboard with a galley kitchen and shower room attached, free Wi-fi and just enough space for a desk. But it was sufficient for the needs of a closeted writer and close enough to his former marital home that he could easily walk over to fetch Oliver from his house or collect him from school. For the time being, he had reached some kind of truce with Francesca, a workable stalemate within which he felt that as long as their relationship was not regressing there was hope for a proper reconciliation. Until such time, he was going to devote himself entirely to the completion of his novel. To inspire this task, he began each morning by googling Adam, checking in on any fresh press reports, reviews on Goodreads, festival appearances, his Amazon ratings and details of his second novel, piggybacking on the fabulous success of his debut outing, *The Red Herring Murders*. Suitably galvanized by jealousy and resentment, not to mention a desire to take back his stolen jacket and that his ex-best friend was inveigling himself into the affections of his wife and son, Jake started to write.

His mobile rang. Only one possible caller:

'Hey, young man. How's it going?'

'Where are you, Dad?'

'I'm here. At home. Where are you?'

'Outside school.'

'Shit. Is that the time?'

'I'm hurt, Dad.'

'I'm sorry. I was caught up in my writing. I completely forgot. Nothing personal.'

'I didn't mean it like that. I meant physically.'

'Don't move. I'm on my way. And please don't call your mother.'

When Jake finally arrived breathless at the school, Oliver was outside the gates, sitting on the wall, with the lollipop woman – or 'school patrol crossing officer' as he believed they were called these days – standing guard. Despite his lateness and the state of his son – bruised eye, scuffed knee, torn blazer at the elbow – this woman came across as entirely non-judgmental as she handed his son back into his care. He felt like hugging her, or perhaps giving her a tip. Instead, he guiltily muttered a 'thank you' and crouched down slightly to question Oliver at his own height.

'Tell me what happened?' he asked, dabbing a handkerchief wet with his own spittle around his son's eye.

'Patrick,' was all Oliver said.

'Don't tell me you were fighting over that girl?' He looked up at Lollipop Woman who was still hovering and gave her a shrug of 'can you believe what kids are like these days?' He was met with a downward glance over her spectacles which seemed to say: 'Of course, I know what kids are like. I deal with the little fuckers every day.'

'Susie,' Oliver said.

'Who?'

'The girl,' he said, before adding defiantly. 'That I love.'

'And who does this Susie love?'

Oliver looked at him with the downcast eyes of the rejected. 'Patrick.'

'I'm sorry that you're heartbroken, Oliver. I really am. And I know it's not going to sound all that consoling right now. But you're probably going to get your heart broken many times in your life. Susie is just the start. You'll never get used to it. But you'll discover that time will heal your wounds.' Again he looked up at Lollipop Woman who nodded at him in approval, possibly reflecting on her own experience with men. Or women. Or whoever. Who knew these days?

'Don't you think that's a bit cliché, Dad?'

'What?'

'Time heals all wounds.'

Jake didn't know whether to be more impressed by the maturity of the rebuke or his use of the word cliché. 'Come on, son. Let's get you back to mine and cleaned up. Your mother is probably going to blame me for this.'

Francesca didn't exactly blame him. Instead, she came out with the remark: 'Like father, like son.'

'What's that supposed to mean?'

'The two of you fighting over the same woman.'

While Jake felt that she was being unfair in her comparison, he decided not to complain. The upside was that this continued feud between the two boys meant that any bodyboarding family trips to Cornwall this summer with Adam and Patrick were most definitely off.

NOW

'THIS IS WONDERFUL, OLIVER,' Jake said. He couldn't remember the last time, he'd been sitting in such close proximity to his one and only son and heir. Possibly when he used to read him bedtime stories. 'This is pretty damn fantastic.'

'I'm glad I'm here,' Oliver said, his youthful cheeks already flushed from the sponsor's champagne. 'Are you going to be OK? You don't look too great.'

'Never felt better.' Jake poured himself a cup of coffee. On Francesca's instructions, he had been told to move from alcohol to caffeine. To satisfy her demand, he had managed to commandeer a whole cafetière for himself, a large portion of which he'd already consumed. 'And you know what? When all this here is over, you and I, we're going to spend more time together. I want to come and visit you in Hackney.'

'I live in Newham, Dad. And I think you'd find my place a bit too rank.'

'Sure, whatever. Well, maybe we could go out and fly a kite together. We had some good times together with the old delta dragon.'

'I was ten.'

'You're never too old to fly a kite.'

'Life isn't a Mary Poppins movie, Dad.'

'That is most definitely true. Although you wouldn't know it, looking around at this glittering gallery of literati.'

'The indiscreet charm of the bourgeoisie.'

'Wow. Who'd have thought I'd have a son who referenced Luis Bunuel movies back at me?'

'I'm in the middle of a part-time course at the MetFilm School.'

'Your mother tells me nothing.'

'She says you're going to read out some sort of list if you win. At which point, she has insisted she will go to the loo.'

Francesca was off at the loo now and Jake could almost hear the tiny muscle-click of Arabella's ears beside him as they pricked up to the conversation. 'So it is true' she said. 'You *are* going to have your revenge on all of us.'

'I don't think of it as revenge, Arabella. I shall merely be speaking the truth.'

'And what might that truth be?'

'Oh, the usual bitter and resentful writer stuff. You saw my interview with Sylvia.'

'Can I expect more of the same then? The industry is so bland, so stale these days. I hope you'll be naming names.'

'I have a whole Rolodex full of them.'

'Oh dear, Jake. Rolodexes are so last millennium.'

Jake shrugged. 'Such anachronisms are irrelevant. Considering you don't think I'm going to win.'

'Let's hope I'm wrong,' Arabella said. 'I could do with a bit of excitement this evening.' A remark which Jake noted seemed to dismiss the ministrations of Lance, her fawning beau. 'And heads up,' she added. 'The cavalry has arrived.'

Jake felt a hand squeeze his shoulder. He assumed it was Francesca back from the loo but he looked up only to find TV presenter Sylvia, decked out in her faux military attire, hanging on to him for balance. 'I wish you luck,' she said, swaying from side to side. 'And remember, win or lose, I still want an interview. Exclusive.' She licked her finger, pointed it up in the air in a counting gesture Jake didn't quite understand. 'After all, you owe me big time.'

She released his shoulder and marched onwards, probably to make similar drunken demands of the other short-listed authors. She was immediately replaced by Guy, who crouched down beside him and said softly: 'Do you want the good news or the bad news?'

'I thought all news was good news to you.'

'That's not the issue here,' he said, steadying himself in his crouch. 'But I'll give you the good news first.'

'Go ahead,' Jake said, taking another sip of coffee.

'The tabloids appear to have dropped their sexual harassment angle.'

'What fucking sexual harassment angle?'

'The kiss. Alison confirms it was harmless.'

'Who's Alison?'

'The Aussie barmaid.'

'You're on first name terms?'

'We have had conversations. Anyway, the tabloids are moving on.'

'Moving on from what?'

'You know. From their online editions. Their headlines.'

'Stop making me drag this out of you, Guy. What headlines?'

'Well, if you insist on knowing. *Sullied Tully* was one. *The Responsibility of Lust* was another. The Sun had you down as *Jake the Rake.*'

'Ok, ok, ok. I got the picture. What's the bad news?'

'They're moving on to the Mary Strauss incident now. Latest news from the hospital is that she's broken her collar-bone.'

'It was an accident.'

'That's not how the tabloids are portraying it. Following on from your assault on a fan.'

'Alleged assault. It was an alleged assault. What are the muck-rakers inferring now?'

'That you were drunk and disorderly. A consistent pattern of aggression. Deliberately sabotaging the opposition. *Last Waltz for Strauss*? *Outrage at Onstage Damage Rampage.* There are accompanying photographs, of course, thanks to our resident paparazzo, the illustrious Gio Ventura. No doubt adding a nice little publishing licensing fee to his bill for tonight's gig. And Strauss might be bringing charges.'

'More charges? I might as well hand myself in right now.'

'If you recall, you *are* handing yourself into Wood Street Police Station once this night is over. But you might have an unlikely ally though in your fellow nominee, that *Saint Shit!* chap, Wayne Kassova. He says the floor of the stage was unsteady. It was an accident waiting to happen. Which means blame would shift to the organisers. We might have to lawyer-up for this one.' Guy rose from his crouch, patted Jake on the shoulder. 'Must get back to my seat. The business end is approaching. This could be life-changing, Jake. Life-changing.'

As if in some revolving door routine, Guy was replaced by Francesca who sat down next to him.

'I'm so glad Nick managed to sort out Oliver,' she said.

'It sounded pretty routine in the end.'

'Give your brother some credit for once. He was there for him.'

'Sorry. Old patterns die hard. Nick did good.'

Francesca leaned over and took a sip of his coffee. 'Have you spoken to your son about his tattoo?'

'I thought I'd leave it up to you.'

'Don't you think it's more of a father-son kind of thing?'

'What am I supposed to say? It's a *fait accompli*. He's already scarred for life.'

'I think you should still have a word. So at least he doesn't go getting any more.'

'I think once he's no longer a young lad, he'll realise the folly of his *Youth for Truth* logo.'

'Why can't you just agree with me for once? And do what I ask.'

'I'm sorry. Old patterns again. I'm going to try to do better. I promise.'

She placed her hand on top of his. After Nick's sudden bout of emotion back in the Gents, it seemed that hitherto withheld affection towards him was becoming contagious. Such were the benefits of *Jake Tully Day*.

'How are you feeling?' she asked.

'Coffee's helping.'

'I meant emotionally. You must be excited. I certainly am.'

'To be honest, Fran. I have no idea how I'm feeling.'

THEN

THERE WOULD BE THE HUNCHED BACK, the rolled-up shirt sleeves, the clackety-clack of the typewriter keys, the *ting* of the carriage return, the snatched away useless piece of writing from the feed rollers, the build-up of the scrunched-up pages in and around the waste paper basket, the piled-up ashtray, the empty bottles of beer★, whisky★, rum★, vodka★, Jack Daniels★, (★delete as appropriate) rolling around on the floor. These used to be the cinematic tropes that showed a writer hard at work on his (women were hardly ever portrayed in such a fashion in film, if at all) novel in the good old days before computers came along, smoking was vilified and alcohol had to be drunk responsibly. Nowadays these visual clues have been reduced to brisk touch-typing coupled with cut, paste and delete on a computer screen. And sadly, even those keyboard strokes had drawn to a halt for Jake.

His writer's block had persisted for some time now. He sat at his desk and stared at the blank screen. Nothing. He pulled down his bed from its wall space and sat on that. Nothing. He did the Guardian cryptic crossword. Nothing. He had a bowl of Heinz tomato soup and a prawn mayonnaise sandwich from M&S. Nothing. He made himself an espresso with his aluminium stovetop coffee maker. Nothing. He did the Guardian Sudoku. Nothing. He went for a walk in the park. Nothing. He made himself another espresso. Nothing. He had a shower. Nothing. He had an Aberdeen Angus beef and red chutney sandwich from M&S. Nothing. He went to meet Oliver after school even though his role as parental escort was no longer required. Nothing.

'Are you depressed?' Oliver asked.

'I'm just a bit down about my writing.'

'Mum says you're depressed.'

'How would she know?'

'I described your symptoms to her.'

'Oh really? And what are they, Sigmund?'

'Who's Sigmund?'

'It doesn't matter. What did you tell her?'

'That you need a shave. And a haircut. And you're wearing the same clothes all the time.'

'That just means I'm being lazy. Not depressed.'

'They could be the same thing.'

'Not necessarily.'

'You're moody too.'

'Maybe I am.'

'Anyway, she wants to talk to you.'

'She said that.'

'Yeah. That's the message.'

'You took your time telling me.'

'I wanted to create a certain narrative tension.'

'Where did you learn to say something like that?'

'I want to be a writer like you. So I Googled it.'

'How to be a writer?'

'Yeah.'

'I don't recommend it.'

'I can see why.'

'Just tell me what your mother said.'

'She wants to meet. Next Thursday evening. Somewhere neutral. You've to text her the details.'

He felt a dark veil lift from his mood. It was the first time Francesca had reached out to him without Oliver as her reason. Perhaps he should be depressed more often. He sat down at his computer, and with the help of Google Maps he determined the exact distance between his former residence and his current one. He then measured out the half-way point and located the nearest restaurant thereto in the medium price range. Seven or eight pm? Seven-thirty. Everything in the middle, everything neutral. The restaurant was Italian – *La Locanda Del Ghiottone*. He looked up the translation – *The Inn of the Glutton*. For punishment perhaps. He texted her the details. She texted back that she would meet him there.

He felt as if he were preparing for a first date. He shaved, he had a haircut, he bought a new shirt, he cut his toenails. He made a reconnaissance trip to the venue, chose the location of their table. He checked out the menu and the wine list. He thought through very carefully what he wanted to say, what he wanted to achieve from this rendezvous. He made notes. He needed to achieve the right tone – conciliatory, humble, remorseful. Yet he didn't want to make Francesca think that he was a desperate wreck. He had to convince her that he was there to support her, to provide for their family, that she could still trust him. He walked over to the restaurant at 7.10 pm. He had already timed the journey. It would take him sixteen minutes exactly.

She was late. He ordered a small bottle of mineral water. He would have preferred a whisky but he didn't want to get ahead of her in the drinking stakes. After a further twenty minutes, he gave in and ordered a bottle of red wine. He had expected a text of explanation but none arrived. He would have texted her himself but he didn't want her to feel he was hassling her. He was walking on eggshells and he didn't want any to crack. She arrived after a further ten minutes. He stood up to pull out her chair.

'Oliver,' she said. 'Homework duty.'

What could he say? Three words and he already felt guilty.

'Merlot?' he offered.

'If there's any left.'

Four more words and he felt even more guilty. He poured her out a glass. She was wearing her hair up, the same way as when he had first met her. A simple black dress, her favourite Chanel No.5 – classic and timeless, that was Francesca. A silver pendant he had bought her in Morocco – casual addition or hopeful omen?

'You look lovely,' he said.

'Thanks.' She observed him over the rim of her glass. 'I'm sorry I can't say the same for you.'

'I did have a shave. And a haircut.'

'I can see that. It's more the forlorn look that concerns me. How's the writing going?'

'To be honest, not very well. I can't seem to write a word.'

'Maybe the pursuit of literary fame is not for you.'

'It's not fame I'm after. Even if I finish this damn thing, and even if I get it published, I'll be lucky if one person reads it. And if by some amazing good fortune, I do become famous because of my work, I'll be surrounded by people who will be envious of me and hate me for it.'

'Why bother then?'

'Some compelling inner insanity that I cannot explain.'

'What are you doing with yourself then if you're not writing?'

'A bit of journalism.'

'Like what?'

'Features and the like.'

'Features?'

'Where to get the best glazed doughnuts in South London. The correlation between salary levels and erectile dysfunction. The optimum time to purchase a plane ticket for the cheapest deal.'

'You hate doing that stuff. Don't tell me you're writing for Estelle again?'

'Afraid so. I need the money.'

'What about what Nick pays you for your dad's place?'

'After rent and what I give you for Oliver, not a lot left.'

'You've also lost weight.'

'A diet of M&S sandwiches and Heinz soups.'

'I see.' Francesca leaned back and had a look at the menu. 'Dinner's on me then.'

'I wish I was proud enough to refuse. Instead, I shall accept gracefully. Business going well then?'

'Very well.'

They ordered and when the waiter had departed, she told him about the make-over she'd been asked to do on an enormous manor house in Hampshire, the furnishings for an office suite in Mayfair, the interior design of a boutique hotel in Brighton. She'd been forced to get herself a proper central office, hire a receptionist and an assistant as well as outsourcing a lot of the grunt work. As he listened, he tried to come to terms with the conflicting feelings racing through him. He wanted Francesca to be doing well. Of course, he did. After all, he loved her and wanted to be able to support her in all her endeavours. Yet at the same time, he was annoyed that she was managing so well without him (while he wasn't without her). The food arrived and he changed the subject.

'Why did you want to see me? Like this. Away from the Oliver hand-over.'

She delicately cut away the skin from the top of her lemon sole. 'We were worried about you. We just wanted to make sure you were OK.'

'That's very considerate of you.'

'I'm not sure how to say this in a way that won't make you defensive, Jake, but… we wondered if you might be drinking… too much.'

He directed his attention to his seafood linguine – a mixture of baby clams, chewy squid, a couple of scallops and chunks of salmon in a creamy sauce. 'I'm not sure what you're getting at here.'

'It's just that... Oliver says that sometimes when you meet him after school, he can smell alcohol on your breath.'

'That's not a crime, is it?'

'See, you're getting defensive.'

'OK, maybe, just maybe, I might be having a bit of an early start these days. What with the writing not coming as easy as I'd like. Well, not at all actually. But yes, OK, I'll make sure my breath is minty fresh when it's my turn to see him.'

'Whether your breath is minty fresh or not is not the issue. You know what the issue is.'

'Yes, I know what the issue is.'

'I'm just putting it out there, all right. I'm sure you know how to deal with it.'

'Message received.'

'Good. This fish is lovely. How's the linguine?

'Excellent.'

'Smart choice of place. I never knew it existed. It's kind of half-way between both our homes.'

He forked an ample helping of creamy pasta into his mouth, washed it down with the last of the wine. 'What about us?' he asked.

'What about us?'

'You know.'

'I don't know. Tell me.'

'I love you, Fran.'

'I know that.'

'I ask again for...no, I beg for your forgiveness.'

'I've kind of forgiven you. I just haven't forgotten.'

'Does that mean there's a chance we can start over?'

He regretted the words as soon as they had emerged. It was too early, much earlier than his notes for this evening's schedule had dictated. He should have waited. Let his charm (whatever was left of it), the wine and any residual feelings she still might harbour for him take effect. Francesca placed her knife and fork down on her plate. She dabbed her lips with a napkin. For a moment, he thought she was going to leave.

'Listen, Jake,' she said. 'You and I getting back together is never going to happen.'

'I don't know how you can be so sure. After all, we have a son together.'

'Please, don't play the Oliver card with me. This is not about him. It's about us. And what's good for us will ultimately be good for him.'

'So what's good for us?'

'You crossed a line, Jake. There is no going back from that. You should know that. You know my family history.'

Jake had never met Francesca's father – or "the bastard", as she used to call him – he was already dead when he and Francesca had got together. But he had heard the stories of the serial womanizer who had made his wife's and therefore his only daughter's life a misery. Francesca had never trusted mankind again thereafter. Jake's behaviour had merely confirmed that. She was right. There was no going back. 'But is there a going forward?'

'Yes, there is,' she said. 'I can't unlove you, Jake. That is never going to go away. I still care for you lots. I will always try to help you and support you in whatever you want to do. And I hope that you will do the same for me. But you and I as a couple. As I've said, that's not going to happen.'

'You know what really upsets me?'

'No. What?'

'It's this total confidence you have about that. Not even one iota of doubt. One little crack in your wall of defiance. It's like all these years of marriage have meant nothing to you.'

Francesca sat back in her chair, fondled the Moroccan pendant he had given her, her eyes going a bit teary as she considered him from across the table. Eventually she said: 'You know that story about the fox you used to tell me from *The Little Prince*. The "you are forever responsible for those you have tamed" bit. Well, not so long ago I decided to go back and re-read the book in its original version. I thought it would be a good way of brushing up on my French. And what I discovered was that the French word from that scene – the word "apprivoiser" – which has traditionally been translated into English as "to tame" in about a billion books worldwide is actually more nuanced than that. It's not just about taming some wild animal and thereafter being responsible for it. "Apprivoiser" also contains the element of getting to know someone by earning their trust. And by earning that trust, they will open up to you and a relationship is formed. So the thing is, Jake, you destroyed that trust. And by doing so you destroyed our relationship. Or at least, what it used to be.'

He returned his attention to his linguine, poked around morosely for a chunk of salmon flesh, lost amidst the cream and the pasta. 'Are you wanting a divorce then?'

'I don't think we need to go legal just yet.'

'There's somebody else, isn't there?'

Francesca laughed. 'That's always what men think. That it can't just be about them.'

'What about Adam?'

'Adam's not even here. He's in the States right now. On a book tour.'

'That didn't sound like a denial to me.'

'Nothing's going on between us. We're just friends. Honest. He's got his former secretary to keep him happy.' Francesca sliced away the last of the fish flesh from the bone, leaving a perfect skinned-off sole skeleton on the plate. 'So, Jake. What's it to be then? Are we going to proceed like two responsible adults who still love and care for each other? Or are you going to sulk for the rest of your life?'

After dinner, after he had parted from her on outwardly calm and amicable terms while internally he was a churning mass of conflicting feelings, he went back to his studio flat, sat down at his desk and started writing. It seemed there was nothing like a whole load of emotional upheaval to get rid of writer's block.

NOW

Perked up by a pleasant caffeine buzz, Jake watched on, as stiff and sombre, the quintet of judges walked on stage and took their seats behind the podium. They had arrived without announcement. No fanfare. No dimming of the lights. They had just snuck in through a side door, catching everyone off guard. Like that world-renowned rock band that sidles on stage and no-one really notices until they pick up their instruments and the lead guitarist strums the electrifying first chords of *Start Me Up*. But in this case, it was a very different famous five. Led by their illustrious chairperson, a dame of the realm, once a Minister of Education in a previous administration. She was joined by an American academic (male), a previous winner (female), a cultural commentator and broadsheet columnist (female, and former colleague of Jake's), and a literary critic (male). Once the jury had settled and once the general hubbub had reduced, the CEO of the company representing the prize's sponsors – a tall, white-haired man of aristocratic bearing (also in an immaculate suit, Jake noted) – strode on stage and took to the podium. Once sympathy had been expressed for the unfortunate accident that had befallen Mary Strauss (all heads in the room turned to Jake), the CEO proceeded with the formalities. Jake meanwhile looked around the hall for the other nominees. There was Wayne, young, cutting-edge and excited. The calm and elegant Thanda. The shy and retiring Scottish Islander, Shona Murray, hard to spot really, he'd almost completely forgotten about her. He caught the eye of that old rogue Vernon Harper at the table opposite, sitting astride his chair, his hands resting on the cane between his legs. Vernon nodded to him graciously and he returned the gesture.

And then there were the occupants of his own table, hemmed in as he was on either side by the two people he loved most. What a wonderful trick of Fate had conspired to ensure that both Francesca and Oliver were here beside him now. Francesca who had always been there to support him anyway despite no longer being his lawfully wedded wife. Francesca who had tolerated him, who had remained responsible for him, who possibly even still loved him in her own way. He knew she was currently having a long-distance relationship with a French documentary film-maker (she always did love creative types) who was much older than she. A benign paternal replacement perhaps for her own philandering bastard of a father, although it was an observation he would never make directly to her face. Most certainly a replacement for her recovering alcoholic of an adulterous ex-husband. The film-maker's name was Patrice, a wealthy man by all accounts – well by Oliver's accounts – who had an apartment in Paris and a small villa ironically not that far from Cap-Ferret where Jake had once spent a glorious summer with Francesca and Adam and Tina and the two young boys in their own rented house near the sea in what seemed like another lifetime ago. The London-Paris lifestyle suited Francesca, Jake thought, it suited her *sensibilité*. She was happy and he was glad. As for Oliver, since he had left school he had hardly seen him so the fact that his son had ended up here rather than at a student demo or in a central London prison cell, was a wonderful mystery to both of them.

Jake patted his jacket, reassured himself of the slight bulge of his speech that lay there in the inside breast pocket waiting to be revealed should he win. Would he have the courage to go through with it? Or would he be overwhelmed by the emotion of the occasion, the demand for propriety, the corporate authority of it all, the sponsor's generous cheque? Would he give in to the relief, this legitimisation of his work, the gratitude towards those who had helped him rather than the resentment towards those who hadn't? Would, one way or another, all the elements of the earth rise up and proclaim that this was indeed *Jake Tully Day*?

THEN

EVEN BEFORE HE FINISHED WRITING THE NOVEL, Jake had started sending out submissions to agents who were prepared to accept unsolicited manuscripts. A covering letter, a pitch, a blurb, the first three chapters, the first fifty pages, the first ten thousand words, a synopsis, the first chapter and the last chapter, an uploaded file on Submittable. Everybody wanted something different. A few agents acknowledged receipt. Some he never heard from again. Others sent a pro-forma rejection after three months, six months, a year. He kept these letters in a folder. One day when he was rich and famous and on the podium collecting some literary award, he would name names. He called it his Decca List after the record company that according to music legend had turned down The Beatles.

And so it went on. He kept writing and re-writing his novel, he kept sending out submissions to agents, he kept getting rejections, the Decca List was getting longer and longer and he was becoming more and more despondent. The money from his property deal with brother Nick was running out and he was forced to keep begging his former editor Estelle for more assignments on lifestyle features built around his old column which still ran under the title *The Life and Times of a House Husband by Jake Tully* although 'Jake Tully' was now Richard Strange, a thirty-something computer programmer living in Muswell Hill with twin sons and an investment banker wife, a relationship rumoured to be on the verge of divorce. The amount of copy Jake could contribute though was limited as he no longer lived on the cutting edge of what was fashionable for the readership of this daily newspaper and its Sunday supplement. He would be far better suited writing for a column entitled *The Life and Times of a Separated Husband and Frustrated Writer Living in a Broom Cupboard in Peckham*. It was an idea he had even pitched to Estelle but with no success.

He had no friends. Not only had he betrayed his one and only buddy but Adam wasn't even living in the country anymore, having absconded to Monaco or some other tax haven with squillions in royalties accumulated from *The Red Herring Murders* and its various sequels and TV adaptations each with a different colour and species of fish in the title, the latest being *The Blue Marlin Murders* or the *Yellowfin Tuna Murders*, he couldn't remember which. Not that he had read any of them, although he did occasionally (every day) Google their Amazon rankings. He also discovered the truism that on marital separation, women were left with lots of female companions acquired through the sorority of motherhood while men (even a well-known house-husband such as himself) found themselves to be on their own, having abandoned all their previous male comrades for the sake of their marriage. Jake did have two saving graces though. He had a son who still seemed happy to hang out with him. And following on from their dinner together at the *La Locanda Del Ghiottone*, he had managed over time to develop a friendly and supportive rapport with Francesca which had turned into frequent telephone conversations where they could both moan to each other about their respective predicaments. Jake about the futility of his existence that centred around rejections from agents and having to write features on subjects such as the sudden popularity of the tartine (basically half a baguette with a piece of cheese or whatever on top) and whether badger or boar hair was the best choice of bristle for the application of shaving cream now that men's shaving brushes were making a comeback. Meanwhile, Francesca could let off steam about the pressures of working with difficult clients who expected her to source throws made from the wool of the vicuña, a mammal of the camelid species, (Francesca: – Is that a fucking llama or an alpaca?) living high up in the mountains of Peru. Or whether she should be using Carrara or Calacatta marble for a customer's fireplace surround. He relished these telephone conversations in his otherwise sterile, starved-for-conversation existence.

'I'm worried about you, Jake,' Francesca said.

'What is there to worry about?'

'It's nearly midnight.'

'I didn't realise that.'

'I know. That's why I'm worried.'

'I don't have a structured existence like you do. I lose track of time.'

'It's the drinking. That's why I'm worried about you.'

Silence.

'You're drinking now, aren't you?'

'Yeah, maybe.'

'How much?'

'A couple.'

'A couple of what?'

Silence.

'Bottles of wine, Jake. You can't be going drinking two bottles of wine a day.'

'If I had someone to share them with, it would only be one bottle.'

'Stop that. This is what always happens. This is what you always do. This is not about us. It's about you.'

'But me is us.'

Silence.

'OK, I'll try to cut down. I promise.'

'I can't believe after all this time, you're still letting the situation between us get you down so much.'

'It's not just that. It's my writing too.'

'I thought the novel was finished.'

'I'm rewriting and rewriting it, trying to go deeper. And it's taking me places I don't want to go.' Caravan muse Angie had been right in her own crazy, made-up way. In the end, the art was always about the artist.

Francesca went on. 'I know things are tough for you right now. I know you're not happy. But you've got to be more pro-active. You're spending too much time on your own. Go out and meet other people. People with shared interests.'

'I don't have interests.'

'You could join a writing group.'

'I just need a break. A bit of luck.'

'You've got to get out there and make your own luck. After all, you've got a son.'

'What's that supposed to mean?'

'I'm not going to go into this right now. It's late. And I have to work tomorrow.' She hung up.

Jake poured himself a glass of wine.

The next morning he received another letter of rejection. He added it to the Decca List and decided to do something he had hoped he would never have to do. He called Tina.

'Surprise, surprise,' she said. 'Jake Tully. I thought you'd disappeared off the face of the planet.'

'Just to Peckham.'

'Same thing.' She laughed at her own little joke. 'To what do I owe this unexpected pleasure…given that I haven't heard from you since we…?'

'I'm calling you professionally.'

'Don't tell me. You've finally written your masterpiece. What was it again? The great novel about the pleasure of love. The lack of it. The responsibility of it. The pain of it.'

'Something like that.'

'So?'

'Can we talk?'

'Sure.'

'Do you have an office somewhere?'

'Still in my garden hut. Office space is so old-school these days.'

'I thought you had moved to Highgate.'

'God, that little pipe-dream fell through years ago when all our infidelities hit the fan. Do you want to come round later? Say around six. I should have cleared my desk by then.'

After a couple of whiskies and a completed Sudoku puzzle in the snug lounge at a local pub, it was getting dark by the time he arrived at Tina's rear garden entrance, now a solid Georgian door with a proper brass plate announcing her literary agency alongside a video security system. She buzzed him in and as he walked to her office along a paved walkway lined with solar-powered path lights and an herbaceous border, he saw the shutters come down on the floor-to-ceiling windows with an ominous whirr. He opened the door to this sealed-off, softly-lit, custom-built space and Tina swung round on her chair to greet him. A bottle of wine and two glasses stood among the various papers on her desk. Manuscripts lay loose or in large envelopes scattered around the room. Like unread tombstones in a graveyard, Jake thought. Smooth jazz played on a high-end stereo system. No wires anywhere. The place was Blue-toothed to the max.

'Well, well, well. Jake Tully. Looking like a real writer these days.'

'What's that supposed to mean?'

'Sun-starved, under-nourished, drink-sodden. And desperate.'

He realised he couldn't argue with that description so he decided to say nothing. Tina had all the power here and he wasn't going to boost it even further with one of his usual sarcastic remarks.

'Take a seat,' she said, 'and have a glass of wine.'

He did as he was told and waited until Tina poured for the both of them. They clinked glasses.

'You don't think this is a bit weird,' she said. 'Given that the last time I saw you, you accused me of breaking up your marriage.'

'You did break up my marriage.'

'I think you have to take responsibility for that. I was only the messenger. And the fuck-buddy.'

'Talking of fuck-buddies, I see you still have Adam on your client list.'

'I'm a mercenary bitch, Jake. I thought you realised that. A product of the American dream migrated to the great gullible British Isles. Money trumps infidelity in my world. It makes life so much easier. Especially as Adam's books have taken off big time.'

'I heard he'd moved offshore.'

'If you call Ireland offshore.'

'I'd heard Monaco.'

'Nothing quite so tax-free exotic. He's living outside Dublin in a run-down castle with the same red-headed colleen he's been banging since his computer days. Our relationship is strictly business. I used to think the two of you had got it together yourselves the way you were so buddy-buddy.'

'We were never that way inclined.'

'I recall he once saved your life.'

'Once upon a time.'

'You certainly found a way to pay him back.'

'Don't think I don't feel guilty about it.'

'Too many double negatives there, Jake. I get confused. Guilty or not guilty?'

'Guilty as charged.'

'And what about you and Ms High and Mighty Francesca?'

'We're on pretty good terms.'

'No going back there?'

'Not for the foreseeable.'

'And young Oliver?'

'He's coming up for his GCSEs.'

'Same with Patrick. Amazing how fast they grow. I got pot plants that take longer. Some more wine?' Without waiting for a reply, she splashed some more into both their glasses. 'So what can I do for you?'

'I've written a novel.'

'I got that. What's the title?'

'*The Responsibility of Love.*'

'Sounds like a self-help book. What's it about?'

'I'm not brilliant at the elevator pitch. So I've written you a synopsis.'

'On a single sheet of A4,' she said, snatching the piece of paper from his hand. 'That's what we agents like. Conciseness. Considering we never have time to read the actual book.'

She perched a pair of glasses low on her nose and read. He watched as she did so. She was still an attractive-looking woman, he couldn't deny that. Hair fiercely dark, a few more lines etched on her face but he wasn't in a position to criticise. How old would she be now? Early forties? He wondered what her relationship status was. A smart, intelligent, successful woman who knew exactly what she wanted, hard to believe she would be without lovers. Or a second husband, although he noticed there was no ring on her finger. She swivelled round towards him.

'Given our history,' she said. 'I guess I wasn't your first choice.'

'True.'

'And obviously you haven't been getting very far with anyone else.'

He thought of his burgeoning Decca List and nodded.

'I'll be perfectly straight with you,' she said, waving his one-page summary in the air. 'Literary fiction just doesn't sell these days. If you brought me crime like Adam or fantasy or sci-fi or young adult…'

'Young adult?'

'Sales of books to teenagers are going through the roof these days.'

'I didn't think they read anything made of paper.'

'It's a secret passion for them. Under the bedclothes with a flashlight kind of stuff. They're so sick of screens, the printed page is a bit of a novelty. Harry Potter got them started and they've been addicted ever since. But literary fiction? Publishers just aren't interested. Unless as an act of charity. Or to give them some kind of high-brow credibility.'

'Some authors break through though.'

'If you're in your twenties, cutting edge and good-looking. Yeah, maybe. But… how old are you now?'

'Forty-seven.'

'A middle-aged male debut author of literary fiction. You might want to stick to that feature crap you write if you want to make a living.'

'I didn't realise you were a fan of my work.'

'Call it morbid curiosity.'

'Are you saying you can't help me?'

'That depends.'

'On what?' Although with Tina now standing up and undoing the top button of her blouse, he could guess what was coming.

'You see, Jake. I've got dozens of other desperate writers out there dying to get into print. And I'm sure your novel is just as good as anything else that's out in the bookselling world sucking up precious shelf-space. You need a bit of luck. That's what you need. You need to find someone out there who is on your side, someone who believes in you, someone who is willing to use their connections to get your work seen by the right publishers.'

'You haven't even read it yet.'

'You see, Jake. I've always felt that there was this energy between us. Don't you feel it too? A certain visceral connection. A certain tingling of the flesh.'

Tina emerged from behind her desk and slid round the edges so that she was standing in front of him. She had started to go into some kind of striptease routine, letting her cream blouse slip off her shoulders, to reveal a lacy push-up bra underneath, also in cream. Her skin was tanned, more so than her natural colouring and he wondered whether she'd just come back from some sun-baked vacation or a visit to one of these tanning salons that seemed to crowd every empty space on the High Street these days. Tina had now moved in closer and she was writhing exotically in front of him. Her lack of self-consciousness as impressive as it was, was having the opposite effect on him. Rather than being caught up in her blatant sexuality – and it was at this point Jake considered Tina might be stimulated by her cocaine habit and not just a couple of glasses of wine – he felt himself shrivel into his own inhibitions which was probably not a bad thing as he was very quickly going to have to make a level-headed decision on how to proceed with his literary career.

NOW

The Responsibility of Love by Jake Tully. The book cover had just been beamed up on to a screen behind the seated jury on stage as the CEO of the sponsors continued with his presentation of the short-list. Jake noticed that both the jurors and the audience continued to be very democratic in their applause, it would be hard to ascertain if they had a favourite among the titles nominated. He refrained from clapping himself, of course, but dipped his head slightly to the roving cameraman who trained his lens on his face then thankfully and quickly (no doubt appalled by the condition of his subject-matter) swept around to take in the rest of the audience. *The Responsibility of Love*. It was a title he had kept stored in his head from the outset, from the time he had reached a maturity when he could properly verbalise the incident in the toyshop when his mother had told him not to pick up the teddy bear. *The Responsibility of Love*. A lesson he felt he had learned as a young boy from the story of the fox in *The Little Prince*. *The Responsibility of Love*. He was surprised no-one else had used it, even for a self-help book. But he had kept Googling and Googling it over the years and it had still remained unclaimed. Although legally he could not copyright these four words, he had put down his marker by having them published in print as well as scattered digitally into the e-universe. He challenged anyone else to come forward now and employ them. *The Responsibility of Love*. He owned them. It was a good feeling.

The actual cover design though was an entirely different matter. How to visually portray such an abstract concept? Guy wanted to go with the figure of Catherine gazing wistfully into the distance at some landscape described in the novel. Jake nixed that idea immediately. He declared that there must be thousands of novels showing the backs of women staring wistfully towards some dramatic landscape. He came back with a more literal suggestion. A montage of urban scenes in the style of Edward Hopper paintings of the period. In the end, he and Guy had agreed that having such a long word as 'responsibility' in the title, didn't really leave much room for anything else, so best to accentuate the typography in a striking yellow against a blue background and leave it that.

A flattering black-and-white portrait shot especially for tonight's occasion now appeared on the screen. Jake with his hand on chin, pensive pose, probably far removed in the audience's mind from the full-colour, blotchy-skinned, red-eyed author they had seen staggering around in their midst or the viewers had just seen at home. A short, printed biography followed with not much to say considering this was his debut novel, along with, for some reason, the opening line of the book which again probably summed up his current physical state:

Even by the most benign and generous of standards, Max was not a handsome man…

He mused on how remarkable it was that these few words penned in a freezing caravan down in Cornwall several years previously could start off a story that became a completed novel which in turn should end up here as blown-up text on a screen at this prestigious event. And on the shelves of many bookstores around the country. And possibly in other countries too should the potential foreign rights sales proceed. And not only in hard copy but as pixels and electronic strokes on countless webpages and e-readers throughout the universe. As well as being narrated as an audiobook into the ears of motorway drivers, the blind and the too-busy-to-read. Perhaps one day a movie would be made of his work. He would like that and already had his cast of Hollywood A-listers in mind to play the respective parts.

The CEO finished his duties and handed over to the chairperson of the jury – the illustrious dame and former government minister, a formidable woman no doubt made more formidable by having had to constantly put down the male clubbiness of her former cabinet members. Jake had always liked her for that reason. Her presence caused a respectful hush to swoop down on the burble of table talk that had accompanied the previous speaker. She ascended to the podium with authority, put on her glasses that already hung from a chain around her neck, quickly concluded her introductory remarks and then reiterated the names of the short-listed books:

Landlocked by Thanda Masuka
The Responsibility of Love by Jake Tully
Salt and Guts by Shona Murray
O, Jackie by Vernon Harper
China Duck by Mary Strauss
Saint Shit! by Wayne Kassova

THEN

JAKE HATED MALLS. But then again why should he like them? After all, he had been brought up in an area where shops were located on high streets, each with its own defined window of wares. For fish and chips, for meat, for shoes, for medicine, for newspapers, for sweets, for tobacco, for stamps, for banking, for betting, for alcohol. There was no garish lighting or mindless music or bored staff or security guards or stale, circulated air or information boards and escalators situated in the wrong places. Going into town in the rose-coloured, soft-focus light of his childhood imagination was like entering an episode of *Camberwick Green* or *Trumpton* where there were pillar boxes and unvandalised telephone boxes on every corner, everyone was friendly, you were introduced to the mayor, shook hands with the bank manager and you could walk by a policeman without feeling intimidated. Oliver, on the other hand, loved malls. He grew up in malls. He hung out with his friends in malls, he met girls in malls, he went to movies in malls, he went bowling in malls, he ate tacos and samosas and sushi in malls. He wanted his father to buy him a new set of trainers in malls.

'I don't know why you like these places,' Jake said.

'It's warm here, Dad. It doesn't rain. There are clean toilets. And there is a naïve sense of optimism about the place. Like we're going to keep on buying forever. Little do they know that sooner or later the whole capitalist system is going to collapse around us.'

Oliver's maturity of thought and political sensibilities (no doubt honed by years of diatribes on socialism and the welfare state from his Grandfather Albert) never ceased to impress Jake. He tried to recall what he used to think about at his age. Sex and surfing, surfing and sex. Oliver continued with his observations of the human condition:

'Everything has to change, Dad. You know that. There'll soon be no shops at all. Everything will be bought and sold online and delivered by drones. What you knew as the high street will be reclaimed for up-market housing. What I know as malls will become these huge, empty, out-of-town, wind-blown, ghostly, dystopian spaces full of drug addicts, the homeless, criminals and unemployed security guards. You shouldn't be so angry about change.'

'I'm not angry. I'm just disappointed.'

'Well, you're angry about something.'

'What makes you say that?'

'It's ten in the morning, Dad, and I can smell alcohol on your breath.'

A wave of shame and embarrassment swept over him. Before he had time to fumble for a mint or an excuse, his mobile rang. He checked the screen. 'It's Mum.'

Oliver peeled off. 'I'll check out the shoe store then.'

'Hey,' she said. 'How's the father-son bonding going?'

'I feel like I'm out with my own father.'

'I think it's good our son's got political attitudes. Kids can be so passive these days.'

'Letting his father buy him a pair of trainers seems pretty passive to me.'

Fran laughed. 'Listen. I might have some good news for you.'

'That would be a change.'

'Are you still looking for a publisher? An agent?'

His mind flipped for an instant to the recent scene in Tina's office. Her lascivious cavorting in front of him, then his rejection of her and the verbal recriminations that followed, causing him to move away from her, around her desk, accidentally hitting a switch somewhere so that the automatic blinds whirred upwards leaving the lit-up, glass-to-ceiling office space and a half-naked Tina blatantly exposed to the overlooking windows of the neighbouring houses. He left quickly after that, knocking over a couple of solar-powered path lights in the process.

'Still looking, I'm afraid.'

'This might be a bit of a long shot. But I'm doing work for a client right now who's a publisher. Small, independent, one-man outfit, not been going long, had a couple of decent hits. Says he's still on the look-out for new talent.'

'That's what they all say until commercial reality kicks in. Then it's the same old, same old.'

'Guy's different. That's his name. Guy Pemberton. He seems to have some money behind him so he's willing to take chances. Anyway, I told him about you. He said he'd have a look at your first fifty pages. Interested?'

'Sure.'

'Send me over a Word file and I'll pass it on. I don't particularly warm to him myself. He's a bit too driven and money-money for my liking but he could be good for you if you could get him on your side. A bit like a skinny Rottweiler. If he likes your stuff, I'll step aside and let the two of you get on with it.'

'Thanks for looking out for me.'

'I'll let you get on with the shoe-buying. I know how much you love malls.'

Guy did get in touch with him. He asked to see the rest of the novel which Jake forwarded. The weeks passed and Jake was ready to add Guy Pemberton to his Decca List when the publisher called again, gave him the address of a coffee shop where they could meet. One of those places stacked with sacks of beans and shelves piled high with all kinds of coffee paraphernalia unimaginable to the inhabitants of *Trumpton* or *Camberwick Green*. And waiting for him was Guy, just as Francesca had described.

'This your office then?' Jake commented by way of a light-hearted introductory remark after he had shaken hands and sat down opposite.

It turned out it *was* his office. 'Permanent quarters are so old-fashioned these days,' Guy said, confirming what Tina had also told him. Guy tapped a finger to his forehead. 'Everything I need is up here. Anything else, I out-source. Proof-reading, editing, printing, marketing, distribution, digital formatting. All done remotely. No more bricks and mortar, Jake. Keeps the overheads low. Makes for a flexible work-force. Gives me the ability to invest in people like yourself.'

'Does that mean you want to publish my book?'

'It certainly does.' Guy held up a USB stick which Jake presumed held the electronic text of his novel. 'I loved it.'

Jake didn't know what to say. He had become so accustomed to being either ignored or rejected by letter or email that it was hard to respond to an actual person saying he wanted to publish his book. If he had been in a pub, he would have ordered a bottle of champagne or a pint of Guinness with a fine malt whisky chaser. Instead, he asked the waiter for a double-shot espresso macchiato and a blueberry muffin, he would save his drunken celebrations for later.

'You're probably wanting to know about the advance,' Guy said.

'I hadn't really thought about it.'

'I find that hard to believe, Jake. Especially as you are no doubt aware from Francesca that I am spending a fortune on renovating my house. Do you know how much Calacatta marble costs these days? Two hundred pounds per square fucking foot.

Can you believe that? Anyway, I hate to disappoint you but I run my publishing business as a lean, mean machine entirely separate from any of my other entrepreneurial interests within strict budgetary limits.'

'So what are you offering?'

'One thousand pounds, Jake. Which I think if you sniff around is probably slightly north of the industry standard for literary fiction by an unknown debut male author in his ... fifties?'

'Late-forties.'

'Sorry. Anyway, it's five hundred on completion of contract and five hundred on publication. Seven and a half per cent royalties on paperback net receipts. Thirty per cent on ebooks. I'll send you over the contract. You can get a lawyer to check it out if you want but it's pretty much all industry standard.'

'What else are you offering?'

'What do you mean?'

'Apart from the money?'

Guy pointed to his forehead again. 'This, Jake. What's inside here. I spent eight years working for one of the Big Five. I have loads of contacts. Buyers, bookshop owners, reviewers, radio producers, festival organisers, book clubs, librarians, bloggers, loggers and floggers. I can assure you of a high-quality product and the passionate promotion of your work to the best of my ability. I promise you.'

Guy was as good as his word although it took him quite a while to implement it. *The Responsibility of Love* wouldn't hit the bookshelves until about eighteen months later. In the meantime, Jake's five hundred pounds didn't do much to alleviate his financial woes. He had to give up his broom cupboard in Peckham and move back in with his father, into a house in which he no longer had any financial interest.

'In my day, a young man couldn't wait to get away from his parents,' his father told him. 'We'd be out there earning a living as soon as we could'

'You went straight from home into the Army and into a war, Dad. It's lucky you lived to tell the tale.'

'The Army was a proper job. Two-and-six a day we got for defending your right to a future. To free health care. To a free education. And you throw it all away.'

'I haven't thrown it all away.'

'Where is it then?'

At this particular point in time, Jake would be hard-pressed to say. But he did have a secret weapon. 'I do have a son.'

'He's a good lad. You have to thank Francesca for that.'

'Hey, I helped raise him too.'

His father grunted. 'Just keep your hands off my booze. I've marked all the bottles.'

Despite Francesca's diagnosis based on an undergraduate degree in psychology and fine arts, Jake didn't think he was depressed. He was just bored and broke, never a good combination. Workwise, all he had were a couple of features to write a month, and even those commissions were dwindling. And having finished his novel, he had no desire or motivation to start another one until this one was published. He had nothing to do except go to the pub (he could no longer drink domestically due to his father's constant vigilance) or to add to his Decca List with the letters of rejection he was still getting from agents. He also pestered Guy every month to check on the progress of his book.

'Everything takes time,' Guy said. 'That's the problem with book publishing. I should have gone into the music business. You listen to the first few bars of what some drugged-up guitarist recorded with three chords in a basement and you can make an informed decision. Books take weeks and months to be read and edited and proof-read and typeset and reviewed and acquired and adapted. One of these days, there'll be some kind of device you can put in your glasses or eyes or even a microchip in your brain that allows you to speed-read a novel. But until that day comes, Jake, I'd advise you to be patient. If you want instant gratification, become a musician. Or a photographer. Or a porn star.'

A box did arrive one day with six author copies of his soon-to-be-released novel. He picked out one and examined it carefully. He knew he should be feeling excited. He should be taking selfies with it, showing off both the title and his name in yellow lettering, contrasting nicely against the blue background. He should be posting photos on Facebook and Instagram. He did none of this. Instead, he felt quite sad. He tried to under-stand why and he realised it was because the content of this book was now fixed and frozen in time. This was how it would be forever with all its imperfections. Never to be developed or improved upon. An everlasting testament to his inadequacies as a writer. He found a pen and inscribed a few of the copies. One to Francesca, one to Oliver, one to his father, one to Nick. He thought about signing one to Angie, sending it on to her in Cornwall with the inscription: 'You were right, it was all about me.' But he remembered her husband Mike with his jittery shotgun threat and decided against it.

There was an initial flurry of activity when the book came out although he didn't push for a formal launch as he didn't really have anyone to invite beyond his immediate family and some colleagues from his waning feature-writing career. But Guy did arrange a few events for him – a local bookstore signing, an appearance at a small literary festival, a couple of library visits, a few reviews here and there (mostly positive and mostly online) but nothing in the nationals. He followed the progress of his Amazon sales but very soon they too dwindled to a halt. According to Guy, he should be glad to sell five hundred copies with a debut novel of literary fiction unless there was something else to hook it on to. What he needed, if his novel wasn't to disappear down a black hole of anonymity, was a bit of luck. That wonderful piece of synchronicity when an author's work arrives on the desk of the right person at the right time. But that didn't seem to be happening until Guy finally called him. He hadn't heard from his publisher in weeks.

'Jake, Jake, Jake. Are you sitting down?'

'I'm lying down. It's seven in the morning and I'm still in bed.'

'You've been fucking long-listed.'

'What are you talking about?'

Guy told him what he was talking about. He was on the penultimate list of twelve novelists for a major literary prize. 'This is gold, Jake. Pure gold.'

'You didn't even tell me you'd put me forward.'

'That's because I didn't think you had a chance in hell.'

'That's very supportive of you.'

'I'm always looking out for you. You just don't see it. Behind the scenes. Working away like a busy little bee. But this is brilliant, Jake. Beyond our fucking wildest dreams brilliant. Even if you don't make the shortlist, sales will go through the roof.'

Sales didn't exactly go through the roof but they did improve substantially. Jake also found that he was in demand. Reviewers and journalists and festival organisers and bookstore managers and radio interviewers were all approaching him. When he made the shortlist, he called Francesca with the news.

'I am so happy for you,' she said. 'Now you have something to make yourself feel better about yourself.'

'I wanted to ask you a favour.'

'Go ahead.'

'Will you come with me to the event?'

'As long as you behave yourself.'

'What do you mean?'

'Can you please remain sober for the evening?'

'I'll do my best. It's going to be a really stressful occasion.'

Francesca gave out a long sigh. 'We can go from my place.

And bring Albert with you. You know how much your dad loves to watch his programmes on my big TV.'

NOW

HAVING READ OUT THE NAMES OF THE SHORT-LISTED books and their authors, the illustrious dame looked up towards the audience. A cameraman scuttled forward crab-like on the stage with his shouldered equipment, mobile phones flashed as she spoke. 'And the recipient of this year's prize goes to...' She waited for a few beats in the currently mandatory style of any presenter making an announcement on live television. Jake held his breath. As did the entire audience. Publishers and their publicists sat poised with either an exuberant 'win' or gracious 'lose' text message composed on their phones ready for finger-press delivery. The dame ended her dramatic pause and said:

Jake Tully. For The Responsibility of Love.

'What?'

Everyone at Jake's table was standing and clapping. Francesca was leaning over, helping him to his feet. He stood up and looked around in astonishment. A sea of blurry faces. Guy was jumping up and down like some sort of crazed gorilla.

'Who'd have thought?' said Arabella.

Nick was trying to engage him in an awkward hug.

'Fuck, fuck, fuck,' said Guy amidst a barrage of *ping, ping, pings.*

Oliver was giving him a thumbs up.

Francesca was saying something to him too. He couldn't hear above the noise of the applause.

'What?'

'Please, Jake. Please don't do anything stupid.'

He wriggled himself straight, took a deep breath, walked towards the podium, raising his bandaged hand in acknowledgement, it felt like a stupid gesture but what else could he do? – he'd never won anything before. He managed to negotiate the steps to the stage with the help of some female attendant to whom he was immensely grateful. Unassisted, he dealt with the remaining few feet to the podium where he was greeted warmly by the formidable dame. She said a few words to him which were indiscernible above the clapping, handed him an envelope containing a substantial cheque he would probably have to use to pay off damages to Mary Strauss, and then she abandoned him centre-stage. He turned towards the audience, grabbed what he could of the podium with his bandaged hand more for balance than anything else, he couldn't see a damn thing for all the lights shining and flashing. He inserted his good hand into his inside jacket pocket and pulled out his Decca List. He took another very deep breath and on the exhale thanked the jury, the organisers and the sponsors (and secretly thanked himself for still having the presence of mind to remember to thank them) and apologised (without prejudice to any subsequent legal claims) to Mary Strauss and her publishers for the unfortunate accident that had caused her to end up in hospital. He also mentioned how honoured he was to be included along with such wonderful co-nominees. 'We are all winners here tonight,' he said.

He realised he should have stopped there, that's what any sane person would have done. But no, this was *Jake Tully Day* and he carried on.

'I'm not going to pretend I hadn't thought about what I was going to say if I won tonight's award.' He brandished his two sheets of notepaper in the air. 'It's all written down here. This is my speech. My Decca List. Named after the record company that famously turned down the Beatles. A list of all the people who rejected or just plain ignored me and this book. You see, I wanted to have my revenge. To name names. To stop pretending that all the rejection and humiliation and simple lack of courtesy didn't mean anything to me or to all the countless other writers who have had to suffer the same.' He paused for dramatic effect for despite his heightened emotional state, he was aware that he was on national television, even if only a tiny proportion of the nation was watching. 'But you'll be pleased to know I've changed my mind.'

A large portion of the audience – but no doubt excluding many of the agents and publishers present – actually let out a collective 'Aw' of deflation that almost made him reverse his decision.

But he went on: 'You could say I've had a bit of an epiphany. Or perhaps I've just had a bit too much to drink.' He paused and looked around him, not that he could see anything, the lights were still dazzling him. He felt as if he was in some kind of white-out zone, no sense of the ground he was standing on or what was in front or to the side of him. That he was floating inside a snow cave of blinding illumination.

'As writers, we are just trying to find answers or give meaning to the issues that trouble or torment us whether they be public or private. Isn't that what all writing is about? Trying to find a vehicle in which to express, disguise or even rectify some kind of loss. Whether that be the loss of love, or self-esteem, or faith, or hope, or trust. Or even a parent.' He returned his Decca List to his jacket pocket, shielded his eyes against the lights with his bandaged hand. 'Thank you, thank you. And if you'll excuse me now, I have to attend an interview at Wood Street Police Station.'

★ ★ ★

Albert Tully turned off the TV with the remote, sat back in his armchair and let out a sigh from the depth of his withered lungs. He winced to a slight twinge in his chest, just below the top of his rib-cage, put it down to the spicy casserole that Francesca had left for him washed down too quickly with a couple of bottles of beer. His innards, so much of a mystery to him for decades, were now a constant source of observation and examination, each crimp, spasm and pinch the potential herald of the Grim Reaper. But he had to admit, men had it easy compared to the females of the species. At least, that's what Jean used to tell him, reminding him that women became obsessively attuned to the inner workings of their bodies as soon as they hit puberty. With their periods, their ovaries, their smear tests, their fearful search for breast lumps, childbirth of course, prolapses, hysterectomies and then the menopause.

'Men have a naive external awareness of their bodies,' she had insisted. 'With only their dangly bits on the outside to worry about.' To which he could now reply: 'You never knew the ache of growing old. That's one thing you can be thankful for. That, and the bloody mess this country has become.' He had been talking to Jean like this for over forty years. While he had promised to love her till death us do part, how was he to know it would turn out to be much longer. Jake and *The Little Prince* had been right about that. Such was the responsibility of love.

Behind him on the gramophone, the violins ceased to weep, the clarinet disappeared with a final sigh, the music faded to a halt, yet with the automatic arm now broken, the needle continued to hiss and crackle on a never-ending loop. He gripped his gnarled fingers around the arm-rests, heaved himself upwards, stood and swivelled, walked to the turntable on the side-board. He lifted the needle from the record. Enough of Debussy, he said to himself. And then out loud: 'Yes, Jean. Enough of bloody

Debussy.' He replaced the arm on its bracket, and as he did so, he thought of Nick and Jake's constant arguing for possession of this mahogany box of an heirloom and its accompanying collection of records. Who would have thought vinyl would come back into fashion? 'What goes around, comes around, Jean.' He smiled, knowing that in his old age his conversation was now reduced mainly to proverbs, clichés and well-worn catch-phrases. 'Yes. What goes around, comes around.'

He returned to his armchair and sat down again with another elongated sigh. Jake's acceptance speech had brought him back again to the reality of Jean's tragic death and he felt the same sadness and overwhelming sense of grief as when he had first been told the news on that fateful day. It had come from two constables at the door of the hut that served as an office down at his forge, youngsters they were, he had almost felt sorrier for them than he did for himself. There wasn't really any sensitive and delicate way of telling someone his wife had killed herself by throwing herself under a train. No police academy courses to give you words for that, at least not back then. Probably got proper classes for dealing with those kinds of situations now. He assumed it would be the same for the army too. Better than those boys with their telegrams – those delivery angels of death from his wartime days.

He supposed it had made sense that Jean had decided to take her life in this way. After all, she was a child of the Blitz, six-years-old during those eight bomb-blasted months between September 1940 and May 1941. That whole period down in London's underground now mythologised into cosy British wartime history – the camaraderie, the bulldog spirit, the serenading musicians, the children's gas masks manufactured to look like a Mickey Mouse face. That was not how Jean had experienced it. For her, it was the hot and airless tunnels; the stench of piss and shit and sweat and alcohol and intestinal wind; the selfish clamour for every inch of space; the fear of being gassed or drowned from a blasted pipe; adults arguing; couples surreptitiously having sex; her mother weeping and shaking; the bomb blasts up above, pounding the earth like the heartbeats in her chest. How could she forget all that? PTSD they would call it now. No name for it back then though, so all the trauma was buried deep inside her until it surfaced again on a platform at Balham tube station, thirty years later. He had wondered at first why she had chosen Balham on the Northern Line. Was it because she considered it was a decent distance from where they lived? Or because she had always thought of that line, delineated in black on the tube map, as the Line of Death? And then he remembered how the station had been hit by a German bomb early on in the Blitz, a burst water main flooding the tunnels, adding to the deaths already caused by the blast. He looked it all up in the newspaper archives on microfilm at the British Library. Sixty-six people killed on the evening of 14th October 1940. Now another death had been added to the toll. And how was he going to tell his boys? He was just a simple working man, a dutiful husband and family provider, a mere moulder of metal, not a compassionate harbinger of bad news.

Of course, he was sparing with the truth. 'Your dear mother has eventually passed on from the illness that kept her confined to the darkness of her room,' he had told them, crouching down to their height (Jean had always instructed him to speak to them thus) as they sat on Nick's bed, their little legs swinging, clad in sandals Jean had newly bought for them. While what he had said was not exactly the truth, it was at least a correct statement of fact. The boys had witnessed her condition and decline, no doubt attributing her malaise to some physical ailment, not the mental one that it was.

He had kept the numbers of the funeral small, the mourners primed not to mention the cause of death. Nick, being the older, had been more suspicious of the explanation, a few awkward questions needing to be swatted away. But Nick, like his parents, had always kept his emotions hidden, didn't want to show himself soft and weak in front of his younger brother. Nick just got on with things after that, put his head down, studied hard, made a good career for himself in the law, was a success in monetary terms even though his marriage was a disaster and his two girls had left home and disappeared to the far corners of the earth as soon as it was legally possible.

Jake was the one most affected by his mother's death. He always did have a difficult relationship with her. Perhaps 'difficult' wasn't the right word. He had a more intense relationship with her, a reflection of her own mood swings that could plunge from pure joy to the deepest depression and then back again. He shared her love of reading, was way ahead of his peers in that skill and loved being read to. Jean always had a stack of books piled high on her night-stand, her own Leaning Tower of Pisa she called it, a visual testament to her appetite for the written word. But the two of them could fight too, Jake often kicking out at her in tantrums, scratching her face and arms like a vicious cat.

When he had decided Jake was old enough, he eventually told him the truth about his mother's death. It was a day when he felt his own relationship with his son began to wane too. Understandably Jake wanted to know why she had done it. What his father had done to drive her towards suicide. Or what had he, Jake, done to push his mother over the edge, both literally and metaphorically? Was it the fights, the arguments, the scratching? Albert had no real answer for those questions, except to try to reassure the boy that he was not to blame.

He didn't see too much of Jake after that, sent him off to a boarding school, being the more practical solution for a motherless household. His progress there remained a mystery, hidden behind monosyllabic answers to questions, except when Albert was called in to see the teachers over disciplinary issues. 'Always with the female members of staff,' he was told. Albert could see the logic of that. And in the summer holidays, the lad had preferred to go off to Cornwall with his best friend Adam, and his parents, rather than spend time with his own father. He could see the logic in that too. By the time Jake had gone off to study at St. Andrews, he felt he didn't have a younger son anymore.

He thought again about Jake's book and the award ceremony. *The Responsibility of Love*. It was strange seeing everything written down like that for the world to see. Distributed in bookshops across the country, translated into different languages, available electronically at the press of a button. Of course, all these readers would absorb the narrative differently, it was just a story to them, set in America during that post-war period he thought Jake had managed to capture so well. A woman trying to deal with the consequences of her bitter actions, whether she was forever responsible for the death of the man she had manipulated into falling in love with her. But Albert could see the fragments of Jake's life buried underneath, his son's search for meaning and truth.

THE SUNDAY TIMES

Serialisation of *The Responsibility of Love* © by Jake Tully (abridged for publication with permission of Guy Pemberton Publishing)

New York, 1959

Even by the most benign and generous of standards, Max was not a handsome man. His bulging, frog-like eyes crowded either side of a flat, boneless nose. There was his almost non-existent chin. The blubbery lips that glistened with nervous spittle. Straight, greasy hair that no amount of expensive conditioner could flatter. A physical repulsiveness that, reflected back at him by observers, caused his shoulders to hunch, his chest to cave inwards, his thin body to stoop, his whole being to shrink in readiness for the next insult or look of revulsion that was sure to come.

It was a great pity that even the kindest of people would hardly ever venture beyond this veneer of distaste for if they did, if they actually talked to him, they would make the most wondrous of discoveries. That Max had a beautiful voice. Not a singing voice but a speaking voice. A deep yet soft, gentle, well-mannered, soothing, charming tone. A wooing voice. A voice that could pontificate on even the most boring of subjects and still enchant an audience. With one's eyes closed, it was possible to believe that it was the most gorgeous of men who was speaking.

Max was an only child of elderly parents who had both passed away when he was still in his early twenties, leaving him a decent sum. He continued to live in their spacious Victorian brownstone apartment, the one he had been born in. He lived a secluded existence, he had no friends and the idea that he might attract a girlfriend was fanciful and remote. He was resigned to a life without love, sexual pleasure or companionship. But that did not mean he could not enjoy other worldly aspects of his presence on this planet. He loved music, he loved books, his inheritance allowed him to indulge in fine food and expensive wines. He arranged to have most of his essentials delivered where possible so that he hardly ever needed to go out. Why should he? When all that would happen was to be laughed and stared at.

His apartment boasted a south-west facing balcony, just broad and long enough for a small table and chair, with a view out on to a park, a rare half-block of green space in this part of the city. It was on this balcony that he sat reading, drinking wine and nibbling on expensive delicacies when the weather was clement. Being located in an apartment building, there was a neighbouring balcony, but it had never been used, as the occupant for as long as he could remember was an elderly widow confined to a wheel-chair. It was therefore with some surprise that one day as he was outside reading, a young woman should emerge on the adjacent balcony and introduce herself as his new neighbour.

'I thought that...' Max stuttered. 'I thought that Mrs...'

'I believe she passed away a few months ago,' the

young woman told him. 'I am the new tenant. Catherine. Catherine Vance. And you are?'

'Ah yes, I'm sorry… Max.'

'Pleased to meet you, Max. I just wanted to let you know that I am a piano teacher. Pupils will come to my home for lessons. I sincerely hope I shall not disturb you.'

'I like music,' was all that Max could muster in response.

Catherine was not a beautiful woman but not an unattractive one either. She was petite with dark wavy hair that she wore unstyled, the kind of hair that Max felt demanded to be tied up with ribbons. She was neat and precise, all her movements performed with short, sharp gestures. Catherine liked everything to be in its proper order. Like notes on a piano score.

From next door, Max could hear Catherine's pupils stumbling over their assignments, especially the beginners, of course. He quite liked these faulty, repetitive sequences, possibly because they reminded him of his own imperfections. He had compassion for these students. And his tolerance was often rewarded by the occasional gifted student, or even Catherine, who would play for herself later in the evenings. As he sat on the balcony, reading his book, sipping on his wine, nibbling on his cashew nuts, he looked across at the park opposite while Catherine played her Debussy, always Debussy, and thought that a life such as his, devoid of the usual social and physical intimacies, could have its pleasant moments as well. This rare moment of positivity was further rewarded when Catherine stepped out on to her balcony with her own glass of wine. She kept many plants on her little patio, so there was no room for a table, just a chair. She sat down and said as she often did:

'I hope my students don't disturb you.'

'Not at all,' he replied. And that would usually be the end of their interchange as he would then be compelled to retreat inside. But feeling somewhat buoyant this evening, no doubt egged on by the uplifting qualities of a rather pleasant Grand Cru Beaujolais, he added: 'I actually enjoy their efforts. It gives me hope.'

'Oh. In what way?'

'That playing the piano is still relevant.'

'It has been for hundreds of years.'

'But these days there are so many other distractions.'

'I know what you mean.'

And so the conversation continued. The sun went down and despite the sudden chill, neither of them decided to leave or even to go inside to fetch a jacket or a cardigan. She was mesmerised by his voice, of course, and he was seduced by the fact that another person, one of the opposite sex even, did not seem repulsed by his looks or his company.

Max and Catherine. They started to spend more time together, on those summer evenings, after she had finished up with her students. He found space for another chair on his balcony and she would step over the low dividing railing and there they would sit, weather permitting.

'Will you read to me?' she asked him one evening.

'Why would you want me to do that?'

'You have a beautiful speaking voice.'

'Really?'

'No-one has ever told you that?'

Max shook his head. 'My mother used to. But I never believed her.'

'Why wouldn't you?'

'I just thought she was saying it to make me feel better.'

'Oh, Max,' she scolded.

He smiled sheepishly. He loved it when she used his name like that.

She went on: 'Your voice... it's so... what's the word? Mellifluous. Yes, that's it. You could be one of those people that do voice-overs for advertisements. Or promoting the latest films. Or speaking the news.'

'That's very nice of you to say so.'

'I'm not just being nice, Max. I honestly think so. As a fact.' She stamped her foot on the metal balcony floor. A childish gesture, he thought, that endeared her to him even more.

'Well, thank you,' he said. 'I shall accept the compliment. And what would you like me to read to you?'

It started off with Tolstoy, after that they alternated with their choices, mostly the classics. He introduced her to Orwell. She came back at him with Woolf. He countered with Kafka. And after that, she went all American on him with James and Steinbeck and Hemingway. Then, on a particularly warm and pleasant evening, she said to him:

'Let's go over to the park.'

'The park?'

'Yes, why do we need to sit in this cramped little space when we can stretch out over there? I'll find us some fruit and snacks. You can bring the wine.'

'Yes, I can do that. Bring the wine. Of course.'

He managed to find an old picnic basket of his parents which they packed with glasses, a bottle of his finest Burgundy, a small jar of caviar. Catherine contributed cheese and olives and crackers and pears.

'A moveable feast,' she declared.

For Max, this was a huge adventure. To go out in public like this. With a woman. He carried the hamper. She brought her book of choice. Madame Bovary. Together they emerged from the elevator, then crossed the road and entered through the wrought iron gates. They decided they would head for the far side where there were benches, trees for shade and beds of seasonal flowers. As they moved towards their destination, he felt her body close to his and she took his arm in hers. The feeling of exhilaration, of sheer joy, that passed through him at that moment was overwhelming. He actually felt his heart leap. It was a sensation that he always thought was exaggerated in novels – his heart leapt to her touch – but now he realised that such a thing could exist. His heart soared. It beat that little bit faster. His skin tingled. His footstep was lighter. He could feel the weight and heft of her arm on his. He started to hum. When they reached their destination, they found a bench in a shady bower. He commented on the vibrant colour of the geraniums, she on the lovely pink blooms on the butterfly bushes. She had let go of his arm but he felt that she was sitting closer to him than perhaps ordinary decorum allowed. He realised he was shaking with delight. He read to her. Madame Bovary. How appropriate. A woman in charge of her own destiny. A woman willing to take risks. A woman who didn't care what others thought of her. He was transported. He was in ecstasy. He took her hand. She didn't pull away. He had never held a woman's hand before. The skin was cold, even though the day was warm. So soft to the touch. He could feel himself become aroused, even though he didn't want to think of this moment as sexual but as sensual, as loving. He put down the book. She was staring out towards the broad avenue that led to the heart of their city. That dainty little face with those dark waves that he wanted to tie with ribbons. He still held her hand. He couldn't help himself, some instinct propelled him forward, to overcome his fears, a lifetime of being rejected, mocked and humiliated. He leaned his face in towards hers.

'I love you,' he said as he kissed her on the side of the mouth.

She jumped. Her body actually lifted up an inch or two off the bench. She began screaming. He wasn't even sure if she was saying actual words. There was just this high-pitched shriek. She was up on her feet now, pushing him away. And just as before his heart had leapt with joy, it was now shrivelling and shrinking and hardening against the pain. Now he could hear the words she was saying: 'What did you think was going on here? Did you honestly believe I would want to kiss someone like you? I was just being nice. Can't a girl just be nice to you without you wanting to take advantage of her? Get away. Get away from me. You disgust me.'

Later that summer's evening, Max threw himself off his balcony. Not so much as threw, but by just allowing his body to fold and collapse, he dropped over the railing, all reason for loving and living having drained out of him so that there was nothing left to hold him up. With a glass of fine wine in hand. Catherine heard the scream of a passer-by above her piano playing. Debussy. Always Debussy. The last wondrous and exquisite sounds Max ever heard. She rushed to the balcony. She saw the splayed and twisted body lying on the pavement below, blood and wine pooling vermillion on the concrete. It was her turn to scream.

★ ★ ★

Unbeknown to Max, Catherine had a boyfriend. His name was Ernest Rigsby, a member of faculty at Columbia University's Department of Music, a music theorist, specialising in the influence of Celtic culture on the folk music of Appalachia. Ernest by name, earnest by nature. Ernest adored her, fawned over her, did everything she asked. He thought this was love, she thought it was weakness. It was a relationship she could control with the snap of her fingers, the flick of an eyelid, the hitch of a hem above her calf. In the aftermath of Max's death, she married Ernest.

Thanks to Columbia University's extensive property portfolio within the vicinity of the campus, Ernest was able to rent an apartment for them from his employer on the fashionable Upper West Side, overlooking the Hudson River. She was happy at first, the ring on her finger lifting the pressure and fear of being left on the shelf while all around her women of a similar age were settling down to a life of husband, children and modern kitchen appliances. She enjoyed being shown off at faculty receptions or strolling along the waterfront of Riverside Park arm and arm with her husband. She continued to give piano lessons but without the same economic imperatives as when she was single and trying to survive. She tried to forget what she had done to Max.

She and Ernest attempted to have children. Their coupling was awkward, she being the more experienced thanks to a short-lived affair with a saxophone player she had met when she had gone for an audition at a club down on 52nd Street. She realised Ernest felt intimidated by her in bed which caused him to be shy and unadventurous with her body, leaving her bored and frustrated. But she was willing to persevere with that marital obligation for the sake of having children. Yet pregnancy evaded her and she blamed Ernest entirely for this failure. Ernest, in turn, had no idea what to do except to keep trying which ended up dissatisfying Catherine even more. In her head, she decided to give the marriage one more year. Ernest was on track for tenure and if he was successful perhaps the extra money, security and status would provide the contentment that she lacked. But the year went by and nothing changed. Tenure and pregnancy were just as elusive as they always had been.

Matters all came to a head one steamy July night. The temperature had reached into triple digits during the day and she had spent the afternoon downtown browsing in a department store just because it had air-conditioning. Back in the apartment, she waited for Ernest to come home. All the windows were open to the sounds of radios blaring and neighbours squabbling in the heat. She had a kerchief in the icebox and one on her head that she kept swapping around. There was a bottle of bourbon on the kitchen table and she had neither the strength to make dinner or to go out onto the fire escape to smoke a cigarette. Her usual ploy to achieve calmness was to play the piano but the humidity caused the keys to stick together and dulled the hammers on the strings. Ernest came home with his shirt sticking to his back, an empty belly and a foul mood in his mouth. The deference he used to have for her had disappeared a while back along with the sex, the love and the ambition.

'Are we eating?' he asked, taking in the sight of a barren table.

'I've no appetite.'

'I see you've a thirst.' He picked up the bottle of bourbon, scrutinised it as if he could tell how much she'd drunk. 'Drinking alone in the afternoon. What kind of a woman does that?'

'The whore that you married,' she snapped back. She knew the thought that he had not been her first lover irked him deep in his bones, tormented his fragile ego. She was itching for a fight and she knew how to start it.

'Look at you,' he sneered. 'You're a disgrace. A disgrace to me. A disgrace to yourself.'

'And you're a nothing. Nothing as an academic. Nothing as a husband.'

'Whore,' he yelled then hit her sharp across her face. She had seen it coming and let her cheek ride with the blow. It wasn't the first time he had hit her but it was certainly the hardest. She didn't react, just let him stand there with the guilt of his violence hanging in the hot, humid air. With the windows open, she might have worried about the neighbours hearing his insult but they weren't the only ones letting steam off their marital woes that hot New York night.

'It's over,' she said, with a calmness that surprised her. 'We're over.'

Ernest was down on his knees, pleading now. She watched the top of his balding, sweaty head as he kept saying, 'I'm sorry,' over and over again.

She was sorry too. Sorry she hadn't made the decision sooner. 'I want a divorce.'

'I'm not giving you one,' he smirked back at her, with that male look of entitled possession that irked her even more.

'We'll see about that.'

He hit her again. He hit away at his marriage, he hit away at his tenure, he hit away at his sexual impotence and incompetence. He knew there was no way back.

She took on more students, squirreled away as much cash as she could until she was ready. Six months later, she contacted a New York attorney who arranged for the necessary papers to be prepared and served, then contacted a local lawyer in Reno, Nevada to act on her behalf over there. She bought a train ticket, packed a couple of suitcases, and set off for the Silver State where she needed to spend six weeks to establish residency before she could have her quickie divorce. She took a Greyhound to Chicago and then the California Zephyr out west. When she alighted off that train after three days and 2,000 miles of tracks at the Southern Pacific Railroad Station, Reno, Nevada, she breathed in the dry, desert air, scanned the arid horizon-wide mountain range, put on her sunglasses against the bright blue of a sky and the glare of a light that was unknown to the residents of

New York City and thought to herself: This is the beginning of a new me.

* * *

Catherine was met on the platform by the attorney-at-law instructed by her New York lawyer to act on her behalf.

'Harold Cornelius Starr, at your service, Madame Rigsby,' declared the rather dapper gentleman in a grey, lightweight pinstripe suit as he doffed his hat, and held out his hand.

Catherine put down one of her suitcases and accepted the greeting with her own gloved hand. 'How did you recognise me, Mr Starr?'

'The description wired was most accurate.'

She hesitated to think what that description might have been. Another bitter widow, in her late thirties, with dyed-black hair, unshapely calves and sagging features.

'And please call me Harry. I am here to help you with "the cure" in whichever way I can.'

She smiled at his remark. A cure was indeed what she sought. 'Accommodation is my first priority. Can you direct me to some kind of property agency.'

'I am deeply offended, Catherine. May I call you Catherine?' Without waiting for her response, he carried on. 'As previously mentioned, I am at your service. Not just in matters of law and all its necessary procedures. But also in matters of housing, employment, and entertainment during your move to Nevada.'

'But I am only staying here for six weeks.'

'Ah, there you are,' said Harry, taking her suitcase and calling for a porter to take the rest of her baggage. 'You must not talk of such a temporary sojourn. The intention to permanently reside in this wonderful state is a crucial condition of your cure. Of course, whether you end up staying here after you have been cured is entirely up to you. A woman has the right to change her mind, has she not? In fact, that is why she is here. Because she has changed her mind. And so, in the matter of accommodation, I can offer you a wide range to choose from depending on your means, your standards and your inclination.'

The out-of-town dude ranches that Harry listed she left to the rich and famous while downtown the Riverside Hotel was way out of her price range. She opted for renting a room in a small boarding house on Ralston Street where she would share a kitchen and bathroom with three other divorce-seeking women. The place was run by an elderly matron, Mrs Amelia Walsh, who had come to the town thirty years previously seeking her own divorce and was therefore well-versed in the needs of her clientele. This included the taking of a daily attendance register at the breakfast table.

'What is of primary importance,' Harry informed her,' is that while many people across our great nation believe that our moral attitude to divorce is rather lax, the same cannot be said regarding our approach to its legal procedures. It is absolutely essential that you meet the requirement of six weeks consecutive – and I mean consecutive – residency in the state of Nevada. I do not care what you end up doing the night before, Catherine, but you must be at that breakfast table at eight o'clock for Mrs Walsh's register. She will be your witness under oath as to your continued residency in Nevada on the day of your court hearing. And she will not be diverted from her task by persuasion, flattery, cajolery or bribes. Perjury is a serious offence in our courtrooms punished by a lingering confinement.'

Catherine rather liked Harry but her boarding-house companions quelled her of any ambitions in his direction. 'He's a friend of Dorothy's,' she was quietly informed. When she confessed to not knowing why that was important, she was told that 'Harry is a bit light on his loafers. His taste does not deviate from his own gender.' And that was the end of that little heart flutter for Catherine.

She enjoyed the company of the other three lodgers though, an ever-changing trio at various stages of satisfying their residency requirement. They came from all parts of the country, from various backgrounds, but Mrs Walsh's girls were always white. Black and Asian women took up residence in the east part of town, frequented their own clubs, gambling joints, restaurants, bars and places of accommodation.

When Catherine realised she would need to find a job to fund her stay, Harry got her work at the Mapes Hotel. She had actually applied for a behind-the-scenes role, helping out as a simple ledger clerk in the casino's accounts department so she was surprised to be taken on as a Keno girl. She always thought that these kind of jobs on the casino floor were for pretty young things but as her line manager told her when assigning her a uniform and a locker: 'Most of the guys that come around here are middle-aged and older. Yes, they'll have an eye to start off with for the young flesh. A pat on the ass, a pinch of firm tit, gives them a little bit of a rise. But once they've settled down for the evening and the games are flashing by and the drinks are flowing, it is a woman like yourself that they like to socialise with, in the wee small hours of the morning.' Catherine didn't know whether to take the explanation as an insult or a compliment. What it did mean though was that she was assigned to work the graveyard shift.

She quite liked the work though, the novelty and its temporary nature making the long hours more than tolerable. After all, she was a simple piano teacher, the dowdy soon-to-be ex-wife of an East Coast academic. And yet here she was in high heels, sleeveless black top and black slacks working in a glamorous hotel that could boast famous guests such as Marilyn Monroe, Frank Sinatra and John Wayne. The work was easy too. All she had to do was collect the Keno cards from the tables of the various customers, take them to the Keno desk to get the selected numbers recorded, return with a copy for the customer, then wait to see whose numbers came up. If any of her customers won, she would double-check the card, confirm the win and then could rely on a generous tip. Sometimes she would be called on to bring drinks and food to the tables as well. As the night drifted on into early morning, a few sleepless customers, men and women alike, would be left in the lounge, automatically going through the motions with the cards, testing their luck against the numbers, trying to distract themselves from the boredom and the loneliness. As her manager had predicted, many of the older men were happy to chat with her. The more they chatted, the more they drank, all the better for the profits of the lounge. She was quite happy to oblige these late-night gamblers, listening to their marital woes in the timeless vacuum of her windowless world. It helped her shift go by until she was blasted back into the sunny reality of a red and orange dawn tinting the Sierra Nevadas and the 8am roll call at Mrs Walsh's breakfast table.

The first thing that Catherine noticed about Cy Walker was that he had beautiful hands. But then again, she was a piano teacher and as such the span of the fingers to cover an octave or more was important to her. As was the depth of skin on the distal phalanges which would dictate the pianist's delicacy of touch, especially when executing a Debussy composition. Cy had long-tapered fingers that apart from their piano-playing potential could wrap themselves around a tumbler of Tennessee whiskey, enclose a Pall Mall cigarette in their vice or tap the back of her hand as she reached down to collect his card. The one other thing that Catherine noticed about Cy's fingers was that as soon as they came into contact with her skin, they sent a tremor up her arm. She pressed a hand to her chest, took in a breath, re-checked his numbers then signalled to the desk that the card was indeed a winning one.

'You bring me luck,' he told her as his fingers then went on to clasp her own. 'Cy Walker's the name. Why don't you stay awhile? I'm going to sit out the next game.'

Catherine looked around the lounge. There was only one other customer, another middle-aged man who was being suitably entertained by her shift-partner, Darlene – a twenty-five-year old stenographer from Ohio who was desperate to find another husband, preferably very rich, very old and very impotent, as soon as the ink had dried on her divorce decree at the Washoe County Court House. Catherine moved her attention from the exquisite hands to the rest of Cy Walker – he was probably in his early fifties, with thick, dyed-black hair, a Clark Gable style moustache, not overwhelmingly handsome but something quite charmingly roguish about him that appealed to a sensibility and a sexual desire that she never knew she possessed.

'If I can get you another drink,' she said.

He nodded his understanding of the trade-off. 'Another Jack. A double. On the rocks.'

She went up to the bar, completed the order, felt her legs shaking as she walked back to his table, placed the glass of whiskey on his table. She then sat down and sighed as she kicked off her high-heeled shoes.

'Nothing for yourself?' he said.

'House rules. No drinking on the job.'

'Pity. I don't feel like drinking alone.'

'I can still be fine company. Even without a drink in me.'

'I'm sure you can be.' He toasted her with his glass, then downed half the contents. 'Here's to drinking to drown out the memory. But unfortunately, the memory keeps drowning out the whiskey.'

Normally, she would have followed up that little opening gambit. Getting a customer to talk about their soon-to-be exes was a good way of running up a sizeable bar tab, but Mrs Cy Walker was of no interest to Catherine at this point. 'I'm Catherine,' she said. 'If you'd like to know.'

'I know that already. Darlene told me.'

'What else do you know then?'

'That you are a most desirable woman.'

Cy Walker wasn't the first customer that had come on to her in the small hours of the morning through a whiskey haze. But this time, she felt herself redden. She wouldn't mind taking a swig of Jack Daniels herself. In fact, that was what she did. She reached across, picked up Cy's glass and gulped down the rest of the whiskey until the ice rested on her lips. She replaced the glass on the table, took in Cy's wide grin, felt herself go all warm and shivery when he said: 'That's what I call a real woman.' He asked if he could call her 'Cat', 'Catherine' seemed too prosaic for a woman as sleek and sensuous as she. How could she refuse.

She learned quite a lot about Cy Walker that night in between her work on other tables. As with the whiskey, he came from Tennessee, from the town of Chattanooga where he had been the proud proprietor of two shoe shops. Like Catherine, he was biding his time waiting to fulfil his residency requirement. He had sold up his business to pay for his divorce and the time he needed to spend in Reno. He had been extremely lucky with his gambling when he had first arrived, using his winnings sensibly to pay upfront for a six-week stay at a decent downtown hotel. He spent the nights drinking and on some low-key gambling at the roulette tables or in the Keno lounges to stave off the boredom and the memories of a marriage in which he had been happy until he discovered his wife's infidelities. Given his background in the shoe business, he confessed to having a love for feet. To prove his point, he picked up one of Catherine's, placed it in his lap and massaged the aching sole through her nylon stocking until she had to hold back her moans of pleasure.

With the first light of dawn, he rose from his table, kissed her hand in an exaggerated gesture and stumbled off into the morning. She finished her shift, went back to Mrs Walsh's boarding house for breakfast and the 8am roll call. By 10am, she was walking past the chambermaids at the El Cortez hotel as if she had every right to be there and was knocking on the door of room 305 with her high-heel shoes in her hand.

She was still in bed with him eight hours later, thinking about getting up and ready for her shift while Cy lay there smoking a cigarette.

'I'm going to tell you something I've never told anyone before,' she said.

'I'm listening, baby.'

She told him about what had happened with Max.

'Why are you telling me this?'

'Because I want you to promise that what I did to him, you will never do to me.'

Catherine's life settled into a comfortable yet exciting routine. She worked the graveyard shift at the Keno lounge of the Mapes Hotel while Cy played the roulette tables on the casino floor. Early morning, he would come into the lounge for a drink or two, play a few cards, keep her company, talk about his winnings or losings (he played to pass the time rather than for high stakes). He would then retire to his hotel room, she would check in at the breakfast table at Mrs Walsh's in order to satisfy her residency requirement and then she would be off to share Cy's bed and his body at the El Cortez hotel. She couldn't remember feeling happier. She had a court date coming up that was going to release her from a dreary marriage, give her back her independence and, dare she wish it, a life with Cy, who would also soon be free from his marriage. She was still young enough to conceive a child. Everything seemed perfect, everything seemed possible.

* * *

Catherine knew that something had happened as soon as she saw Cy enter the lounge. Even from where she was standing, she could see he was breathing heavily, the sheen of sweat on his brow reflected off the harsh casino lighting. He spotted her, came striding over, pushed her down on to a seat by one of the Keno tables.

'What's going on?' she asked.

'We're just talking natural, all right?'

'Sure. But what's happening?'

'It's good news, babe. I've just won big. Huge.'

'That's wonderful,' she said, her mind already racing forward to a more luxurious future than the one she normally had in mind. She wanted to ask how much he'd raked in but she kept her mouth shut. She licked her lips, could feel the little dry flakes on her skin, the air-con a perpetual dehydration hazard for the staff.

'You got that big purse of yours?' he asked.

'It's in my locker.'

'OK, this is what we are going to do. We're going to stroll over to the bar, just like I'm a normal customer, right?'

'Sure, honey.'

'I'm then going to slip you the rolls of bills I've got stuffed in my pockets and I want you to take them to that purse of yours in your locker. At the end of your shift, I want you to walk that purse straight over to my hotel.'

'You know I can't do that. I need to be at Mrs Walsh's for eight.'

Cy's eyes widened and he looked at her as if she were executing the biggest betrayal he could imagine. He clenched a fist and he made to slam it on the table but seemed to think the better of making a scene. Instead, he hissed: 'If you hurry over, drop off the bag and head straight back, you'll get there in time.'

'I won't. I'll be late. And you don't know, Mrs Walsh. She's a stickler. If I'm not there at eight, she won't mark me down. And then she won't testify under oath as my witness to residency. She swears by Almighty God, and God won't allow her to lie.'

Cy wiped the sweat off his brow with the back of his hand. 'All right, all right. I'll have a cab pick you up here. Straight to my place, then yours. You'll have plenty of time.'

She leaned over, patted the back of his hand. 'Thank you.'

Together they walked over to the bar. Cy ordered a double Jack, and surreptitiously fed several bank-wrapped bundles of bills into the pocket of her apron that she used for Keno cards, pencils and a notepad for drink orders.

'Now go,' he said.

Off she went back through the staff room door and straight to her locker. Her fingers shook as she fiddled with the combination lock. The six numbers of the date of her birth. Only a few days away. What a birthday present, she thought, as she scooped the packs – several crisp bundles of twenty-dollar bills – into her locker, snapped shut the lock, and turned to rest her back against the metal. She was trembling. She held a hand to her chest and took deep breaths. The amount of money she had just locked away was way more than she had ever dreamed of. She imagined putting down a deposit on a Cape Cod-style house, all in white, a steep slate roof with a couple of gabled dormers, a fine lawn out front. A car parked in the drive. A Plymouth Valiant or an Oldsmobile. Or a Buick Skylark convertible. In mint green. She smiled to herself. Who the hell did she think she was? Princess Grace? She smoothed down her apron, fixed her brassiere straps and with a shake of her shoulders walked back out to the lounge. Cy had already left.

The rest of her shift was a disaster such was her distracted state. She spilt drinks, mixed up cards, got orders wrong. But what did she care? She figured there was at least six thousand dollars stashed away in her locker and she was going to be walking out the casino at the end of her shift and never coming back. She would have disappeared even earlier but she didn't want to leave co-worker Darlene in the lurch. And anyway, Cy had warned her not to draw attention to herself. So come seven-thirty in the morning with the sun creeping up over the hills, she was out in the car park her purse stuffed full of her future when the car pulled up in front of her, the door swung open, she crouched down and began to slide into the backseat. It was only when she was about half-way into the vehicle, that she realised someone else was sitting there too. And it wasn't Cy. A hand reached out, grabbed her wrist and dragged her the rest of the way inside the car. The driver pulled off quick with a sharp swing to the left that caused her door to slam behind her. A push from the guy beside her– a skinny man with sharp features and a pencil moustache – forced her upright as the vehicle itself righted itself and they sped away. The man shoved her again.

'Money in the bag?' he said.

She recognised the accent straightaway. Why wouldn't she? It was straight out of New York. Long Island. She looked straight ahead at the back of the driver's head, didn't say a word, clasped her hands together to form a loop around the handle of her purse.

The punch came quick to the side of her jaw. Somewhere within the pain, she felt one of her teeth move, tear into skin, as her head jerked to the side, hit the passenger window. At the same time, her bag was wrenched away from her, twisting her wrist awkwardly in the process. From her slump by the car door, she watched as the contents of the bag were emptied onto the seat. The man picked out the wads of bills, collected them into his lap and then swept most of her other possessions back into her purse.

'Pull over, Vinnie,' he said to the driver.

The car stopped, the man leaned over her, pulled down on the door handle, and her own weight against the panel had her falling backwards, out of the car and on to the sidewalk, her upper back and neck connecting hard with the concrete as she hit the ground. Her purse was thrown out after her, then she heard the car speed off.

She lay there on the sidewalk staring up at a cloudless sky. Her jaw ached, she tasted blood in her mouth, her tongue raked over a loose tooth. She turned her neck slowly to make sure she had movement there. She would have loved for a pair of caring hands to reach down and pick her up but it was early morning in God knows what part of town, and the streets of Reno were always deserted, even in the middle of the day, never mind now in the dawn hours. She eased herself up into a sitting position. Her stockings were ripped, the skin on her legs scraped, her dress covered in gravel and dust. She picked up her purse, opened it and found her pocketbook. Remarkably the contents were intact – a couple of dollar bills and some loose change, her social security card and her staff card for the casino. She pushed up and on to her feet and looked around. It wasn't a part of town she recognised. She saw the neon sign for an Al's 24Hour Diner, a couple of blocks further up. With the sun already blazing down on her, she staggered up the street.

She realised she had been abandoned on the east side of town when she pushed open the door of Al's and all the customers were black. A breakfast clientele out of the clubs on East Commercial Row and Douglas Alley – late-night gamblers, jazz musicians, casino workers. A few raised their heads but it seemed that a beat-up white lady in ripped stockings didn't seem to draw much attention in this part of town. She met the eyes of the large woman serving behind the counter who gave her a sympathetic nod. She proceeded towards the restroom where she immediately threw up into a toilet bowl inside a cubicle. Once she felt there was no more bile left to surface, she went over to a sink, rinsed her face, plucked out her loose tooth, spat out the blood. Her cheek had come up in a bruise and her neck and back had stiffened up so she could hardly move her upper body. She went back out to the dining area where the woman behind the counter slid her over a cup of black coffee. She whispered her gratitude, took a couple of sips, noted with dismay the time of eight thirty-five on the wall clock, retrieved a dime out of her pocketbook and called a cab to take her to the El Cortez hotel.

Shaking and distraught, she knocked on the door of Cy's hotel room. The door opened immediately and she fell into his arms. She wanted him to hold her, to comfort her, to never let her go, but instead he walked her over to the centre of the room and sat her down on the edge of the bed.

'What the fuck happened to you?' he screamed.

'I got rolled, Cy. I got rolled.'

'What do you mean?'

'Two guys outside the hotel. They drove up, dragged me into the car, took the money and threw me out on to the sidewalk.'

Cy started pacing the carpet, slamming his fist into his palm. 'Fuck fuck, fuck.'

'You knew about this, didn't you?' she said. 'You knew you were putting me in danger.'

'I didn't think they'd touch you.'

'Who are "they", Cy? Who are they?'

'I owed some guys some money. They were watching, waiting for me to win big, then pounce. That's why I needed to get the money out all secretive. Like I said, I didn't think they'd touch you.'

'Look at me, Cy. I don't care about the money. I'm cut and bruised. I've lost a tooth. Why don't you hold me?'

Cy didn't stop his pacing. 'I've just lost six fucking grand.'

'Forget about the money. You've still got me. I'm here for you. And you need to be here for me.'

Cy stopped pacing and stared at her. 'What are you talking about?'

'You and me, Cy. I love you.'

He laughed. An hysterical laugh, a dissonant mixture of distress and disdain. 'Are you kidding me, Cat?'

'What about us? Our future? Your divorce?'

'There is no divorce. I've never been married. Only a sucker gets married. This whole fucking town is testament to that. This is where I live, Cat. Every few weeks, I move from casino to casino, chasing after skirt looking for the cure. You're just another desperate divorcee. You're just another Reno fuck to me.'

She stood up and walked out of the room, walked out of the hotel, walked away from the river, the casinos, the bank, the courthouse, the newspaper offices, the motels, the gas stations, the water towers, she just kept walking north out of town. After she passed the university campus, the broad streets narrowed, the fancy colonial revival buildings thinned out until all that was left of Reno was the odd mobile home popping up here and there on otherwise barren hillsides. There were no more roads, just dirt tracks, leading to mountains and desert. The sun was beating down on her back, she had no water with her, she just kept going. There were no paths now just endless stretches of parched grey earth punctuated with clumps of sagebrush, sometimes pockets of fine sand, difficult to walk through, sapping her strength. Her tears dried as quickly as they came, the salt irritating her bruised skin even more.

But as she struggled on into the wilderness, it wasn't just thoughts of Cy that occupied her mind. It was an accumulation of pain, anger and frustration acquired over her still-quite-short lifetime – her fearfulness that had prevented her pursuing a career as a pianist, a loveless and abusive marriage to Ernest, her unfulfilled desire for a child, and most of all, her overwhelming guilt for the way she had treated Max. That poor desperate man, how she had teased him, lured him in. At the time, she had pretended to herself she had been doing him a favour, providing him with the pleasure of the female company that he craved. But she knew also that she was taking out her frustrations on him, basking in her power over him, power that she eventually abused. Even after all these years, she still felt responsible for his death. And here she was now, stumbling out into the desert towards her own oblivion, consumed by her own humiliation and rejection. How ironic was that?

She slowed down, her steps beginning to falter in the oppressive heat until she came to a complete halt. Was this the spot on which she was to die? And as she contemplated her predicament, she found herself possessed with immense clarity. Was this the light before the darkness? The final epiphany? And in this blissful state she realised that inasmuch as she hated Cy for what he had done, his actions alone weren't the reason for her despair. It had been a process of accumulation. He was merely the cruel icing on a very unhappy cake. Just as she would have been for Max. And if she were to take her own life as a consequence, then that was her decision to make and hers alone. No-one else was responsible. And by admitting that, she realised that she was also not responsible for Max's death. That too was Max's decision and his alone.

And with that understanding, she felt a weight disappear off her already aching neck and shoulders. Muscles that had been tense for years loosened and relaxed. A tight knot within her whole being unravelled. She spun around on the spot, arms outstretched. She felt light, she felt redeemed. She held her head back and gazed upwards. The sky was the same relentless cloudless blue. The Sierra Nevadas continued to line the landscape to her west in shades of burnt umber. To her east, a small shiny silver, single-engined plane came up over the hills above the Stead Air Force Training Base hidden away in the next valley. She watched it carve up the air far above her, the sun glinting off its wings, its throaty growl breaking the silence as it performed turns, drove up vertical corridors before looping down again. She undid the top two buttons of her blouse, reached into the cleave of her brassiere and pulled out two rolls of twenty-dollar bills. She wiped her face with the hem of her blouse and turned around.

Back on the edges of town, she managed to hitch a ride to her boarding house. She was grateful that Mrs Walsh was discrete enough not to ask any questions about her bruised and dishevelled state. At the same time, she was not going to throw herself on her God-fearing landlady's mercy and beg her to ignore just this once this gap in her continued residency. Catherine had no intention of staying another minute in this town, never mind another six weeks. She had no intention of ever marrying again either so what did it matter that she would go through the rest of her life legally linked to her weasel of an academic husband. Instead, she took a long hot bath, dressed in her best clothes, packed her two suitcases, paid off her rent then took a cab downtown to the law offices of Harold Cornelius Starr where she paid her bill for expenses incurred to date. Another cab driver took her to the east side of town, waited for her as she left a five-dollar bill for the woman behind the counter at Al's 24Hour Diner, then drove her to the Southern Pacific Railroad Station.

* * *

When Catherine set foot in San Francisco in the spring of 1965, it was a time of great change for her and for the nation to which she belonged. She was caught in the cusp of transition between the great post-war innocence, morality and optimism that had been shattered by the Kennedy assassination, and the cultural revolution heralded by the arrival of the Beatles, the civil rights movement and the injection of psychedelics into the counter-culture. For the first time, the US Government had committed ground troops to its war in Vietnam, a move initially backed by a patriotic public whose mood would soon sour with the rise of the death toll. Disillusioned youths, poets, writers, musicians, students and draft-dodgers were flocking to San Francisco where rental property was cheaper, hair was longer, skirts were shorter, music and drugs were experimental. The city itself was in the midst of an urban renewal. Construction of a new public railway transportation system had just begun, new bridges were being built, old-time neighbourhoods were being bulldozed and replaced with modern housing complexes.

Catherine was initially unaware of any of this. She booked herself into a downtown hotel and spent her first few days doing what most visitors to the city did. She rode the cable car up to Nob Hill for a view of the bay, she enjoyed a mug of clam chowder and a stack of crab sandwiches down on Fisherman's Wharf, she shopped for new clothes at Macy's in Union Square, she ate dim sum in Chinatown, she walked among the dahlias and palm trees in Golden Gate Park, she sipped ocha from a tiny cup in the Japanese Tea Garden and discovered a fortune cookie buried within her bowl of rice crackers. It read: 'Happiness yet to reach you but arrives from unexpected place. Lucky number: 10.' She contemplated this prophecy in meditative mood as she sat by a small pond within the gardens, observing the tourists on the Drum Bridge and the flashes of sunlight on the orange-pink skin of the koi swimming below the surface of the water. Yes, happiness was yet to reach her. She had no doubt about that. But at least the message of the cookie gave her hope. She opened her purse, took out the daily paper and scanned the classifieds. Rental property was indeed cheap in San Francisco. A furnished ground floor apartment in a Victorian building in Telegraph Hill, two bedrooms, electric kitchen, fireplaces, carpets and drapes throughout, outstanding view of the bay and nearby gardens. $55 per month. That was less than she had been paying at Mrs Walsh's boarding house in Reno. She went along to have a look. It was on the corner of Bay and Stockton. The building number was 10. As long as there was space for a piano she would take it.

She paid two months rent upfront, bought a second-hand piano through the classifieds, then made an appointment at a local bank in order to open up an account. The manager's name was Frank Jackson, a kind-mannered man about twenty years her senior with a fleshy face, greying hair combed back from his forehead in crinkly waves and a soothing voice that could accept your money and reject your loan application in equal measure. His office was all wood panelling, brass-studded leather chairs and cigar smoke. A bag of golf clubs stood in the corner. She opened her account in her maiden name while he took her bundles of cash with soft, powdered hands but with no questions asked and provided her with a receipt written out in a fine script with a silver fountain pen.

'I wonder if you would do me the honour of having dinner with me,' he asked in such a gentle way that she did not find his sudden approach forward or offensive.

Honour? When was the last time a man had said he was honoured by her presence? Certainly not smooth-talker Cy Walker when he inveigled his way into her life and her underwear. Or when her husband Ernest Rigsby was making up for his sexual inadequacies with drunken slaps across her face. She was sure dear Max had been honoured by her presence but she preferred not to think about him. So why should she refuse Frank Jackson this honour? After all, she was a Keno lounge girl fresh out of Reno who knew how to handle men. And anyway, she didn't know another soul in town.

Frank picked her up from her apartment in a black Oldsmobile, a vehicle of restrained elegance, she thought, and entirely appropriate for a bank manager. He took her to a plush restaurant, told her his life story as middle-aged widowers with grown-up children and no greater ambition than to play more golf tended to do. She thought he was a pleasant man who made her (and her money) feel safe and that they could be friends. She told him so as they sat in his car at the end of what had been a delightful evening and he appeared happy to agree.

'In which case,' he said. 'I wonder if you would mind helping me out tomorrow with a task I have to do at the bank. It should only take a couple of hours or so.'

'I hope you're not asking me to help you rob the place,' she said.

'Oh my, Catherine,' he said, patting her knee. 'How could you possibly think such a thing?'

As parishioners piled into the white-stone Catholic church opposite for Sunday prayers, Catherine waited as Frank opened up the heavy wooden doors of the bank then escorted her inside. More locks were undone to take her through the tellers' section and then into a rear room where the vault was situated. Frank looked at his watch.

'Ten o'clock,' he announced. And right on time, she heard the sound of hydraulic bolts unlocking. Frank spun the metal spindle at the centre of the steel door then pulled it open. He told her to wait as he went inside. He came back carrying three teller trays of coins which he laid down on a wooden table and repeated the process until he had brought out ten trays.

'What's this all about?' she asked, thinking that they were indeed robbing the bank.

'Up until a few months ago,' Frank told her, 'quarters and dimes contained 90% silver. Thanks to our dear president, Lyndon B. Johnson, signing the Coinage Act, all the newly minted ones for this year onwards will contain no silver at all. What I would like to do here is to separate the wheat from the chaff, putting all the 1964 coins and earlier to the side.'

'And then...?'

'Then, my dear, Catherine. As your bank manager, I would advise investing a prudent amount of your savings in precious metal. I reckon any increase in the price of silver over the next few years is going to outpace the interest on any deposit you might have in this here bank.'

For the next two Sundays, she and Frank managed to sort out over one thousand dollars' worth of silver quarters and dimes, two hundred and fifty dollars of which she then purchased from the bank and stored in her very own deposit box.

But Frank's concern over her financial well-being didn't end there.

'You gotta be owning your own property,' he told her. 'Prices are dirt cheap at the moment because there are plans for a freeway that nobody knows where the hell it's supposed to be going. But it isn't going to be passing through Telegraph Hill, I can tell you that. I'd be buying your own place, Catherine. With that view out over the bay, some green space nearby and tucked in close to the Powell-Mason cable car line, you got nothing to lose.'

Catherine felt she had everything to lose. But with Frank's reassurance and with all the money she had, he helped arrange a long-term loan to purchase the apartment she was originally renting. And when another apartment came up in the same building, he helped her to acquire that one too, and then another, until two years into her residency in San Francisco, she found herself to be the owner of a fine three-storey Victorian building, mortgaged up to the hilt but within which two of the properties rented out for an income sufficient to repay the interest on her loans. On the day she concluded the final acquisition, she walked up the central staircase linking the various apartments until she was able to open a small attic door leading out to a balcony set into the tiled turreted roof. She looked out across at the sun glinting off the famous bridge, its towers and suspension cables shining as if indeed they were made of gold.

★ ★ ★

For Catherine, it was as if all the undercurrents of rebellious American youth – its essence, its emotion, its idealism, its heightened consciousness, its spirituality, its political activism, its sexual liberation – had erupted in one place in an orgasm of hope and music and drugs and art and love and peace. And that place was the Haight-Ashbury district of San Francisco in the summer of 1967. The Hippies were wearing flowers in their hair, Timothy Leary was urging them to turn on, tune in and drop out, Allen Ginsberg was mesmerising them with Sufi chants while The Grateful Dead and Jefferson Airplane supplied the music. Although Telegraph Hill was around four miles from the happenings at Haight-Ashbury and very much on the periphery of all this counter-culture, Catherine could not help but be affected by the spirit, the mood and the fashion of the times. The best way she could describe it was that there was a 'loosening up' inside herself. There was less tension in her muscles, there was more of a flow in the movement of her limbs, she let her hair grow longer, her clothes became shapeless and more colourful, she wore beads and bangles and bracelets, she even experimented with a little pot. She found herself opening up to different kinds of music so that not only did she teach classical piano but she was also happy to cater to her students' requests for songs by The Beatles, Simon and Garfunkel, and Bob Dylan. Many of her tenants were wandering minstrels themselves from all over the country and very quickly her apartment became a venue for impromptu musical evenings with guitars, drums and sometimes even herself on keyboards. She felt she was too old now to paint her face, wear short skirts and trip out on acid, to pretend that she was really an integral part of this youthful rebellion but at the same time she hoped somehow she could be some kind of a mother to it all.

She still saw Frank. She went out with him for dinner at least once a week but despite setting quite firm boundaries for their friendship, she was aware he was very slowly attempting to trespass over them. He was a patient man and no doubt felt that these slight encroachments might at least go undefended if not unnoticed. The request that she should link her arm in his as they walked. That 'goodnight' peck on the cheek that lasted slightly longer each time, moving in almost imperceptible adjustments from the outside of her cheek to the corner of her mouth. The gifts that seemed to become more regular and more expensive each time. It was a slow assault that culminated with a card that arrived by post one morning inscribed with a verse from Robert Browning's Lost Mistress:

Yet I will but say what mere friends say
Or only a thought stronger
I will hold your hand but as long as all may
Or so very little longer

It seemed this card was a preparatory tactic, a softening-up, a subtle note of intention that was followed by a visit from the man himself later that evening. She sat on the sofa and watched him silently prowl the Persian carpet in front of her fireplace until he eventually sat down beside her.

'I've been offered a promotion.'

'That's such good news, Frank.'

'Yes, it is.' He clenched his hands on his lap. 'There is only one problem…'

'Which is?'

'The new job's in Vancouver.'

The slight sinking feeling she experienced in her stomach surprised her. 'Vancouver?'

'The bank is expanding into Canada. It wants to put me

in charge of total operations for British Columbia. It would mean going from branch to regional manager. It would be a wonderful way for me to sign off on the last few years of my career.'

'You deserve it.'

He took both her hands in his. 'I would like you to come with me.'

She saw the pained look in his eyes, as if she could see right through to the heart of him. The hope and the fear all rolled up into one. The sheer vulnerability of it all. That his future happiness could be so totally dependent on this moment. So totally dependent on her. All she could say was:

'How far is Vancouver?'

'About a thousand miles from here.'

'I see.'

'Catherine. It must be obvious to you that I have feelings for you. Very strong feelings. And if I can be so presumptuous I believe you have feelings for me too.'

'I am very fond of you. You've been a wonderful friend to me.'

'I can be so much more.'

'You're a good man, Frank. Please don't make me do this to you. Please don't make me hurt you. I couldn't bear it.'

He ignored her pleas and went on. 'I appreciate I am a good deal older than you. But there's a lot I can offer you. This job will provide me with an excellent salary, I am due a very good pension when I retire. I can provide a very comfortable lifestyle for us both. I know you've had a rough, tough time with men. Let me give you a gentler, a more loving life. Let me be responsible for you. Let me look after you.'

'I don't need looking after, Frank. And I don't want looking after. I don't need a knight in shining armour. I am happy here.'

He let go of her hands and stood up. She thought he was going to leave but instead he appeared to re-think his strategy and sat down beside her again. 'After all I've done for you.'

She felt her whole body stiffen. 'I never, ever asked you for your help. Or your gifts. You offered and I accepted. I never expected there to be some kind of... of intimate trade-off.'

Frank shook his head. 'I don't know what happened to you, Catherine. You used to be such a sensible woman. I put it down to all that pot you smoke with these youngsters.'

She laughed at that remark, perhaps a little too loudly given the delicacy of the situation. For Frank responded by gesturing with his hand to the expanse of her Victorian lounge. 'I could bring all this to an end,' he said. 'I could call in all your property loans.'

It was her turn to take both his hands in hers. 'But you wouldn't do that to me, would you, Frank? You're too much of a gentleman for that.'

* * *

As Catherine watched Frank's black Oldsmobile pull away from the sidewalk with its U-Haul trailer attached, bound for his promotion and his new life in Vancouver without her, it was not without a wave as well as a certain sadness. But it was a feeling she quickly dismissed. She decided there were a couple of things she must now do with her life if she were to move on without Frank's benign patronage. The following day, she set these two plans in motion. First of all, she signed up for a course of lessons at a local driving school. She then went down to the animal rescue centre on Sacramento Street with what she hoped was an open mind and an open heart. She returned with a three-month-old male German Shepherd. She named it Max.

Her desire to adopt a dog had surprised her. She had never owned one before, or any other pet for that matter. Was her puppy Max a substitute for the child she never had? Was Max a substitute for the absence of a meaningful relationship in her life? Was Max a substitute for never having found love? Was Max a substitute for Max? Whatever the reason, she had found it hard to refuse the dark, beseeching eyes of this black and tan puppy as she walked the aisle of cages within the rescue centre. She couldn't help herself be moved by that slight sense of fear and mistrust in the creature's eyes she felt her untapped love could soothe. And when she picked him up and she felt his frightened heart beating fast into the palm of her hand, and then finally the warm, raspy lick of his tongue on her chin, these were sensations she could not resist.

Criteria for adoption required she should be able to provide adequate space for this type of dog to thrive and she reassured the staff at the centre that her house in Telegraph Hill was an excellent place in which to rear her pup. She installed a kennel in the small secure yard at the rear of her property where Max could run freely during those hot summer months when there was a pleasant breeze floating in off the ocean. For the winter she set up a basket for him in the kitchen by the stove. She took him on daily walks to nearby Russian Hill or when she was feeling more energetic, she tackled the steep hills and stairways of the dizzying descents down to Fisherman's Wharf. Once she had learned to drive, she let him roam among the redwoods on the trails behind Oakland or further up the coast where he loved to tear up and down the sand, frolic in and out of the waves. She enjoyed watching him grow, learning how to train him, getting to understand his personality. He was a confident, attentive and intelligent dog, loyal and affectionate to her but aloof and uninterested in strangers. He was a bit of a chaser too, quick to run after balls and sticks and mice and cats and squirrels and sand crabs, but always obedient to give up the hunt and return to heel on her command. She discovered in herself that she wasn't particularly fussy with her attention towards him in the way she had seen other dog owners smother and wrestle their pets. It was almost as if she and Max had an adult relationship. She went on with her life and he with his until desire and necessity brought the two of them together in an understanding, affectionate and sympathetic kind of way.

It occurred to her in a rare moment when she actually stopped and thought about how she was feeling that she realised she was happy. Perhaps not as some achieved, permanent state of being, but as a fleeting sensation of contentment that she could enjoy at this particular time and in this particular place. She had been out walking with Max, enjoying the sunny crispness of late autumn, taking in the views over the bay, greeting neighbours, chatting with other dog owners, planning her day in her head. She came to a halt, brought Max to heel, let him lick her fingers as she breathed in the salty air. She was in good health. She had a waiting list for piano students while her tenants were much more reliable now that the Summer of Love had passed and the city had settled down to attracting – how could she put it? – a more traditional clientele of professional types and graduate students. She had a car, she had financial independence. She had Max whom she loved more dearly than she could have ever imagined. What more could she want? She started to hum to herself as she walked with her canine companion at her side. Was this the happiness from an unexpected source that her fortune cookie had predicted?

Owning a dog had also made her much more aware of local green spaces and the city's development plans. She became involved with the People for a Golden Gate National Recreation Area, a coalition of conservationists, civic-minded organizations and citizens such as herself who were concerned about the proposed commercial development of unused military land the Army wished to dispose of along the Golden Gate headlands. The group wanted the areas for public parks while the federal government wanted it for high-rise apartment blocks and upscale housing. It was a time of environmental activism, her community was coming together over the issues, she was meeting and being impressed by strong-minded women who were willing to lobby and negotiate with the State politicians. As she sat down one afternoon going over the latest reports and the agenda for the next meeting, the front doorbell rang. At first, it took her a while to recognise the figure that stood grinning before her on the front step. He seemed shorter and with a shock of grey hair, no longer dyed the black of his Reno days. His bravado seemed to have gone too along with the sharp cut of his suit that now hung crumpled from a skinnier frame. The Clark Gable moustache was still there though, looking rather tired and old-fashioned in her eyes.

'Not going to ask me in?' Cy said, waving a lit cigarette in front of her.

'Why should I?'

He pushed passed and into her living room, spun around to face her. 'Nice place,' he said, looking around, then stubbing his cigarette in one of her seashell ashtrays. 'How about some coffee? Or have you something stronger?'

'I don't want you here,' she said, annoyed with herself for hearing the quaver in her voice.

'I won't take up much of your time,' he said, sitting down on the sofa. 'Once we've tidied up a little matter.'

'And what might that be?'

'Why don't you get me a little something from that bottle of Jack you got over there. You know it's my favourite.'

She knew she should have thrown him out there and then, but some kind of shadow impulse overtook her. It was those memories of their sexual encounters in that Reno hotel room – so wild and so… so satisfying. It had been years since a man had last touched her…and that man had been Cy. She went over to the sideboard and poured him a measure of whiskey into a crystal glass. She noticed her hand was shaking and she wasn't sure if it was from fear or excitement. She poured one for herself and when Cy patted the space beside him on the sofa, she found herself sitting down exactly where he had indicated. He clinked his glass with hers and said:

'How long's it been?'

She shrugged. 'Four years maybe.'

'Five,' he said. 'You look different. I hardly recognise you in these clothes. And your hair. It's much longer.'

'How did you find me?'

'Wasn't difficult. I knew from the start that you came here. That fixer lawyer fellow – what was his name again?'

'Harold Cornelius Starr.'

'Yeah, Harry. He told me where you were headed.'

'So much for attorney-client privilege.'

Cy smiled at that. 'It's amazing what a couple of green-backs will do to a man's tongue. It was a piece of information I thought I'd store until the time was right.'

'I'm using my maiden name.'

'Yeah, I thought you might do that. I checked out your details at the Washoe County Courthouse before I left. Prospective divorce proceedings are of public record. Lucky for me that you didn't remarry.'

'I've never even gotten divorced.'

'Reno was a bit of a waste of time then. Figured too you would probably go back to teaching piano. A quick look in the San Francisco telephone directory for a Catherine Vance, piano lessons, and here I am.'

'What do you want, Cy?'

'I want that thousand dollars you stole from me.'

She let out a throaty laugh. 'You played me, Cy. That money I took was well-earned and well-deserved.'

'So was its absence.' He held up his arm. For the first time, she noticed that two of the fingers on his left hand – the fourth and the pinkie – were horribly disfigured. She remembered those hands, their long, tapered elegance, the way they used to touch her, the thrill that they gave her. For a moment, she wondered how she would feel if they touched her now. Cy went on: 'My creditors didn't appreciate the fact I was a grand short.'

'That was your problem to sort out.' She made to stand up but he grabbed her arm, forced her to sit back down.

'I want that money, Cat.'

She looked at his desperate face and considered her options, especially some of the rent money she kept stashed under her mattress. 'I've got a hundred dollars here in the house. I'll give you that. But only if you go away. For good.'

'I'll take it as a deposit.'

'That's all you're getting. I mean it.'

'I don't think you're in a position to make demands.' He tightened his grip on her arm. 'Like I said, I'll take it as a deposit. And maybe there's something else you could do for me. He reached across with his damaged hand and stroked her cheek with his three good fingers. 'For old time's sake.'

It happened quickly. A blurry leap of canine bulk from the back of the sofa. One moment Cy was there in front of her, touching her face, the next he was on the floor, his whiskey glass flying out of his hand, its contents spilling before it smashed against the base of the fireplace. Max was on top of him, gripping his shoulder with his slobbering jaws as Cy twisted around on the carpet, trying to shake off his captor, his hands up around his neck and face for protection. She screamed, then began calling off her dog but he wouldn't let go of his clamp on Cy's shoulder. She grasped his collar, leaned forward, whispered in his ear as Cy writhed underneath. 'It's all right, Max,' she whispered. 'Good dog. Good dog. It's all right. I'm all right.'

She pulled him back and he let go of his prey.

Cy pushed himself to his feet, stepping back and away from the dog's growling stance. There were deep pressure marks in the cloth of his suit at the shoulder but no rips, no blood. Max had just done enough to hold Cy down rather than sink his teeth into his flesh. She felt the creature straining against her arm, the tension in his body, his long pink tongue hanging out, panting.

'You didn't tell me you had a fucking dog.'

'Get out, Cy. Get out.

'Give me my hundred bucks. And I'll be out of your life for good.'

'Just get out.'

He tried to sort out his jacket as best he could with trembling hands. He took stock of her dog straining on her arm, gave a shrug, picked up the bottle of Jack Daniels as he passed the drinks tray. 'This isn't over,' he said. 'I'll get you for this.'

The door slammed, she sat back down on the sofa with Max's head in her lap. She bent over and pressed her cheek against the wiry fur of his neck. 'Thank you,' she said, over and over again.

The next day, she drove out to the beach by Fort Funston, part of the land area that her conservation group was trying to get incorporated into the public park system. It was Max's favourite spot where he would scamper up and down the dunes until he was all heated up before diving in and out of the freezing ocean to cool off. She had brought a whole bag of treats for him – a piece of raw liver from the butcher's, bones to chew on, dog biscuits smothered in peanut butter. It ended up being a good morning for the both of them, the walk on the windy beach helping to purge the memories of the day before. But it was hard not to think of Cy when she turned the car into her street and saw the flames pouring out of the ground floor windows of her building.

* * *

'Frank, I need your help.'

'What happened?'

'There was a fire in my building.'

'Jesus, Catherine. Are you all right?'

'I'm fine. I wasn't there when it started.'

'What about your tenants?'

'They're OK too. It happened in the afternoon some time. Everyone was out at work or at classes.'

'How did it happen?'

'I don't know yet. But I don't think it was an accident.'

'Somebody would do this on purpose?'

'I don't want to talk about it right now.'

'What about the damage?'

'Pretty extensive to my place, superficial for the tenants once they air out the smoke. I said I'd arrange for any redecoration if they can't get rid of the smell.'

'How are you coping?'

'That's why I wanted to talk to you. I assume I have insurance.'

'I wouldn't know the answer to that, Catherine.'

'What do you mean? You arranged the loans.'

'I authorised the loans. But the actual paperwork would have been done by someone else. Sometimes the bank insures the property and charges you for it. Other times, it is up to you to take out the insurance and note the bank's interests as lenders on the policy. Do you remember if you've been paying annual premiums?'

'I just make the monthly payments. Doesn't that include insurance?'

'Look, let me check for you. Give me a couple of hours or so and I'll call you back. Where can I get hold of you?'

She gave him the number of the hotel and her room.

'The important thing is that you're OK.'

She put down the receiver. She wasn't sure if she was OK at all. She hadn't been allowed back into her apartment even after the fire crew had subdued the blaze. The chief fire officer said that he couldn't be sure but it looked like arson, some kind of flaming object thrown through a rear window of her ground floor apartment. Fortunately, the fire had been caught before it had spread upwards. As for her own place, the front living room had escaped most of the blaze but her other rooms were severely damaged and the officer had deemed them currently unsafe for her return. She only had the clothes she was wearing and those smelt of smoke.

She ran herself a bath, undressed, led the phone into the bathroom and laid down in the hot water to soak. She was asleep when the ringing of the phone woke her.

'I'm sorry but the news doesn't look good,' Frank told her. 'It seems it was your responsibility to insure the property. Given that the bank doesn't have any notification from you or your insurers that they are noted on any policy of yours as lenders, indications are that there isn't any insurance at all.'

'What does that mean?'

'Look, I might be able to sort something out. After all, I think the bank needs to take some responsibility for not making sure you had taken steps to put a policy in place. In the meantime, what are you going to do?'

'I have no idea. All I've got is a car and the clothes that I stand up in.'

'You've got a car?'

'I learned to drive since I last saw you.'

'You've also got a bag of silver in a safety deposit box.'

'I've got you to thank for that, Frank.'

'It was always going to be money for a rainy day.'

'It's certainly been pouring down here.'

'Why don't you come up here for a while. I've got plenty of room. Vancouver is a beautiful city. And it looks like you need a place to stay.'

'I've got a dog now.'

'I wouldn't worry about that. I love dogs.'

The next morning, she checked out of her hotel. It wasn't so much that she wanted to see Frank, although she knew he would be reliably helpful and comforting. It was just that she couldn't face having to deal with everything else – the police, the fire damage, her tenants. And she did need a place to stay. She stocked up on some beer and dog food, bought herself a cheap sweater and pair of slacks, filled the car up with gas and headed out of the city for the Interstate. It was early winter and she was travelling a further thousand miles north to snowy Canada. She just hoped her seven-year-old Rambler Classic would be robust enough for the trip. She figured she could do the journey in two days, three tops.

It was good to drive, it gave her time to think. Or talk. For she found herself chatting away to Max curled up there on the front seat beside her, nodding and whimpering as she voiced her worries. And she could imagine him talking back to her in that beautiful mellifluous voice of his namesake, just as they used to do on those summer evenings on the balconies of their New York apartments.

'There I was only a few days ago musing on how happy I was. And now this.'

'Hubris,' Max said. 'That's what they call it. Hubris.'

'You're right. I was getting too cocky. So along comes that bastard Cy and then the fire.'

'It would be hard to disassociate the two occurrences.'

'The fire officer said he would mention my suspicions in his report.'

'You should contact the police yourself.'

'Yes, yes. I'll do that when I get back. But what happens if I'm not insured.'

'You still have your stash of silver.'

'I doubt that'll be enough to cover all the damage.'

'Why don't we wait until you have a chance to go over it all properly with Frank?'

'Yes, Frank. Frank will sort it all out.'

'Frank's a good man.

'He's always been kind to me.'

'It's important to have someone like that on your side.'

'Yes, it is. But I need to think of our current needs right now. Like where we're going to spend the night.'

After around seven hours and 350 miles into her journey, she found a budget motel off the highway, just south of a small town called Medford, not far into the state of Oregon. She had hoped to have driven further but she was too weary to go on although at least having crossed from California into another state gave her a certain sense of achievement. The Paradise Motel was a typical two-story collection of around twenty flimsy, run-down rooms built around a small, empty swimming pool. The heater struggled to keep her warm and the place stunk of cigarette smoke and disinfectant. Ordinarily, she would have been terrified staying in such a place by herself with doors banging at all hours, raised voices, footsteps in the corridor outside her room, and the sound of various TV and radio programs competing for attention. But she had Max with her and she knew she was safe. She picked up a takeaway menu for a local restaurant from reception, ordered in a pizza, sipped on a beer she'd kept cool in the trunk of her car, and called Frank.

'How are you feeling?' he asked.

'I don't feel anything.'

'You're probably in shock about what's happened.'

'Probably.'

'I know it's not the best of circumstances to be saying this but I'm looking forward to seeing you again.'

'It will be nice to see you too.'

'I'm sure we can sort things out.'

'I hope so.'

He gave her detailed directions to his place which she noted down on a Paradise Hotel notepad. She hung up, watched back to back episodes of the *Here's Lucy* show and fell asleep with the TV still on.

The following morning, she had a huge breakfast at a local diner and looking at a map, she figured she still had around 600 miles to go to Vancouver. She didn't fancy spending another night in a motel but if she had to, she'd like to have at least reached Seattle. She fed Max a hamburger and some hash browns off her plate, got herself a takeaway coffee and set off on the highway again. The further north she drove, the colder the weather became. The rain turned into sleet and a light layer of snow frosted the ground alongside the highway. She had the heater on full blast, she had the radio on up high, Max was asleep in the back and she moved on. She drove past Eugene, Salem and Portland, out of Oregon and into Washington State. The sky was getting darker, the weather was getting bleaker and she was dying for a pee. She decided to get off the highway and find some deserted spot where she could relieve herself in privacy. It would also be an opportunity to let Max have a bit of exercise before the darkness and what looked like worsening weather kicking in. She exited at the next off-ramp and headed into the countryside for a few miles before she found a place to pull over. Max was as eager to jump out as she was. She dived behind some trees, pulled down her new slacks and knickers and urinated among the long frosty grass, one eye on the road for passing cars, the other on the look-out for Max who seemed to have found some animal to worry and chase. Once she'd wiped herself off with a tissue, pulled herself back into some form of decency, she called out for her dog and waited for him to come. When he didn't respond, she moved further away from the road and into the trees. What she thought might have been a wood was simply a couple of rows of pine trees and beyond that an enormous frozen lake, the light of dusk and a rising moon reflecting eerily off its surface in a kind of icy blue haze. As her gaze skimmed across the glazed top, about fifty yards in from the edge, she saw the hole in the ice and the struggling form of her dog in the freezing water.

She screamed his name, the sound of her voice echoing back at her across the empty, frozen landscape as she ran. She could feel the give on the thin ice as her feet slipped across the surface. She could see Max's paws struggling for purchase on the ice at the rim of the hole into which he was submerged. She reached the gap in the ice and cursed herself for not bringing a stick or a branch or something for Max to grab hold of. But the dog seemed very stoic about its fate. He wasn't barking or yelping, there appeared to be no sense of panic in his eyes. There was a task at hand – the clawing at the ice to gain a grip in order to heave himself out. And even as he thrashed about, failing in his efforts, his head and body dipping under the water only to reappear again icy and shivering, he continued trying to wriggle himself out of his predicament devoid of any panic. She laid herself flat on the ice at the edge of the hole, stretched out her arms to him. He thrashed towards her and she grabbed his head, then scrambled her arms down his neck to his collar. She pulled and pulled but she just didn't have the strength to drag him out of the water. She could feel the ice beneath her beginning to sag and crack but she held on to her dog.

'Come on, Max. Come on. You can do it.' She looked down at him, the slicked back fur and those dark beseeching eyes that had drawn her in the very first moment she had seen him in the cage at the rescue centre. 'Oh, Max, my love. Come on. You can do it.'

And in one swift movement, the dog was somehow able to clasp her around her shoulders with his paws, drag himself up and over her head. As he swept himself out of the water, she could feel the cold, wet fur of the underside of his body and tail slick against her forehead and hair. But as her dog escaped, his weight on top of hers forced the ice in front of her to give way and she toppled into the water. She went under head-first, then managed to right herself, come up quickly to the surface. She gasped for breath, feeling the icy air penetrate her frozen lungs before she went under again, her heavy clothes pulling her down. She kicked away madly, forcing herself up to the surface, spitting out the water she had involuntarily swallowed when her lungs had automatically demanded air. Max was at the edge of the ice-hole, barking like crazy, slipping and sliding on the rim, trying to figure out what to do. She was flailing, losing strength, losing breath. Her dog was just a whimpering, steaming shadow against the wan moon rising behind him. He was testing the waters again with one paw and then the other, getting ready to pounce.

'Stay, Max,' she shouted. 'Stay, Max. Don't jump. Please don't jump.'

ACKNOWLEDGEMENTS

This book was written during a period of three years while I travelled around the world as a digital nomad. I would like to thank the kindness and generosity of Jennie Emerson who provided me with the time and space to write at Casa Nava, Bella Orxeta, Spain and to Manjula Spears and Rich Panico who hosted me for several months at their tranquil Satchidananda Mission property in Athens, Georgia, USA.

I am also grateful to those many other friends who provided me with shelter from the storm as I journeyed along the way:

Jette and Arne (Copenhagen, Denmark)
Richard, Mel and Gill (Toronto, Canada)
Helene (Montreal, Canada)
Chris (Monterey, California)
Alan and Taku (Berkeley, California)
Barry and Mary; Sven and Linda (Qld, Australia)
Chris and Tim   (Brisbane, Australia)
Marty and Sonia; Nurit and Frank (Sydney, Australia)
Debbie and Steve (Perth, Australia)
Kazuki and Taeko; Mark and Keiko (Kamakura, Japan)
David and Lev (on a boat, somewhere in the Bahamas)
Narve and Age (Villajoyosa, Spain)

Steve and Sabine; Ellis and Karen; Jonny and Jean (London)
Stephen and Judy (North Berwick)
Patrick and Melinda; Randy and Jackie (Oxford)
Michèle and Neal (Stroud)
Anne and Andrew (Lewes)
Jackie and Nick (on a boat, Shoreham-by-Sea)
Sofia (Glasgow)

Special thanks to my sister Judith and husband Steve for their
hospitality in Perth, Western Australia; to my brother Michael
who had to put up with me for seven months in Glasgow
during lockdown; and to that person I can never truly repay for
her gift of life and love, my mother, Rose.

For technical support at various stages on my writing journey,
I am also grateful to Judith Sher (reading and copyediting), Sara
Sarre and Iain Maloney (reading), Ron Grosset (publishing),
Andy Bridge (cover design) and Laura Jones (typesetting).

ABOUT THE AUTHOR

J. David Simons is a Scottish novelist whose works include *The Credit Draper* (shortlisted for The McKitterick Prize); *The Liberation of Celia Kahn*; *The Land Agent*; *An Exquisite Sense of What is Beautiful* and *A Woman of Integrity*. He is also a previous recipient of the Robert Louis Stevenson Fellowship.

He lives, works and writes as a digital nomad.